Christmas Cookies Mysteries

An Anthology Inspired by
THE OAK RIDGE BOYS'
CHRISTMAS COOKIES ALBUM

Patricia Bradley and a baker´s dozen
of award winning authors

ALLY PRESS

Table of Contents

Hark the Herald

Patricia Bradley

Angels Sing

If glaring at the ledger sheet would change the numbers, Jane Albright would do just that. Finances had never been this bad at CrossPointe Fellowship Church in Woodpine, Alabama. A sigh came from behind her.

"At least we're not in the red."

Ever the optimist, Chris—not Brother Chris or Reverend Holley—just plain old Chris who changed Cross Point to CrossPointe-with-an-e—reminded her of an ostrich with its head in the sand. "It's in the pink, and by Friday—"

"Don't borrow trouble, Jane."

"Hmph." There he was calling her by her first name again when she'd told him it didn't sound professional. She supposed she should be flattered a man young enough to be her grandson called her by her first name. "Any thoughts on how to change these numbers?"

Jane certainly didn't have any. First the pandemic had shut them down, and now that it was over, people just weren't coming back. Oh, sure, the sermon was on the "web," and there were plenty of viewers, but many never thought to send in their tithes and love offerings.

Even though Chris held down a good job at the paper mill working nights, he still needed to be paid for his pastoral duties. And he'd worked hard with the rag-tag kids choir on the upcoming Christmas program to debut in three weeks on Christmas Eve.

Chris cleared his throat. "I, ah, think we may have a solution. A miracle, actually."

Jane widened her eyes then narrowed them as she studied the young pastor. He had that same gobsmacked look her boys had when they came to her with a request they knew was going to be denied. And the quiver in his voice mimicked her boys', too. "A miracle?"

"Yes! I was at the Java House, discussing our financial problems with one of the deacons when a gentleman approached me. Said he couldn't help overhearing our discussion, and he wanted to help. He's offered to bring the Oak Ridge Boys here for a Christmas Eve concert. And they will even donate their fee."

Jane managed to keep her jaw from dropping. Of all the harebrained—the very idea that they could get the Oak Ridge Boys to do a concert at their little church—she took a deep breath and opened her mouth to tell him so.

Chris held up his hand. "Before you start putting up roadblocks, hear me out. Or better still, just think about it until Elliott gets here to lay out the plan."

"Elliott?" She squeaked out.

"Elliott Broussard. He'll be here in…" Chris checked his watch, "Five minutes."

Jane could hardly wait. While Chris retreated to his office, her fingers flew over the computer keyboard, entering Elliott Broussard into a DuckDuckGo search.

She scanned the bio that the search engine returned. It billed him as a free-lance publicist and named several groups that he worked with.

The Oak Ridge Boys were one of them, but when she checked their website, his name wasn't listed.

Footsteps approached from the hallway. Had to be this Elliott Broussard, and Jane looked up from her computer, fully expecting a suave, thirty-something con man. Her breath caught.

"You must be the indispensable Ms. Jane Albright," he said with a voice as smooth as molasses.

He was suave all right but closer to her age than thirty. She reined in her runaway heart—it didn't matter how handsome or distinguished-looking Broussard was, he wasn't pulling a con on her.

"And you can be none other than Elliott Broussard," she replied sharply.

"Elliott W. Broussard." He bowed from the waist. "At your services, madam."

Chris entered the room from his office. "Oh, good. I see you two have already met." He looked over at Jane. "Would you please join us and take notes?"

Indeed she would. She grabbed a notebook and followed the two men into Chris's office.

Jane kept quiet as she took notes. She'd learned a long time ago to make herself almost invisible—like a piece of the furniture. That way the participants usually forgot she was there and often disclosed information they wouldn't have normally.

But that didn't seem to be working with Elliott Broussard as they sat around the table in Chris's office. Broussard continually tried to draw her into the discussion as he laid out the plans for the concert.

"Ms. Jane, don't you think an hour is a good length for the concert?" Or "Ms. Jane, what do you think about starting the concert at eight p.m.?"

He'd asked this last question only seconds ago, and she'd paused her note taking. "Seven would be better—it'll be Christmas Eve, and most families have a lot to do that night."

He steepled his fingers to his lips and nodded. "Oh, yes, I see your point."

Finally she'd had enough. "Mr. Broussard—"

"Call me Elliott." He graced her with a gentle smile.

She pursed her lips then continued, "Mr. Broussard...why would the Oak Ridge Boys do a concert for our church for free?"

He placed his hands on the table in front of him. "I hate that you doubt me, Jane, but those boys have a heart of gold. When I told them about your predicament and pointed out your church is right on their way home, and that all they had to do was stop off for an hour, they were completely onboard."

She studied his face. If something sounded too good to be true, it usually was, but she wasn't sure how to call him on it. "Just what do you do for the Oak Ridge Boys? I didn't find your name anywhere on their website."

"Oh, I do a little of this and a little of that. Nothing official and usually work through their manager. I tell you what—why don't I give you their manager's number before I leave. You can call him and verify everything I've said."

Jane would do just that. She waited for him to give her the number, but instead, Broussard turned to Chris. "I think your idea of having the children sing before the Oaks is a brilliant idea. That will get the kiddos' families there."

Jane sniffed. "I would think the Oak Ridge Boys would be enough incentive."

"Of course, just thinking about the kids. Chris said they'd worked really hard, and I wouldn't want to disappoint them."

Jane leaned forward. "How do we handle ticket sales? Will people purchase them here at the church?"

"It's been my experience that it's better to sell tickets online," Elliott said. "It's much easier for people to click a button than to get in their car and drive here."

Jane noted his response in her notes. For once he made a good point. And if they sold tickets online, they would have an idea beforehand how much money they would take in—they desperately needed enough to see them through the winter.

"Will we take money at the door?" Chris asked.

"That's not a good idea. I took a gander at your auditorium and looks like the most you can seat is 400 people—"

"Actually, 450," Jane said. As hard as it was to get folks to come to church nowadays even for their cantata at Easter, it would surprise her if they filled that many seats, in spite of it being the Oak Ridge Boys.

"Four-fifty," he amended with a nod. "You wouldn't want to sell that many tickets on line and then have people at the door and not be able to admit them."

Another good point that she noted.

"I'll handle all the communication with the Oak Ridge Boys and their manager." Then Elliott rubbed his chin. "Do you want to set up the app for purchasing the tickets or do you want me to do it?"

"I'm sure I can handle that," Jane said.

"I'd much prefer you do it, Elliott." She and Chris had spoken at the same time, but his voice overrode hers, and he offered her an apologetic smile. "I think since Elliott is familiar with this sort of thing, he'd be better suited to handle it."

The older man beamed. "Glad to do it."

Jane eyed him thoughtfully. "And how much will your take be?"

The look in his eyes reminded her of one of her boys when their feelings were hurt. Then he drummed his fingers on the table and looked toward the window. When he brought his gaze back to Jane and Chris, he smiled. "I don't normally do this, but I like you people and you have a real need. I feel led to forgo my fee."

"We couldn't possibly impose—"

"What a generous thing to do." This time Jane's voice overrode the pastor's.

When Jane called the number Broussard left for the Oak Ridge Boys' manager, the voice on the other end verified everything Broussard had told them, and that the Oaks would be at the church at seven p.m. sharp. From there everything snowballed.

The local newspaper ran a story on the concert, and by the week before Christmas, sales had soared for the event. They were only fifty tickets from being sold out. If the remaining tickets sold, they would clear enough to keep the church going through the winter and even be able to pay Chris a small bonus. He had worked so hard and deserved it.

Jane checked the PayPal app, and her heart warmed at the sight of almost $10,000. But more than the money, she prayed the concert would be the catalyst that brought members back to church on a regular basis.

Elliott, as she now called him, had taken to dropping by the church a couple of times a week, and she'd grudgingly accepted he might be a decent sort. She'd even started looking forward to visits from their "benefactor" as Chris called him. The front door jingled open, and her heart lifted at the sight of him in spite of the teensy-weensy bit of suspicion that just wouldn't go away.

"Ah, the lovely Ms. Jane," Elliott said, placing a small vase with a single yellow rose on her desk.

Her cheeks heated up. She looked pointedly at the rose. "What's that for?"

"I hope it's an enticement to celebrate by having coffee with me today—we just sold the last ticket."

"You're kidding!"

He beamed at her. "I kid you not. So how about it? Coffee at the Java House?"

The temptation was great. Elliott had a way of making her feel like she was the only person in the room even when others were around. But…even when he was smiling at her, like now, a tiny warning flitted through her thoughts.

"I'd like that." Maybe she could learn more about him if they were away from the church.

Jane pulled her down jacket close against the north wind as they walked the short distance to the coffee shop. She welcomed the nip in the air since the unseasonably warm weather the last few days had made it seem more like September than Christmas.

Just as they reached the door, a whirling dervish of a boy barreled into Elliott, hugging his legs. "Mr. Ewiott, tank you!"

"Jeremy!" Jane pried him loose, looking up into Elliott's startled face. "I'm so sorry." She turned to the boy. "What's gotten into you, son?"

Tears threatened to spill down the boy's face. "I just wanna tank him. Mama said I couldn't go to Sunday school 'cause it'd be too cold, but Mr. Ewiott is gonna fis it."

She looked up to give Elliott an apologetic smile, and her breath caught. For a second, she thought the man was going to bolt down the sidewalk. Then Jeremy wiggled out of Jane's grasp and wrapped his arms around Elliott's legs again. "You gonna come hear me sing?"

Elliott's eyes blinked rapidly. "Ah, I, ah…"

The poor man was touched beyond speech. Had to be a first for him. "Of course he'll come," she said, stepping in to rescue Elliott.

After Jeremy and his mom left, Elliott was uncharacteristically quiet as they entered the coffee shop. He got quieter still as different patrons greeted him like he was an old friend. After they ordered their coffee, Elliott pulled a chair out for Jane, and she settled in it.

He raised his eyebrows. "How about one of Miss Betty's scones with that cup of coffee?"

No one made better scones than Jane's friend and owner of the Java House. "Make mine blueberry."

He seemed to be back to his old exuberant self as he stood in line to order and talked with those around him.

Jane couldn't help but compare Elliott Broussard to other men his age. So many of them sported double chins and receding hairlines, not to mention a paunch hanging over their bellies. Elliott could be a walking advertisement for a fitness center. And that head full of silver hair… it was enough to make a woman swoon.

Silver-tongued, too. There was that little twinge of warning that made her sit upright. She knew so little about him—he could even be married…or worse.

"Here you go, love," Elliott said and handed her the coffee.

The words spoken in his velvety voice wrapped around her like a warm blanket. Even so, her hand quivered as she took the cup. What if he wasn't on the up-and-up?

"Be right back with the scones."

Jane stirred her coffee as she waited for his return. He returned empty-handed, and she raised her eyebrows in a question.

"Miss Betty is bringing them. Said she had some 'special' scones for us."

A few minutes later, the rail-thin owner of Java House set a plate of pastries in front of them with a flourish. "These are right out of the oven."

"You shouldn't have gone to any trouble," he said.

"Listen here, young man—" Jane almost giggled. Betty was at best only five years older than Elliott, "Nothing is too good for the man who's saving our church! And they're on the house."

Elliott's face turned the color of Betty's Santa hat, and once again she had the sense that he might bolt.

"You give me too much credit," he said softly.

"I don't think so," Jane said when Betty returned to her kitchen. "God is using you to grow our faith—You've given us hope again."

His eyes widened, and he swallowed hard. "How are the scones?"

She broke off a corner piece and nibbled it, her tastebuds exploding at the perfect combination of butter, sugar, and flour with the blueberries and lemon zest. "Excellent, as always!"

Neither spoke while they enjoyed the coffee and treat. Jane laid her fork on the plate beside a few crumbs. "You've never talked about your family...you do have one, right?"

He stared at his empty coffee cup, then looked up with a gentle smile. "Oh, yes, I have a family. A son who's married. Trey and his lovely wife have given me three beautiful grandchildren."

"And there's no Mrs. Broussard?"

Elliott peered at her over his cup. "The sainted woman passed away eight years ago. And you? Is there a Mr. Albright?"

Heat flashed up her neck. He thought she was interested in *him*! Jane gulped her coffee, sending it down the wrong way. Once the coughing stopped, she fanned her face. "Sorry. And no, there's no Mr. Albright. He passed over twenty years ago."

"That's terrible. A woman as fine as you should have someone looking after her."

His words sent a flurry of heartbeats crashing against her ribs. *Focus.* "So, uh, your children, do they live near you?"

The twinkle in his eye told her she hadn't fooled him. "Sadly, no. They live in Florida."

"What part? I've often thought of moving there myself."

"Oh, the Tampa area."

"Why, that's close enough for you to join them for Christmas."

He frowned. "No, I plan to be here in Woodpine—at the church on Christmas Eve. Wouldn't have time to drive there."

"So, you'll be alone on Christmas Day?"

"It won't be the first time."

Evidently, he didn't normally spend Christmas with his family. "Then you're invited to come to my house."

"Why, Jane--"

She palmed her hand toward him. "It won't be just the two of us. My boys will be there with their families and Chris, the pastor, his girlfriend...maybe even a couple more people. I never know how many will show up."

She was talking too fast, but she couldn't seem to stop.

"You'll never know how much your invitation means to me, but I'm afraid I'll have to decline."

The wistfulness in his eyes caught her by surprise. His words might be saying no, but his eyes said otherwise.

All day Christmas Eve, Jane kept checking her phone. In the week since she'd had coffee with Elliott, she'd found no less than three Broussard's living in the Tampa area. She'd reached two of them who assured her they were not related to their "benefactor."

She'd left a voice mail for third one who had the same velvety timbre to his voice as Elliott, asking that if he was related to Elliott W. Broussard, would he please call her. So far she'd heard nothing, and something told her time was running out.

Not that she had any proof that anything was wrong. She'd checked the PayPal account, and everything seemed all right there. Maybe it was because she couldn't reach the Oaks' manager. She'd left three voicemails on the number Elliott had given her but no return call.

What if they didn't show up tonight?

The thought, like a pesky mosquito in the summer, wouldn't go away as she paced her living room. Jane checked her watch. Four-thirty. She might as well go on to the church—she could pace there as well as here. And maybe Elliott would be there—he'd said he'd be at the church by five, but perhaps he'd be early, and then she could ask him why she couldn't get in touch with the Oaks' manager.

Gray clouds hung low over the darkened church, and a cold north wind blew as she climbed out of her Taurus. It wasn't supposed to snow, but who knew. The conditions were certainly right.

What if the roads became slippery and the Oaks couldn't get to their little town? What if they had to return all the ticket money? At least they had it to return, but then how would they pay the power bill come January?

Shivering, she unlocked the church and flipped on lights in the sanctuary as she walked to the choir room. The children would be here soon to prepare for their part in the program. Her cell phone rang as she unlocked the church, and she yanked it from her purse and frowned. It wasn't a number she recognized. And it certainly wasn't the manager's number either—she'd put that name and number in her contacts.

"Hello?"

"Uh, I believe you left a message on my answering machine asking about an Elliott W. Broussard."

There was that velvety voice again, and her heart leaped in her throat. "Yes? Is this Elliott?"

"Uh, no, ma'am. I'm Trey."

"You…sound just like him."

"I've—" static garbled the line. "…before."

"So you do know him?"

"I'm sorry, you broke up there. Look, whatever you do, don't—"

Reception was terrible in the choir room, and she'd lost him again. "Hold on, let me move to a better spot."

When she reached the sanctuary again, the call had dropped and Jane quickly rang him back, but it went to voicemail. She left a message asking him to call.

That seed of worry had mushroomed into a full-blown tree. What had the caller been trying to tell her?

"Jane! Are you here?" Chris called from the back of the church.

"I'm in the sanctuary." She turned as the front door opened, and several children and their parents hurried inside.

"Ms. Jane, where's my song?"

"And where's my robe?"

Little voices clamored for her attention—it was showtime and utter chaos would reign until she got them organized. Half an hour later, with everyone in place and Chris practicing their songs with them, Jane slipped outside to try and contact Trey again. Once more it went to voice mail.

She checked her watch. And where was Elliott? He'd said he'd be here by five, and it was almost-five thirty. Jane punched in his number, and it went straight to his message center. That only happened when a phone was turned off...or on do not disturb...

"It came upon a midnight clear...," the pure sounds of the children's voices rang through the church.

They were nearing the end of their program, and sweat bloomed on Jane's hands as she stood in the wings of the stage. The church was full—standing-room-only, and she hadn't seen even a shadow of Elliott

Not only that, there'd not been a word from the Oak Ridge Boys or their manager, and they were due to take the stage in twenty minutes.

Her cell phone buzzed in her hand. The same number from before—Trey Broussard! She stepped away from the stage. "Hello?"

"I'm sorry I couldn't get back to you before now. Can you hear me?"

"Yes. Do you know where Elliott is?"

A loud sigh came through the phone. "What con has he pulled now?"

Jane's heart sank. She knew it. Had suspected it from the beginning. "Your father? He's in the habit of pulling cons?"

"I'm afraid so. How much did he take you for?"

Time slowed. The PayPal account. Elliott had access to it. Buzzing started in Jane's ears as she swallowed down the nausea rolling up her chest. "I don't know…we sold tickets for a concert featuring the Oak Ridge Boys."

Trey groaned. "I'm so sorry. My father doesn't know even one of the Oaks or their manager."

"Thank you for calling me back," she mumbled and hung up. What were they going to do? There were 450 people waiting for a concert…

Suddenly Chris appeared at her side, waving his phone. "The money. It's gone. Every penny."

"What do you mean?" *Don't say it. Don't say it…*

"Elliott cleaned out the PayPal account."

He said it.

"Let me think." She paced the short hall. "Have the children sing more songs. Maybe we'll get a miracle."

Elliott W. Broussard walked toward the bus station, the music coming from the church haunting him. He was getting too soft for this line of work.

He shouldn't have gotten close to the people here. For the first time in his life, he wished he could undo what he'd done. But it was too late. If the church people found him, they would tar and feather him before running him out of town.

"O, little town of Bethlehem
How still we see thee lie
Above this deep and dreamless sleep
The silent stars go by…"

He closed his heart against the music. Where was that bus? Elliott peered down the road and took a step back, and then he rubbed his eyes. What in the world? Four men, dressed in black, walked toward him.

"Hey, buddy!" The one with a long white beard called to him, "Know where we can find a landline? Our bus broke down, and there's no cell service around here."

"Yeah," a deep bass chimed in, "And there doesn't seem to be anyone around town."

"Everyone's at the church," Elliott said, swallowing hard. "Come on, I'll show you the way. I'm Elliott Broussard."

"And we're—"

"The Oak Ridge Boys," he finished for Joe Bonsall. By now they were nearing the church.

"Oh, wow!" Joe said. "Listen to those voices!"

A chill raced over Elliott as the children sang.

> *"Hark! The herald angels sing,*
> *"Glory to the newborn King!*
> *Peace on earth and mercy mild,*
> *God and sinners reconciled."*
> *Joyful, all ye nations rise,*
> *Join the triumph of the skies,*
> *With th'angelic host proclaim:*
> *"Christ is born in Bethlehem."*

"Man, they're good," Duane Allen said.

"Indeed they are," Elliott said. "Too bad about what happened."

"What happened?" Four voices asked.

"The church was struggling to pay their bills, and this con man came through town, promised he could get you boys to do a concert."

"You're kidding." Golden folded his arms across his chest.

"Afraid not. The con man skipped town with the money. The concert was supposed to be tonight…now the church will have to come up with the money to refund the tickets."

Richard Sterban rubbed his jaw. "Maybe not. Seems like we might have had bus trouble just so we could do this show."

They exchanged glances with one another, then Golden said, "We'd have to do it acapella, but I say, let's go for it."

Duane Allen turned to Elliott. "You want to go in and introduce us?"

Elliott released the breath he'd been holding. "Why don't you just surprise them as soon as the kids finish their song?"

> *"Hark! The herald angels sing,*
> *"Glory to the newborn King!"*
> *"Hark the herald angels sing*
> *Glory to the newborn King!"*

He took out the phone with the number he'd given Jane to call the Oaks manager and texted: Boys are on their way.

With peace washing over him, he turned to listen to the children. When the song ended, he heard Chris address the church. "Well, folks, I'm disappointed to tell—"

Duane Allen opened the church doors and walked down the aisle with the others following him, singing "Silent Night, Holy Night…"

While the Oak Ridge Boys were singing, Elliott slipped around to the back entrance of the church and eased into Jane's office. He took out his checkbook and stared at the balance. Eleven thousand, eight-hundred and fifty dollars. He quickly scribbled out a check and tore it out, placing it in the center of Jane's desk.

Then he pocketed the checkbook and slipped away from the church. He already had his bus ticket to Lake, Florida. Fifty dollars should get him to Tampa. Maybe he could make things right with Trey.

He walked toward the bus station with "Hark the Herald Angels Sing" playing in his head.

Ollie Bramlett

Joseph S. Bonsall

(aka Christmas Cookies)

ONE

Oliver Bramlett was a bit slow. He moved slow and he talked slow. But those folks who thought he was not the sharpest knife in the drawer would have been dead wrong.

As a small boy growing up in Tomkinsville, Kentucky, little Ollie loved just two things: books and banjos! He probably read more than 200 books before he turned fourteen and proceeded to win every banjo-playing contest held at the Monroe County Fair since he turned six. Yep... It was all books and banjo to Ollie. When he wasn't picking, he was reading. When he wasn't picking or reading, he was putting in a hard day's work at the Pennworthy farm.

Ollie's dad had just 'run off' according to his mom so it has always been just Oliver and Fran, and it worked out well for them both as Fran Bramlett was not exactly a socialite either. She cooked and served up food at Monroe County High School for the students and did some candy striping at the Medical Center. She and her son were never close, but they coexisted as well as could be expected.

It was Fran who bought him his very first banjo when he was just five years old. She had found it while browsing around at a yard sale. She just loved yard sales, and there was always one happening on an any Saturday within' driving distance. The previous owner of the banjo had passed away, so he obviously didn't need it anymore. Therefore, the old 5-string Vega ended up in Ollie's hands and right from day one the boy could pick and roll a bit. And as years would pass Ollie would become quite proficient at Scruggs-style bluegrass pickin' Yeah… the boy could play.

For the most part though, Ollie had no real friends at all. Oh, he had played some banjo with a few local pickers from time to time, but he never really bonded with any of them.

Most folks around Tompkinsville and all around southern Kentucky just believed that he was on the stupid side, and even now, at the ripe old age of twenty-nine years old, he was still pretty much ignored by most everyone except for old Oscar Pennworthy who owned around 1000 acres of pristine farmland over in Fountain Run by the Kentucky / Tennessee state line.

Pennworthy had been a tobacco farmer just like his daddy and his grandfather who started it all, but tobacco farming was on the outs these days. So now Oscar was in the process of turning his crops into the lucrative hemp growing business. Unlike the illegal (thus far in Kentucky) THC in marijuana plants that made one high as a Georgia pine tree, the legal hemp plants contained an active chemical called CBD that many believed contained healing properties of all kinds. It seemed people all over the world found themselves rubbing CBD oils and such all over themselves, and it wasn't cheap either.

Old Oscar didn't give a flying flip about any of that. He was just looking for a new way to make a living, and this hemp thing was providing a darn good buck or three. He was also preparing for the eventual legalization of the good stuff; for when and if that were ever to happen, he was ready to go. Although thoughts of everyone being stoned all around him all the time was a frightening thought.

Oscar was still an old school conservative, Pentecostal, and born again Christian and really couldn't imagine pot being legalized here. But if it meant food on the table and paying a bill or two, he guessed he could make that work. After all, he figured tobacco was an evil drug as well; but again, a man has to make a living and there weren't many other options around these rolling hills.

Oscar had lost his wife, Hattie, years ago to breast cancer, and only he and their one son lived on the farm. Oscar, in the old white farmhouse that had stood for generations, and his son, Eric, in a small log cabin that Oscar had built for him on an upper ridge, by a tree line and an old underground stream. Thankfully, the county was able to run some electric current to the ridge as well.

Eric Pennworthy was a rugged looking and sturdy boy who had graduated Western Kentucky University with a bachelor's degree in Agriculture and a Masters in Kentucky women. However, Eric had learned more from his father and grandfather than he could have EVER learned up in Bowling Green.

After college, Eric came back home and went right to work for his father. He loved working for his dad who no doubt paid him a lot more then than he was worth, but Eric figured that one day this place would all belong to him, and he would be growing the good weed until Jesus came back. He might even settle down if he could ever find that perfect woman to marry. They could live happily ever after growing pot and making babies, but for now he would help dad grow hemp, and on the weekends, he would head on up to Bowling Green or down to Nashville, Tennessee and party his brains out.

The only other employee of Oscar Pennworthy besides his son was one... Oliver Bramlett. *"The boy was a might strange,"* thought Oscar, *"But he worked his fanny off"* Oscar appreciated that and actually cared quite a bit for Ollie. Eric just figured Ollie was some kind of weirdo and told him so quite often. He even nicknamed Ollie 'Deliverance' and would sing DADA DA... DA DA mocking the banjo kid in that long ago Burt Reynolds flick. Oliver loved the old man, but he quite honestly hated Eric's guts.

So when Oscar Pennworthy and his ambitious son were both found dead on a crisp, early December Saturday morning on the dirt floor of one of the Pennworthy barns, the blame naturally fell on Oliver Bramlett.

TWO

Old Oscar Pennworthy had been a fixture down at the local Farmers Co-op every morning since the Earth began to cool. He would sit around in a semi-circle with several other old timers, and they would pretty much solve all of the world's problems. Whether the object of the conversation revolved around politics, religion, women, or more politics, someone always had a solution... or at least a good joke.

When Oscar didn't show up at the Co-op, everyone was a bit worried. Cootie Steel went to the phone behind the counter and called Big Mike's Eating Table down near Fountain Run. Oscar ate a family style breakfast there on most mornings, and sometimes he was accompanied by his son.

Big Mike answered the call and told Cootie that he hadn't seen Oscar OR Eric and that alerted Cootie's spidey-sense, so he immediately called Sheriff Raymond Sprinkles.

"I'll run on down there and take a look," Sprinkles told Cootie and so he did.

The Sheriff had his own key to the gate of The the Pennworthy farm, so he drove down there, noticed that the chain on the gate was unlocked as usual, so he just swung open the gate and entered the property. It was about a half mile down a gravel road from the gate to the farm and as he approached the farmhouse, the very first thing he noticed was that Oscar's Ford F150 blue pickup was parked where it usually was. Glancing left toward an old lean-to building full of rusty old implements, he saw Eric's mustard colored Jeep Wrangler with the "GIRLS and GRASS" bumper sticker. Sprinkles approached the barn, saw two dead bodies, drew his sidearm, and called for backup.

The sound of sirens filled the air as two Monroe County Sheriff deputy cruisers, a Tompkinsville Police car, and a Kentucky State patrol car all made their way down the gravel driveway that led deep into the Pennworthy Farm. Sprinkles was examining the bodies in the barn as the other law enforcement officers arrived.

"What have we got, Sheriff?" asked Trooper Neilson of the State Patrol.

"Two dead bodies I'm afraid, Jim. It's old man Pennworthy and his son Eric, deader than Lincoln, I'm afraid. Better call the Monroe County Coroner and Fitzgerald's funeral home, but don't nobody touch or move a thing until state forensics goes over the scene."

Sheriff Sprinkles just figured it HAD to be Bramlett. *That boy just wasn't right… never WAS! But why would he do this?"* He thought. *"And just HOW did he do it? There was no sign of a struggle, no wounds … no nothing!"*

"Deputy Stevens, go pick up Ollie Bramlett and bring him in for questioning. He is the only other one that works down here."

"*This one makes no sense at all … not that they ever do,*" he muttered under his breath while fighting back tears as the late Pennworthy father and son were zipped into body bags.

Oliver Bramlett found himself sitting in a dank, gray room in a dank, gray uncomfortable chair. There was very little light given by a hanging light bulb, and Ollie was fidgeting around nervously when Sheriff Sprinkles walked in and sat himself down in a similar chair that was turned backwards and pulled it up in such a way that the two men were facing each other.

"Ollie, do you know why you are here?" The Sheriff's voice sounded all echoey to Ollie.

"I believe I do," said Ollie, choking back a tear. Word of the Pennworthys' demise had sped around the small town and county like wildfire. Ollie's mom was telling him all about what she had heard as the patrol car was pulling into the driveway of the small Bramlett home.

"Ollie, do have any idea who might have done such a thing?"

"It's usually the butler," Ollie answered, thinking about Agatha Christie novels from childhood readings past.

"Pennworthys' didn't have no butler, Ollie," answered Sprinkles sarcastically. "Where were you last night and early this morning?"

"I was home with mom last night, Sheriff, and this morning I was picking some banjer. And then I was fixing to head on down to the farm for work," Ollie's sing-song cadence trailed at the end there, and it didn't go unnoticed.

"But you did NOT go to work this morning did you, Bramlett!" shouted the Sheriff.

"Sheriff, I ain't never had a special time I had to be at work. You could ask Mister Penn… umm sorry. It's just I always knew what had to be done down there, and he never cared when I did it, AS LONG AS IT GETS DONE!"

"When was the last time you were down there, Ollie?" asked Sprinkles.

"Yesterday? Day before for a little while," his voice trailed off a bit.

"Ollie... who might have done this?"

"Sheriff, sir, I really don't know. I mean old man Pennworthy was a great guy, and he always looked after me. I worked there just three days a week, but he paid me enough that between me and what momma makes at school and working part time at the hospital, we are doing just fine. Sometimes Mister Pennworthy would get his mandolin out, and we would sit on the porch and pick. We would even sing a little, and sometimes he would share stories about Mrs. Pennworthy. That Eric though was a real butthole but Mister Pennworthy was more like a hero to me... a hero... like a father..."

"Eric could just suck it no matter where he is now," he thought. The Sheriff opened the door to the gray room and told Ollie to go on home and stay there!

THREE

Sheriff Sprinkles studied the forensics report and was as dumfounded as ever. Both deaths were the result of absolutely nothing. Time of death was around 10 hours before Sprinkles found the bodies. The Monroe County coroner could only ascertain that both men died of respiratory failure and appeared to have somewhat suffocated to death, but tox screens showed no noticeable abnormalities. To read this report, Oscar and Eric and Ollie should be working right now and getting those pastures ready for next Spring, because there was no reason that they should be dead, but they WERE dead. A father and his jerk of a son just walked out to the barn the evening before and just died, together, at the same time and of the same symptoms?

"Sounds like murder to me," thought Sprinkles, *"but who and why and how?"*

The Sheriff called the coroner and asked, "What was in their stomachs?"

"Looked like some Kentucky Fried Chicken, mashed potatoes, sweet tea, and what appeared to be several Christmas Cookies," the coroner responded.

"Christmas Cookies?" Sprinkles hung up the phone and thought of Ollie Bramlett. He really didn't think that Bramlett could be responsible. There was no motive at all unless Ollie just went nuts? Nah… Sprinkles sat in his tiny office in his comfy chair with his feet up on the desk and allowed his mind to drift off into total police mode. Things just did not add up. He still believed that Bramlett held the key to solving this mystery.

Just then, Deputy Marie Wilson walked in and brought the very unexpected news that there were two FBI agents out in the foyer waiting to see him!

FOUR

The two men looked straight out of a Hollywood casting call for guys that looked like FBI agents. Sprinkles thought, *"Why do FBI guys always look like FBI guys?"* The thought almost made him laugh, but he was not in a laughing mood of late and wasn't sure when he may ever be again. Besides, FBI in T'Ville?

The two men were very cordial. "Hello, Sheriff. I am special agent Cookie Gilchrist, and this is special agent Marc Dougherty. Everyone shook hands, and the two men then took a seat in the small conference room that was adjacent to the Sheriff's office.

"Are you men here about the Pennworthy deaths?" asked Sprinkles hesitantly. He didn't want to use the words murder until he heard from the agents as to just why the FBI was interested.

"Sheriff," answered Gilchrist, "We have been investigating Eric Pennworthy for well over a year now. It would seem that he had communication with a drug cartel working out of Memphis and Nashville."

Well now, THAT certainly came out of left field. Sprinkles didn't know what to make of this revelation. "So, um, what? Didn't see that coming... what do you think Eric was into and did this involve his father?" asked the Sheriff.

"We have no evidence that the old man had any idea about the son's ambition to sell and distribute opioids all over southern Kentucky with cartel backing," answered agent Dougherty. "We were going to arrest Eric just after Christmas after he provided just a little more rope to hang himself with. We have surveillance video and taped conversations of Eric. The cartel has even visited the Pennworthy farm on several occasions, and we believe big plans were being made and Eric was included in all of them."

"Well, it's not like we don't have a lot of drug problems around here already, agents," answered Sprinkles. "Meth labs back in the hills, Oxycontin coming in by the truckload. God knows we don't need any more of that kind of crap. Do you think the cartel murdered Eric and Oscar Pennworthy? I mean, Eric was a real jerk and maybe he ticked them off?"

"We just don't know, Sheriff, but we'd like for you to keep us in the loop if you would. We really need to bust these cartel guys if possible, and Eric was our big lead. We will happily share any info from our end as well."

Just like that, special agents Gilchrist and Dougherty were gone, leaving Sheriff Sprinkles more bewildered than ever.

FIVE

Alejandro Francesca Cortez was the Tennessee point man for the Juarez drug cartels, whose tentacles spread farther and wider across the US of A than anyone might have dared to imagine. Dealing in drugs and death for huge amounts of money was the Juarez style, and God help those that got in the way or tried to thwart them by throwing a wrench into their plans! A wrench was indeed thrown at the cartel when the news of Eric Pennworthy's strange demise reached Alejandro. The Juarez cartel really wanted that Pennworthy farm, and nothing was going to stop them from getting it!

The farm was just north of the Tennessee state line about a dozen miles or so and would have made a perfect front as well as a storage facility and passing off point for running drugs from Nashville on up to Louisville, Kentucky. One thousand pristine acres of supreme land, including twelve pastures and four tobacco barns, and hardly anyone ever went down there. In some ways, the Pennworthy place might as well have been on Mars! Alejandro also figured that pot would be legalized in Kentucky way before Tennessee, and that would have made for a nice legal and lucrative operation as well, which would have been a perfect front for the cartel.

Alejandro made tons of promises to young Eric and had been grooming him for over a year now to act as point man for the entire operation. Eric Pennworthy was promised drugs, women, and more money than he could ever make growing hemp. The only obstacle was the old man Oscar, but Alejandro even had a plan to work that out eventually. But now that was a moot point. The old man and his son were both dead, and it's all getting harder to process by the minute, but Alejandro was a patient man and so were his associates. They would figure out a way to get that farm when the dust settled, and some of that dust was about to settle...

SIX

The honorable Judge Boyce Burrows had called Ollie Bramlett and his mother Fran as well as several other friends and acquaintances to the reading of the Oscar Pennworthy's last will and testament around a week or so before Christmas. There were no other living relatives, so the Judge was anxious to get on with the reading. He had known Oscar for many years and acted as his legal attorney and would be executor several years before he was elected to the office of Monroe County Judge. Also in attendance was Sheriff Ray Sprinkles and special agents Gilchrist and Dougherty of the Federal Bureau of Investigation. All three men had spent a few moments in Judge Pennington's chambers about thirty minutes before the proceeding to let the Judge know that they would be there in an official capacity to listen and to observe, just in case there were any clues that might be revealed in the reading. Sprinkles was more interested in what he now considered to be a double murder case, and the agents were smelling around for anything that might incriminate Eric and reveal his relationship to the Juarez cartel drug-running operation.

Everyone stood as His Honor entered the small anti-room that was adjacent to the Monroe County courthouse. Judge Burrows took a seat and everyone sat down almost humorously at the same time, but other than that there was not very much in the proceeding to laugh about.

"Thanks, everyone, for being here. We are all saddened by the loss of Oscar and Eric. I am honored to share the final wishes of one Oscar Pennworthy, and, as executor, I plan to see that his wishes are honored and respected under Kentucky law. This will be short and sweet. Oscar has requested that his remains be interred at the Fountain Run Baptist church cemetery beside his late wife, Hattie Pennworthy, and a small insurance policy of ten thousand dollars will be cashed in to cover funeral costs. If there is any money left over that amount will be donated to the American Cancer Society in the name of Hattie Pennworthy. Oscar has bequeathed that all of his possessions, including the house, the land, the acreage, his truck, his savings, and all of his farm equipment including tractors, tools, and implements be left to son Eric and one Oliver Bramlett. As Eric Pennworthy is also deceased and his having left no instruction, it would seem that Ollie Bramlett will inherit all of the above."

Ollie seemed dumbfounded. He could not even find his breath. He thought he might faint dead away with the news that he now owned an entire farm and all that went with it.

"Mister Pennworthy really DID love me," he spoke out loud as his emotions got the best of him. He even started to cry but what caught the eye of Sheriff Raymond Sprinkles was the stupid and knowing smile spread across the face of Ollie's mother Fran. The Sheriff was not sure why this bothered him, but the hair on the back of his neck was tingling and that had never let him down before.

Judge Boyce Burrows closed the meeting with a word of prayer and asked Ollie to follow him to chambers to read over and sign all of the documents that the Judge had prepared for him.

The FBI agents learned nothing new at the reading, except for what they knew already and that was that nobody in this county cared anything about Eric Pennworthy. One thing they also knew for certain was that they must alert Ollie Bramlett to the Juarez cartel and their desire to claw their way into the state, possible using the now Bramlett farm as an entry point. However, they still didn't have quite enough evidence to make a case without Eric, but they would keep on observing for sure.

The Sheriff caught up with them before they entered their very descript, black Ford Expedition SUV. "Agents, I need a favor." He called out as Gilchrist and Dougherty turned to look back his way.

Sprinkles continued, "Beings your case and mine are sort of connected, could you have your people at Quantico or wherever go over the autopsy and toxicology reports for me? There seems to be a piece missing in this puzzle, and your people are the best there is. So can you help me?"

"We would be happy to help, Sheriff," answered agent Cookie Gilchrist, and that little conversation was about to set off a completely new chain of events in Monroe County.

SEVEN

The Federal Bureau of Investigation's Toxicology and Chemical Labs report appeared on Sheriff Sprinkle's desk just two days after the reading of the Pennworthy Will. The red flag noted in the report was important enough to have had it delivered in person by a government courier. And as the Sheriff began to read it, he realized just why his neck hairs had bristled at the reading. A drug known as Suxamethonium Chloride or in short Succinycholine or even shorter Suxxi was discovered in both bodies The chemical is literally undetected in the system unless a very high degree of professional toxicologist knows just how to look for it. The human body breaks the chemical down very quickly, but it can still leave a clue or a byproduct that can be detected by the trained eye. Suxxi is actually used in medicine as a part of the general anesthesia process. And in professional hands and in a controlled environment, it is quite useful. But used as a poison in the wrong hands, a slow paralysis ensues, and the respiratory organs can just shut down and lead to death by asphyxiation. And there was a fair amount of Suxxi found by the FBI in what was left of the lungs of Oscar and Eric Pennworthy.

The Sheriff swung his feet off the desk, donned his hat, walked outside the municipal building to his patrol car, and drove straight to the Monroe County Medical Center. An hour or so later, he and a deputy arrested Fran Bramlett for the murder of Oscar Pennworthy and his son Eric.

EIGHT

Ollie's mother found herself in the same small gray interrogation room that her son had been in a week or so earlier. Yes, she had known that Oscar would leave the farm to her son and Eric, and yes, she had made the cookies for the Pennworthy's as she was always baking something for them and taking stuff down there. Truth be known she had a crush on Oscar. Sheriff Sprinkles had evidence from the Medical Center Hospital that there was indeed a small vial of Suxxi missing from the office of the anesthesiology department. The staff there had told him that Fran pretty much had the run of the place when she was there and could have easily made off with it. The FBI got involved to a small extent because of their ongoing investigation of Eric and the Juarez Cartel, so they took Fran's laptop. After going through it, they found that Fran had Googled info on poisons and Suxamethonium Chloride in particular, so it seemed that Fran's goose was pretty well cooked. She had poisoned the Pennworthys so that her son would inherit the entire place and that seemed like a rock-solid motive.

Her trial was quick and succinct. Her appointed counsel could not make a good defense case for her no matter how hard he tried. A jury found Fran Bramlett guilty of murder in the second degree, and Judge Boyce Burrows sentenced her to thirty years in the Kentucky State Penitentiary in Eddyville, Kentucky. Fran never said much on the stand to the District Attorney or anyone else for that matter. The evidence seemed to be against her, and she seemed to accept her fate willingly. She was a simple and stoic Kentucky woman, and the only thing that seemed to matter to her right now was that her son would be ok.

The Sheriff thought it a bit strange that Ollie Bramlett just vanished during the proceedings and never even showed up for the sentencing.

Sheriff Sprinkle went to visit Ollie just before New Year's Day and found him moving all of his stuff from his quaint little house that he had shared with Fran to his new home... now known as The Bramlett Farm.

"I just wanted to occupy my mind, Sheriff," said Ollie. "I remembered that small box of cookies and wondered what had happened to them. Good thing I didn't eat one. I guess mom got her wish with me now owning the Pennworthy farm, but I sure hate how it all went down."

With that, Ollie began to weep, and Sprinkle put his arm around the young man.

"I am sorry, Ollie, but I wish you well. If you need me, just call... Happy New Year!"

Sprinkle drove back to the office where reporters from the Tompkinsville News were waiting to get the entire scoop on the Pennworthy Murders.

NINE

It was a bright New Year in Monroe County. The weather was unusually mild, and Oliver Bramlett found himself sitting on his new front porch picking banjo as he stared out on to exactly one thousand acres of pristine farmland that would be bristling with activity come Spring. It seemed that Kentucky was about to legalize Cannabis as Oscar always thought they would. Oscar and his obnoxious son were long gone, and now it was Ollie who would be planting and hiring and building a very lucrative business. Pennworthy had also left a decent amount of savings to Ollie as well as the farm, and he figured he would reinvest that money into some newer state-of-the-art tractors and implements. *"Who is a weirdo now, Eric,"* he thought.

His thoughts were interrupted by the big black SUV that was making its way down the driveway towards the farmhouse.

"Well, this is entirely expected," thought Ollie. He had known well and good what Eric was up to, and he figured the Juarez cartel would show up sooner than later.

Alejandro Francesca Cortez got out of the SUV and much to Ollie's surprise, the man with him was one Manuel Vargas Juarez himself. Ollie kept picking as the men approached the front porch and took a seat. Ollie put the banjo back in the case.

After introductions, Juarez himself spoke. "Mister Bramlett, we have an offer."

"That I can NOT refuse?" answered Ollie with a smile as he pondered the Mario Puzo novel, The Godfather. He had never seen the movie, but he had read...

"We can provide cheap labor, utilize the farm for our own purpose, and pay you more money than you can possibly imagine if you will work with us," said Alejandro.

"Same offer as you made Eric Pennworthy?" asked Ollie.

"More perks for you, Bramlett, as real pot growing has become part of your future. And if you do as you are told and keep your mouth shut about our involvement here, you will live a long and fruitful life," answered Juarez.

"OK, DEAL... let's celebrate," said Ollie.

Ollie went to his car and opened the trunk. Underneath the carpeting, there was a small compartment from which he carefully retrieved a small box of Christmas Cookies. After he had added the SUXXI to his mother's recipe, he had brought this very same box to work one day and shared it with Oscar Pennworthy and his son. That worked out quite well now didn't it. It was easy to score the Suxxi at that podunk hospital, and it was Ollie who used his mother's laptop to research the drug. Fran had no idea he even knew how to use it. Ollie opened the box and offered a few cookies to the men who were still sitting on his front porch like they already owned the place. Alejandro and Manuel helped themselves to the cookies, shook hands with Ollie, and drove on up the driveway and away from the farm, promising to stay in close touch.

TEN

The headline in the Tompkinsville News read "SPRINKLES solves CHRISTMAS COOKIE caper"

A very innocent Fran Bramlett was now baking cookies... in the Kentucky State Penn.

Oliver and Eric Pennworthy were rotting in the ground.

Special Agents Cookie Gilchrist and Marc Dougherty found the charred bodies of Alejandro Francesca Cortez and Manuel Vargas Juarez in what was left of a Cadillac Escalade that had crashed on Interstate 65 south, just twenty miles outside of Nashville, Tennessee. Witnesses reported that the car never slowed. It just drove off the highway and smashed into an abutment at a speed of around seventy miles an hour and exploded on impact.

Oliver Bramlett had become George Bailey from the movie *It's A Wonderful Life*.

"OLLIE… you are the richest man in town," he thought as he picked a little Earl Scruggs banjo from the front porch of his thousand acre cannabis farm.

From Love

Lisa Preston

to Love

For all I could tell, the kid trying to hitch a ride had sixteen to twenty-something years on him. My thirty-four still feels young—I stroke lip gloss on several times a day due to my outdoor job and ought to use more sunblock—yet I can't guess ages with any real skill. In the half mile I had a bead on him, the hitchhiker waved by the only traffic ahead of me, an 18-wheeler, then a sedan. He wasn't likely to see many other cars after I drove Ol' Blue past him and his thumb. The stretch beyond Redmond Hill sees less traffic than a goat path.

Picking up hitchhikers is not my cup of coffee on a good day and today was a bad one. Any month heading into January is a dread for me, has been since I was a fourteen-year-old tussling with my first and worst boy trouble, and this week had been unsettling. Weird stuff kept happening at our little one-bedroom house at the end of Vine Maple Lane.

Yesterday, we were pretty sure our mail had been snooped through 'cause it was in the box way too tidy, all facing the same direction and in a squared-up perfect pile. Our nuttier-than-squirrel-poo mail carrier doesn't ever lay letters that way. She more tosses 'em in piñata-smacking-style.

Kind of creepy to contemplate someone rifling through our mailbox.

Charlie Two barked up a storm after dusk the last couple days. Guy had stepped out last night and thought there was a prowler. He even went so far as to say we should lock our doors. I hadn't known our doors had working locks.

The day before, winter squash—apparently harvested from our garden—had been set on our back porch. We accused each other at first, but both Guy and I were dead sure we didn't pick the last of the butternut. I asked my best friend Melinda, but she said no way did she sneak over and fondle our vegetables.

This morning, a battered wind chime of little copper bells appeared on the old nail where our carport's corner used to hold a broken thermometer. The bells startled me enough that I'd lost my footing, slipped, and ripped open the edge of my right hand against our rough wood porch.

The hand wound was going to make shoeing a horse less than delightful. I'd hollered to ask Guy about the wind chime before I remembered that, number one, he'd left for the diner already, and B, we were still fighting. So, I'd lost my lunch over the porch rail. Now here I was, clamping my teeth on my sore hand and driving badly in a bad mood.

Trying to concentrate, I checked my mirrors and saw the kid standing in the lane watching Ol' Blue leave him behind.

Letting off the diesel's accelerator dropped my speed considerably. The weather was turning to sleet—this part of central Oregon doesn't get too cold too often, but it was clearly making an exception this afternoon— and Ol' Blue's four-wheel drive was out. Getting it fixed was going to cost two thousand dollars, at least. Meanwhile, I'd have to negotiate the Redmond Hill road in two-wheel. The weight of my tools and shoe inventory would have to give my old pickup traction on the ice.

The dark figure in the lane behind me was still there, getting smaller as I motored on.

It *was* Christmastime, after all.

I slam shifted into reverse and backed up hard enough to make the young man jump to the shoulder.

"Look tough," I suggested to Charlie Two, the golden furball snoozing with his head on my thigh, "He might be a serial killer."

The kid pulled open my passenger door and knocked back his black raincoat's hood. Dark wet hair. Quick, nervous, fake smile.

"Dale's Horseshoeing," he said, demonstrating his ability to read my truck doors, which bore nice big decals with my business name and the house phone number. "Is your name Dale?"

"Rainy Dale," I allowed.

Proving he had the manners of a killer, he didn't offer his name. His black rainsuit covered whatever he wore for real clothes. A black backpack was slung on his right shoulder. He shifted the pack to his feet and reached to pat Charlie Two, ruffling my good dog's haunch.

When I'm driving, I use Two as an armrest so the young man's fingertips brushed mine. The effect was a zingy charge like nothing I'd ever felt. Tingly. Hot and cold. Strange and familiar.

I eased my hand away from his and put both palms on the wheel.

The hitchhiker squared his back against the truck door facing me, seatbelt still unfastened.

Being belted-in myself, I now felt like a prey animal in a loose lion's cage. "Where you trying to go? There's a good diner in town. I'm heading down the road a ways to shoe a couple horses."

"So you're not driving far?" His smile widened. "You're local?"

I reconsidered how he'd turned down the semi-truck's offer of a ride and didn't like the feeling that he was asking me something he already knew the answer to.

Instincts are a good thing. If a girl even thinks she's in a bad situation, she needs to pay attention and fix it.

Cranking the wheel hard, I made a U-turn and called my Redmond Hill clients.

"It's Rainy. You'd asked me to shoe Shiloh and that little chestnut you still need to name sometime before the New Year. I was on my way, but I'm turning around."

My cell phone was on speaker because otherwise it's too hard to hear in a diesel truck. "Rainy? I didn't catch all that. You still on to shoe my horses in the next week or so? Couldn't quite understand. You're breaking up."

"Yeah, I'm about to go through that dead spot on the way back to town."

"Losing you, girl, but I gather you're not coming out today. Don't blame you. It's turning to hail over here. Stay off that hill." The call ended with a beep.

This made my hitchhiker chuckle and suddenly I saw that part of myself that Melinda—

that's Deputy Kellan if you're not her best friend—calls the people who manufacture work for the po-lice without being themselves of the criminal persuasion.

I had just allowed a stranger into my truck then created a situation where the person whose house I'd been headed to no longer expected me to show up.

Two is a good young dog, but protection is not one of his services. He excels at lap warming, naps, snacks, and the occasional spot of herding strays. Now he licked the hand of the hitchhiker, who'd quit laughing and pointed to my scraped-up right hand on the wheel.

"What happened to your paw?"

"Slipped and fell."

"Hmm. That's too bad." He seemed genuinely sympathetic then brightened up like a whackadoodle on happy drugs. Gifting me with a sketchy miniature smile, he said, "Still, it's not a . . . you know, a primal wound."

The skin-prickling was unmistakable now as the young fellow eyed me.

I said, "How about I drop you in town right quick?"

He started to respond, stopped himself, half-started again and pursed his lips.

I didn't like it. What butters my toast is predictability. This situation looked set to go haywire at warp speed.

Ol' Blue rumbled while I shoved my boot into the accelerator, failing to attract the wanted attention of any deputy.

Hitchhiker Boy mumbled on about how he'd been making his way across the west. Texas, New Mexico, Arizona, Nevada, California, then north. Blah blah.

Ten years back, I'd followed a similar jagged path, tracking down my childhood horse 'til I finally found him up here in Cowdry, Oregon. Buying him back had been my mission. That first night, I'd met Guy, and one thing led to another. Got enough clientele as a horseshoer to make it in this town. Over many months, Guy and I grew close, more than close.

One dusk, literally at the end of my rope, I'd shared my shame and told Guy everything.

Right away, my sweetheart had said I'd done a brave thing, a good thing. But every year ends with me remembering what signing my name to that paperwork felt like.

Stuck in my thoughts, I didn't take in much as the hitchhiker blabbed about his travels. We made the miles. Not one word escaped my mouth until I pulled in at the new 24-Fuel on the southeast end of town.

"You said there was a good diner in town. Why don't you take me there?"

"They've got food inside this 24-Fuel." The grease from the convenience store's fry-all vat where they crisp up frozen corn dogs, chicken fingers, and taquitos wafted over to mix with the stink of spilled diesel dregs and gasoline.

No way was I going to take him to the one restaurant in town that felt like an extension of our living room.

He pointed at my blue-checked flannel sleeve. "You wore that same shirt yesterday."

That's when I knew I was sitting next to the prowler from last night and maybe the night before.

He'd watched our house, watched me, touched our things, done it for days.

And this afternoon, he let the other vehicles pass while he waited to thumb a ride in Ol' Blue.

We sat there eyeing each other over Two's warm body, me wishing the stranger would get out of my truck right that second, him thinking whatever scary plan he'd concocted.

Must have been the cop car pulling into the parking lot that made him shoulder his pack and dismount Ol' Blue, but he eyeballed me all the way as he closed the door with both hands, shifting his jaw before he turned to walk off at the pace of a three-legged spider.

Christmas Cookies Mysteries

He glanced back again before going into the 24-Fuel's store.

Then he watched me from behind the glass door.

Bang. Melinda's fist thumping Ol' Blue's side made me jump. She wrenched open the passenger door that had been closed too carefully. She wore jeans, sneakers, and a roomy flannel shirt over her tank top.

Off duty.

Mel's ponytail is a tad darker brown than mine. We dress almost the same, though her flannel shirts stay unbuttoned to conceal the pistol on her hip while leaving her with ready access.

She banged on Ol' Blue again. "What's up?"

"Not me." I buried my hand in Two's fur so she couldn't see me shaking.

"You and Guy still fighting?"

Direct, my friend Melinda is.

"Little bit," I allowed.

She shifted her gaze. "How ya doing, Eye-Eye?"

She used to call Charlie Two *Junior* and then *The Second.* Her latest nickname for him seems to be trying to use the Roman numerals in this awkward way. He forgives her everything, wags and licks.

"You're quiet," she said.

I nodded.

She doesn't know why I hate January—its approach, its past. And the strange hitchhiker? Should I say anything to the law about him? He was history, right?

Melinda pointed a finger down the road. "I could use a double burger. Let's go over to the Cascade and let Guy feed us."

Guy knows of course. We've been together nine years, married eight. I told him that one time. Isn't once enough?

I never thought this thing would stay so hard for me.

"Rainy? Come on. The baby needs some chili fries."

It's not that I told Mel I'm preggers. She guessed. But now Guy knows that she knows, and he sees this as all the more reason why he should get to tell the world that we're going to have us a baby come Memorial Day or early June.

I nodded again. "See you there."

The Cascade Kitchen was hopping. You'd think people would go home for the holidays, but Guy has a way of making the diner the happening place.

He is fit to be tied that I don't want to tell people. Right now, I'm still not showing but

how a pregnant woman shoes a horse is a question I'll be addressing through springtime.

Guy wants to tell everyone in Cowdry. He wants to climb trees and shout the news from the tallest big leaf maple or Western red cedar he can find.

He wants to tell his folks and mine, back in Texas and California, and he wants to have a party.

We don't know if this life growing inside me is a son or a daughter.

I know I'm eating my own heart out.

Melinda hadn't shown up yet. I started to head for the last twirly stool at the counter, but the big group in the corner booth wouldn't have it.

"Rainy," Hollis and Donna Nunn called together. "Come join us."

Donna and Hollis are like our substitute parents since Guy and I live so far from our own. They were sitting with the Delmonts and with

Manny who works as their general hand and a buddy of Manny's. The waitress, Sissy, had both arms loaded when she stopped at their double table. Meat and three, burgers, an extra platter of cheese fries, salads, and that sampler of startling appetizer goodies Guy's added recently. The scents of perfectly seasoned sticks—zucchini, mozzarella, carrots, purple-green onions, and pork skewers— called to all.

Beyond the kitchen's swinging doors, Guy swiveled in his sneakers to eye me. He's a tall one so it wasn't hard to see his expression, that same cranky and wistful look he'd left the house with this morning.

Can't fight in front of other people so sitting with our friends was not the worst idea ever.

Hollis rose and pulled out a chair near Donna. The door jingled and he glanced in that direction. I twisted while sinking down, wondering who had caught Hollis's eye.

Melinda strolled in and snagged a chair from a four-place table where a couple of high school kids lingered over bottomless coffees. She hauled her selected furniture to a sitting place at the edge of our group with her back against the wall.

Wasn't long after the howdys that food-sharing commenced then the door jangled again. Mel took in the new arrivals with a smile and then a Wood Plank Expression. I twisted in my chair again.

It was her honey Biff, followed by the hitchhiker.

My breath caught. I grabbed napkins and wiped fresh sticky sweat off my forehead.

Do it.

"Mel." I slid my chair hard toward hers. She leaned in, allowing me to speak softly into her face. "That fellow who just came in here . . ." I winced, kept my eyes closed, and got the ickiness out. "I think he's kind of been stalking me. Maybe been to our house, gone through our mail. Said some mighty weird things when I gave him a ride to the gas station."

Like only a great friend would, Deputy Kellen saved me. She gave Biff her chair then pulled out her badge and ID that showed the County is her employer and headed for the young man behind us.

"Hey, buddy, you got some ID?"

While they went back and forth a bit on that, I tuned out, needing to listen to something less confrontational. Guy loads up the jukebox with Christmas albums aplenty this time of year. Some of those tunes are joyful, but let's be honest, some of 'em are tearjerkers. A man with a hearth-warm voice was going on now about what made angels sing.

A hand clutched my shoulder, and I gasped over my ice water.

The hand's wedding ring matched mine.

"You're jumpy," Guy said.

"Sorry, it's just nervous—" I cut myself off to eavesdrop.

Melinda's voice filtered from farther away, like she was walking toward the exit. "Okay then, buddy, can I get your date of birth?"

I swiveled in my seat again.

The kid's hand was on the diner door, the one that read: *push*.

"January first, two-thousand." Then he pushed and walked out.

Melinda let him go. I figure she didn't have enough information to allow for putting hands on him.

I did. And I had every reason to choke, which I also did.

Spluttering, I shoved past Guy then Melinda, about knocking the waitress over in my run for the door.

Outside, nothing.

A single set of footprints in the sleet.

It was almost snowing now.

Praise the Lord, because he'd made tracks, that boy. Stepping into the street and squinting hard, I saw a figure disappearing down the block.

Reckon he'd actually run from the diner.

What was that? Anger? Shame?

Hate?

I pelted hard to catch him, started yelling soon as I got in yelling range.

"Stop!"

He kept going.

"Hey! Hold up there."

He didn't turn back.

"Wait, please!"

He stopped, kept his back to me, stayed silent.

"I know who you are!"

He turned halfway around, still wordless.

"You know who I am, don't you?"

His head lifted, and he took a hesitant step backwards like a green horse spooking in the wind.

Tears trickled across my cheekbones, and my voice caught as I explained. "There was a time a few years back when a man tried to kill me and—"

He cut a hand across the space between us to interrupt. "Who?"

I swung my sore hand in the same motion. "That's not the point. What I wanted you to know is that as I was blacking out, the only thing I thought about was you. All I wanted in the world was to know that you were okay."

His eyebrows hiked up.

Words poured out my mouth. "I'm so sorry. I'm more sorry than I can say. I always was. If you knew how old I was then, if you could . . . Honestly, what I did, I did *for* you, not *to* you."

He let me touch his shoulder, and I could have bawled.

Instead, I said, "I did it for love."

I wished I was touching his bare skin, not his wet raincoat. I recollected the distant tingly feeling echoed from our time in the truck and from twenty years ago.

At last, he spoke. "My mother and father—"

Those first two words slayed me, made me wail out loud which stopped whatever he was going to say.

Asking was beyond every kind of hard, but I tried again with all my will. "They're good people?"

He nodded. "They're the best.

My knees were weak, but I knew this was relief.

They're the best.

Thank you, thank you. Lord, thank you.

"Do they know where you are?"

He nodded again. "I have their blessing."

"Please come back inside the diner with me. Can we sit together or with my friends? They're like family. Can't we eat together? The cook is my husband, Guy. Please, come meet him and let me get you some good food. We can visit, or just sit. But please come back inside with me, okay?"

He nodded, barely.

Guy and Melinda were on their toes outside the diner's door staring as I dragged the boy toward my two besties. I bulled right past them and made for the big group occupying the pushed-together tables in the back.

On my heels, Guy murmured in my ear, his breath hot and familiar. "Rainy, who is he?"

I whispered the crushing truth so softly that it could have stayed a secret, like I didn't fully own the words.

Like I'd cheated.

But Guy heard me. He dropped to a free chair beside me like he'd been knee-capped.

"I'd like to introduce you to these people," I told the boy in my clutches. "What's your name?"

He looked me square in the eye. "Fletch. Fletcher Dale Bishop." Then he moved to take a place next to Hollis Nunn when Donna pointed to an empty chair.

Hollis rose, gave his name, shook hands, and it went like that all around the table, folks introducing themselves to Fletch out of mere goodwill. Gave me the minute I needed to look around the room, at all my friends, my husband, my best girlfriend, and then my boy.

I spoke the truth clearly, made sure I was heard. "Fletch is my son. I gave him up the day he was born."

An announcement like that causes quite a lot of, "Well, I'll be," and "My word," and "Goodness sakes."

During that ruckus, I hissed in Guy's ear. "They didn't know my name. It was a closed adoption."

"I know," he whispered back, "You've told me."

"So how could they have put part of my name in his? What is that?"

Guy took both my hands in his and kissed me. "That's grace."

I didn't mean to cry, and I didn't make a sound, but the tears flowed out both corners of my eyes.

And then my son whispered in my other ear. I felt his warmth, marveled in it, then the words. "My parents always said the same thing you told me outside. They said it showed pure love."

Guy had said something similar, that night on the mountain when I broke down and told him the truth about when I was young and scared and heartbroken.

Guy. My Guy. I'd been making him miserable because I was tied in knots.

I dared to slip a few fingers of my right hand into Fletch's palm. *Tingle.* Sometime soon, perhaps he'd tell me how he found me. I'd sure listen to anything he wanted to say, but right now this fragile hope for a future that included Fletch in our lives was kindling.

Guy was still holding my left hand. I squeezed him and leaned in. "You can tell everyone."

His grin stretched as big as it gets. He banged a spoon on a half-full water glass, teased them, got all the mileage out of his big announcement. But my brain went *hummmm,* and I heard nothing more than white noise while he spoke.

Because now what would Fletch think?

That I was replacing him?

Our big noisy group shrieked and shouted congratulations. Biff punched Guy's shoulder. Hollis shook his hand.

"Rainy," Donna said when the din quieted down, "you're going to be a good momma."

Guy and the others thundered agreement at this prediction, but Fletch pulled his hand from mine, shook his head, and raised a finger to correct her.

Every kind of shame and horror and regret trudged through my heart.

The table got deathly still as Guy and this family of friends I've created over the last near decade in this little town quieted uncomfortably, their gazes casting about to each other, me, the tabletop, the floor, and then to the son I'd given up as a newborn twenty-one years back.

"She . . ." Fletch paused to clear his throat, "*is* a good mom."

The smiles, hugs, and pure love that flowed through the room were magical.

Best Christmas of my life."

Characters in "From Love to Love" are from Lisa Preston's horseshoer mystery series that begins with *The Clincher*

Away in

Beth Pugh

a Manger

Some men worry about waist size, preferring six-pack abs over twin-pack cream horns, even on the Saturday before Christmas. Me, not so much, but Wyatt, the newest mall officer under my command and my replacement for the day, seemingly fell into that category. He turned down my breakfast offer with a polite smile but continued to glare at the offensive pastry. Ignoring his obvious disappointment, I held back a chuckle and started on seconds.

Just as I chugged the last of my coffee, screams erupted from the live nativity adjacent to the food court. Jerking my head toward the cardboard stable, I choked down the last bite of cream horn, staggered upright, and started running. As soon as I got to the nativity, a rambling, teenage Mary was by my side.

"I just turned around for a minute. When I came back to the manger, my brother was gone!" Mary swiped her palms down the make-shift robe as she struggled through tears.

Gone. With that one word, my day transformed from common to criminal. I instructed Wyatt to call 911, making sure he knew to cite a possible kidnapping. He took a few steps away from the commotion, phone to his ear. Then, I asked Mary to start over.

She gestured toward her partner—a pimple-faced boy with shaggy hair—and pulled in a ragged breath. "I didn't know Joseph was gone on a bathroom break."

At his name, Joseph, approaching, stopped mid-stride and stiffened, straight as the walking stick he leaned on. "Can you drop the acting bit and call me by my name?"

Mary crossed her arms and frowned at him. "Sorry, *Ethan*. Why didn't you tell me you were leaving?"

"I did tell you.! You were too busy playing with your phone to hear me." Ethan gestured to the cell in her hand. "You and that fake Instagram.! It's so stupid."

Mary's jaw dropped, but she quickly recovered, stomping toward him. "No, what's stupid is you leaving me by myself. Now Jesus—C-Carter—is g-g-gone!"

Holding back an eye roll, I placed myself between Mary and Ethan. *Always the hard way.* I counted to three as I caught her softly by the shoulders, breaking the rule of not touching civilians for Ethan's protection. Mary seemed a bit unhinged and, with her fists clenched, a rogue right hook wouldn't have surprised me.

"It doesn't matter how it happened," I said, bending my knees to get on her level. "I need you to focus. The window to find your brother is tight, so let's focus on him, okay?"

"Okay." As Mary eyed the empty hay, her shoulders sagged as tears started anew. "Please, find my brother. I c-can't lose him."

Mary's plea pierced me like a stake through the chest. Not the pitch or tone or even the volume, but the palpable fear tinting her voice. I bit back a sigh. Though my shift was done, it looked as though my work was just beginning.

"You won't." I tightened my grip on her shoulders. "I've been head of security here for five years and I haven't lost a child yet. I don't intend to start today."

Even from a few feet away, Wyatt raised an eyebrow at my spiel. *Eavesdropper.* I'd just spent the last half hour telling him how easy security at Quarter Mall was compared to the big cities. If it wasn't for visitors from the neighboring, touristy towns during summer and holidays, the mall would have shut down when the coal mines did. Normal shopping days were lazy at best, hectic at worst, but never unmanageable… and rarely criminal. I'd made that point loud and clear this morning, which explained Wyatt's baffled expression. He was probably wondering where my kidnapping experience had come from, especially after I'd confessed that the occasional pickpocket was as crazy as life got.

Since there was no time to explain, I simply shrugged. When Carter was back where he belonged, I'd come clean about my time with the NYPD, the job I'd conveniently kept to myself while the two of us Wyatt and I chatted. That particular position was irrelevant in Quarter, Tennessee. With a 1,569 residential population and leave-your-door-unlocked mentality, crime fighters needn't worry.

Placing a hand on my hip, I stared at the frazzled Mary. "Is your mom here?"

"In the mall, yes." Mary nodded vigorously, nearly knocking the head covering down over her face. She pushed the cloth back and blew at her bangs. "But I'm babysitting while she and Nan do some last-minute shopping."

"Call her."

"I can't. She doesn't have her phone." Another swipe of her palms. "Mom says the ringing bothers Nan or something, so she leaves it in the car. She's coming over at ten when the nativity actually starts." Shaking slightly, Mary pointed behind the manger. "There's a doll over there in my bag. Carter wasn't *really* Jesus."

"I see. What's your mother's name?"

"Teresa Matney," Mary said.

"Ok." Whipping out my phone, I texted the name to guest services with instructions to page her every two minutes. "We'll call for her over the speakers. Maybe we'll get lucky. What about your grand-mother's name?"

"Patty Williamson, but Nan's too wrapped up in her own little world to pay attention to something like that. Don't bother."

"We'll still give it a shot." After sending the grandmother's name too, I squeezed Mary's shoulders once before releasing her, swinging my gaze from her red-rimmed eyes to Wyatt as he approached. "You make the call?"

"Yes, sir," Wyatt answered, circling around the stable area. "Cops are on their way."

"Good." Cupping Mary's elbow, I guided her to a hay bale and urged her to sit. "Listen, Mar—"

"Cindy."

Before I could stop myself, I stuck my hand out to her. "My name's Gordon Duke." As she shook, I went on. "Like I said earlier, I'm head of security at the mall and I'm going to do everything in my power to bring your brother back to you, safe and sound. But you're going to have to help me, Cindy. I need you to stay here with Wyatt and tell the police everything you can remember about Carter. What he's wearing, weight, hair color, whatever you can think of."

"O-okay." She started to bob her head in agreement but stopped short. "Wait, the Insta. I posted a picture of Carter this morning. He'd spit up all over his coat, so I took it off. With his paci and dimples, it was the perfect shot, no filter needed…not that I use them." Her cheeks pinkened as she flipped her phone around. "Here."

After memorizing what I could of the baby—mohawk hair, fair complexion, purplish birthmark along the jawline, candy cane-colored pajamas—I motioned for Ethan to join us. When he was close enough to make eye contact, I straightened to my full height. "You're going to stay here, too, son. I need you to help keep Cindy calm and fill in the gaps where you can. Did you see anything suspicious? Anyone watching you or a shopper that might have talked to you while you were setting up?"

As he sat down beside Cindy, Ethan threw an arm over his pretend wife's shoulders. Without hesitation, she leaned into him.

Smart move. I had to give it to the kid. He had more guts than I did at that age. Better instincts, too. Snapping his head toward me, Ethan's eyes widened. "There was this guy earlier that helped me carry some hay bales. I've never seen him before, so I don't think he's local. He commented on how cute Carter was while I burped him for Cindy."

Now we're getting somewhere. Scratching my jaw, I pressed on. "Do you remember what he looked like?"

Ethan squeezed the back of his neck as he cocked his head to the side. "About my height, but bulkier. Spiky hair, black leather jacket, combat boots. He, uh, wiped his forehead with a bandana just like that."

All eyes turned to the scrap of cloth left in the manger. I snatched it up and tucked it in my front pocket. Not protocol, but it would be safer than leaving it with panicked kids. "Good job. Gives me something to go on besides the photo." Taking a step back, I studied the modern-day versions of the iconic Bethlehem wanderers. Did the real Mary and Joseph wear those same fear-laced faces? *Maybe.* Chances were good they felt the same sort of emotions. Frustration. Worry. Uncertainty. The couples were probably close to the same age, so they likely had a lot in common.

Mary's cell phone dinged.

Then, again, maybe not.

I pointed at the teenagers and tipped my chin toward Wyatt. "If you remember anything else, tell Wyatt. A scar, a brand of cigarette, a logo. No matter how small the detail, let him know. Got it?"

Cindy and Ethan nodded in unison.

I mimicked the motion and headed toward the back of the stable where Wyatt stood. Putting my hands in my pockets, I walked like I was taking a stroll in the park instead of starting a search and rescue. *Keep the kids calm.* I nodded once more, this time to myself. *Keep yourself calm.* After a few measured breaths, my heart rate steadied. Didn't help the quivering in the pit of my stomach as the pastries from earlier attempted to crawl back up. With a hard swallow, I stymied the threat.

I can't believe I'm doing this. Scanning my surroundings, I dug deep to channel my past and the old me that liked being a cop. Catching the bad guys had been everything late-night television made it out to be and more. I loved the rush of the hunt. I craved the thrill of the chase. Until *her.* Erica Clevinger. Three years old with a unicorn backpack and blond pigtails the same color hair as the straw in the manger. Closing my eyes tight, I tried not to think about the way those braids shone against the black trash bags where her body was found, or the stench of blood that rose from the dumpster, or the ripped rainbow tights soiled with moldy scrambled eggs.

Get a grip, Gordon. She's gone.

The perp was gone, too, thanks to me. Six feet under. It'd been self-defense. Deep down, though, the satisfaction of knowing I'd served justice *without* a judge and jury, excited me. But the feeling had quickly faded as the weight of taking a life buried me beneath smothering guilt. I'd still be choking, if not for the forgiveness and freedom of Christ. Washed in

His mercy, the kind that I myself had failed to extend, I vowed never to use a firearm again.

Crossing that line from protector to punisher scared me right out of the badge and the streets of New York. The next week, I quit the squad and started looking for a new home, somewhere that I'd never need to use a gun again unless I was hunting. Quarter, Tennessee, with southern charm, Bible belt morals, and family focus, fit the bill.

Exactly the town I needed.

As I gave Wyatt pointers on keeping the teenagers calm, thoughts of the gun in my holster distracted me. New management had insisted I become certified about a year ago, but until today, I'd ignored the heaviness at my side. Even during training, I knew I would never need the weapon, not when every man and his mama went to Sunday services. That knowledge gave me peace. Carrying the gun didn't bother me. Using it, though? That was another story.

Father, give me strength.

Familiarizing myself with the Glock's placement, I skimmed the handle. The metal felt coolcool metal against chilled my fingertips. Cool Cold and powerful. I shuddered as Wyatt tossed me a walkie. After double-checking the frequency, I relinquished the nativity scene into his capable hands and began walking through the food court. A quick scan of the cafeteria space found mainly empty chairs and clean tables. A few teenage girls sipped on drinks from the coffee place in the corner, but no one else stirred. No strollers, no crouching figures, no black jackets. After giving the court a final sweeping glance, I turned my search further inward.

My thick-soled boots hit heavy on the tile with each step I took. I focused on the rhythmic sound and not the weight settled on my right hip as I surveyed the few people around me. With only a handful of shops open so early, shoppers were scarce. *Thank God.* I headed down the right hallway. It was the wing with the most shops already open. If the kidnapper wanted to hide, it was his best option, not counting the bathrooms.

The lights from Beauty Works shone through the windows and out the propped-open door. Holiday hours made for longer days for the store that was usually closed at this time. I slipped in and grabbed a make-up case off the first shelf I saw. The pink and green plastic screamed nineteen-eighties, but the store stayed quiet as a church mouse. Only a squirt bottle kept silence at bay as the cashier sprayed down the screen with cleaner. I gave the room a quick scan, side to side and front to back. Finding myself and the lone saleswoman to be the store's only occupants, I left and started toward the next shop.

In the two minutes I'd been inside, the hallway had grown gotten busier. More foot traffic meant more civilians. More civilians meant better odds for the kidnapper to stay undetected. *Great. Just great.* I huffed and walked on, past the candle shop and the purse store, both still closed. As I cleared a row of vending machines, a whine, low and muffled, sounded from somewhere to my right, in the direction of guest services and the bathrooms. I breathed deep, in through my nose and out through my mouth, while cutting down the corridor.

Another whine, louder this time. I smoothed my gait, so as not to attract more attention to myself than my uniform already did, and walked casually toward the family bathroom. Wriggling the door handle, I leaned in as much as I could without seeming suspicious.

"Just a second." An annoyed male voice rose over the running faucet.

Muscle memory took over as I positioned myself to the side of the door. From the placement of the hinges, I'd have a clear line of sight when the guy came out. A few seconds later the water turned off. My pulse hitched once before barreling full speed ahead while the fingers at my side stretched closer to the firearm.

"Sorry to keep you waiting, man. It's all yours." Bathroom Boy—smooth-faced as the day he was born—smiled as he cleared the door.

I examined him covertly, keeping my head straight despite the internal shake going on. No leather jacket, no spikey hair, no boots. Instead, a tucked-in dress shirt stretched across the man's tensed right shoulder, where he held the straps to some travel bag, loafers met the hem of his khakis, and a side part any stylist would be proud of cut down his hair. *Not the guy.* Waving off his apology, I placed my hand on the door to give the illusion I was going in. Another whine sounded.

Then, again... Bathroom Boy could have changed his clothes inside, stuffed them in the bag, and laid Carter on top of them. The shoes? Ethan could have been mistaken. Did I think the guy in front of me was capable of such criminal know-how? Not on my life, but anything was possible.

In seconds, I laidhad a hand on his shoulder, directly on top of the bag's straps. "I'm going to need to look in your bag."

Bathroom Boy tilted his head back, averting his gaze to the ceiling momentarily. "I knew this would happen." He blew out a breath and handed me the bag. "I told Celia it was a bad idea, but she just wouldn't listen."

With care, I pulled the zipper back slowly. Before I was even halfway done, though, something wet and cold hit my hand. Two nostrils poked out of the opening and nudged me to continue. Snapping my eyes to Bathroom Boy, I yanked back the zipper. Front paws covered in white curls burst from inside followed by a furry head no bigger than my fist.

"A poodle?"

Bathroom Boy scowled at the animal. "My girlfriend refused to leave Boo at home by himself but insisted we reenact our first date to celebrate our six-month anniversary. I had to sneak him in. You get it, right?"

"Sure." Blinking, I handed the bag back while Boo wagged his tail. "I get it. Don't let anyone else see the dog, ok?"

"You got it. Thanks, man." Bathroom Boy pushed the dog back inside and fiddled with the zipper.

Leaving him to his own devices, I went back to the right wing of the mall, my feet flying faster than before. Time was slipping away. Too much time. A glance at my watch showed a little better than ten minutes had elapsed since I left the stable. I needed to find this guy before he got away, if he hadn't already. Most likely, the cops had the entrances and exits covered by now, but professional criminals understood the system well enough to slip past much better-trained police forces than Quarter's crew who might answer ten robbery calls a year.

Picturing Carter's sweet face front and center on the missing person bulletins hurried my pace, but worrying he might suffer the same fate as Erica shifted my steps a notch higher into a jog. *Not on my watch*. I had no intention of telling another mother her baby's life had been taken too soon. The first time had sent me running for the hills. I didn't want to find out where a second time would take me.

I stayed against the wall as best as I could, weaving between stalled shoppers as I trotted to Tons of Toys. With the Christmas season in full swing, they were the first to extend their hours, and the first to fill up every Saturday. A bell dinged as I crossed the threshold, but the cashier was too busy bagging a light-up caterpillar to notice me. The worker on the floor didn't turn around, either, as he continued to pick up the a Checker set that had been knocked from the shelf.

Studying the room, my gaze landed on the popular story circle in the back. Two short bookshelves stood in front of the rainbow-colored rug where children of all ages sat and listened to the store's newest addition every weekend. Except iIn the month of December., Tthough, the readings were cancelled to make it easier for shoppers to move around. It had been that way since my first year at the mall and even though I expected to see an empty rocking chair, my eyes wandered toward the circle. Instead of an unoccupied glider, though, my stare lighted on a twenty-something man nuzzling an infant into the crook of his neck. His hair was gelled to the heavens.

Adopting my former hand-in-pocket pose, I watched for a moment. The man smoothed the blanket over the baby's back, gently cradling the child's head. His movements displayed familiarity, easiness, practiced care. With nothing more than a rough description to go on, Rocker remained a suspect despite his seeming proficiency with kids. The child threw itself toward the man's right arm and the blanket slipped down. Seeing an opportunity to get closer without giving my mission away, I strolled toward them. I was halfway there to the cover when a petite blond stepped between Rocker and me. She stooped, retrieved the blanket, and placed it back over the child, rubbing the barely-there hair covering the crown.

"Thanks, babe." Rocker whispered as she drew close.

Leaning down, the woman kissed his cheek. "No problem."

The couple's interaction, and the bright pink sleeper the child wore, assured me the trio had nothing to do with Carter's disappearance. I veered to the left and walked behind the cash register. From the vantage point, the entire shop was visible. In addition to the group I'd just witnessed, there were a few more shoppers scattered along the game wall and the block section. None with a baby or a black leather jacket.

Another miss.

I gave my head a hard shake and returned to the hallway, my heart rate spiking as patrons closed in around me. The Christmas crowd was out in full force now. Bodies going both directions passed me as I attempted to give them all once-overs. The futility of the task squeezed my lungs, making my breaths shallow and stilted, but I pressed on. Carter needed me. How long had it been since I was able to say that? Three years? Four? Since New York?

Chewing on the inside of my cheek, I gave up guessing. Sweat dripped down my temple and under my collar as I picked up the pace. I swiped at it with the back of my hand but didn't slow down. I sped up instead, making it worse. A new rivulet rolled over my right brow, catching in my eyelashes. I wiped the moisture away, blinking a few times as I refocused on the seasonal mass on either side of me. As my vision sharpened, a black jacket streaked across my peripherals. The person was too far away to be certain, but from the swatch I saw, it could have been leather.

I sprinted forward, my stomach pitching a fit as I did. *Maybe Wyatt had the right idea.* A swallow sent my breakfast back down to the bottom of my stomach where it belonged as I searched for the coat. *Where are you?*

Moving from one person to the next, I prayed liked my life depended on it. Squinting, I let my gaze linger a moment more before reversing my stare to the starting point. Where a lady's green peacoat had been a few seconds ago, a black leather jacket stood in its place. *Gotcha!* Wrenching my eyes upward, I homed in on the man's hair. The strands were spiked, going every which way, and he walked with an elbow out. The way a mother would with an infant nestled in the bend of her arm.

It was possible he was holding Carter, especially at the almost standstill speed he was going. If I had a stolen baby sleeping in my arms, I'd try hard not to wake him, too. Do a turtle crawl if I had to, which probably would have been faster than Black Jacket's walk. With a deep breath, I worked my way through the shoppers, until I was an arm's length behind the suspect.

Then, I slowed my pace. If I rushed him like a bull the way I wanted to, he'd have no need to keep Carter quiet. He'd bolt and I'd be forced to chase him. Chances of injury for everyone involved, including Carter, skyrocketed, which didn't bode well for reuniting the baby with his family. No, I needed to tread lightly.

So, I did, keeping my sights locked on Black Jacket. If he moved left, I moved left. If he stopped to look at a poster, I stopped to look at a poster. If he sidestepped part of the crowd, I sidestepped part of the crowd. When he ducked into Mountaintop Decorating, I followed with my stare until my feet could catch up. I expected him to pick up the pace once inside the store, but he didn't. He ambled up the center aisle and toward the counter with even slower steps, pausing in front of a vanity to check his reflection. I blinked back my confusion and kept following a few paces behind until he made it to a back door that I knew led to the shop's storage room. The space was full of extra recliners, dining chairs, and lamps. Its side door led to the outside.

Let Black Jacket leave the mall?

Not an option. No way, no how, not when I had the power to stop him and the weight on my hip assured me I did. Praying for strength, I ran towards the storage room, surprising myself with a speed I hadn't reached since my days in the city. *Must be the adrenaline.* My feet hit the backroom tile just as Black Jacket slid between two rows of metal stools.

"Stop!" The yell echoed in my ear as the suspect froze. "Now, turn around and put your hands up."

Eyes the size of snowballs met mine as Black Jacket spun on his heels, his right arm raised. The left stayed put, just as I suspected, but not because of Carter. His forearm pinned three pink boba drinks against his chest, securing the cargo like the bar on a rollercoaster.

"This ok?" Black Jacket ping-ponged his gaze between my face and the cups pressed against him. "My ol' lady will kill me if I spill her tea."

I scrubbed a hand down my face to keep from screaming. "You're good. Sorry. I thought you were someone else."

"No problemGlad I'm not." Black Jacket stretched his arm tighter. "Can I go now?"

Inwardly groaning, I dropped my head, bringing the man's boots into view. Combat boots, like Ethan had said. Slowly, I let my gaze drift upward, taking in the ripped jeans, the leather coat, the spikey hair. No doubt, this was the guy who helped with the manger, but where was Carter? My mind raced with scenarios I'd heard in the city. Black Jacket could have handed the child off to a partner or hid the baby somewhere in the mall or sold the boy already. But in Quarter, Tennessee, he probably never took him.

"Yeah, you can go," I said, waving him on.

"Thanks." Black Jacket pulled out a bandana—red paisley—from his coat pocket and wiped his brow. "You had me sweating bullets there."

He laughed and walked on, but I didn't. That bandana, a perfect match to the one I was carrying, didn't just prove his innocence. It cemented my feet to a new square one. *Lord, guide me.* Slipping the cloth from my pants pocket, I traced each edge, assuring myself it was still intact and in my possession. On the last corner, my fingertips caught on thick stitching. After flipping the material over, a monogram—PWL— stared back at me. *A personalized handkerchief?* Could be.

I dug my phone out of the other pocket and opened my messages, realizing that the texts I'd sent earlier to have the mother and grand- mother paged had never gone through. After hitting resend, I read the names to myself. Teresa Matney and Patty Williamson. The grandmother's name certainly fit the P and W of the initials.

Closing out of the screen, I hit Wyatt's contact but before the call could connect, a baby's cry sounded. My feet instantly unglued from the spot as I sprinted back the way I'd come, between a dining room table and a loveseat. As I made a sharp right, the wailing rose in volume. Before I knew it, I was at the back of the store, where the coffee tables and entertainment centers should have been. The furniture must have been rearranged for Christmas because instead of living room furniture, I skidded to a stop in front of a crib display. Gray curls bent over the railing as an elderly lady scooped up the squalling baby and began to sway.

I tiptoed toward them until I was able to get a good look at the child. The port-wine stain along the jawline was easy to see, even from a few yards away, and identified the child as the missing baby. Carter was safe.

Thank you, Lord. Than—

The phone I still gripped interrupted my praise. Seeing Wyatt's name flash across the display, I hit the green button. "I found him."

A loud exhale came through the speaker. "Where?"

"Mountaintop Decorating," I said as the woman I assumed was Patty began singing about lowing cattle.

"You got the guy in custody?"

"Not exactly.—"

"Well, you might want to, sir." Wyatt's voice cracked in my ear. "We've got another missing person on our hands. The baby's grandma wandered off. She has Alzheimer's and might be a danger to herself or others."

As Patty kissed Carter on the forehead, I smiled for the first time since my morning cream horns. I knew that Wyatt was right, that in her confusion she had the capability to cause harm, but today that wasn't the case. "Sometimes she might be dangerous. But right now, she's loving on Carter, calm as can be."

I described the scene to Wyatt who relayed it to the family. Patty's identity was confirmed based on my description, and, after promising to escort the pair back to the stable, I hung up. Then I opened the camera on my phone, zooming in to catch the awe-filled expression on the baby's face as he tugged on Patty's hair. Another smile slid into place as I whispered 'cheese' to myself and took the picture.

When we returned to the nativity scene, I covertly snapped a shot of the doll in the manger and asked Cindy if I could text her a couple of pictures for her Insta thing. Even though we both knew I had no idea what I was talking about, she nodded and typed in her number. In seconds, both pictures were on their way.

She'd never need the photographs to remember her crazy day at the mall, but maybe the images would remind her of something more than the time she lost her brother. Maybe, in those shots, she'd see the same thing I did.

Two Christmas miracles.

Jesus away in a manger and a grandmother's love.

Aunt Elvira's Jewels

D. L. Havlin

(aka Hay Baby)

"Pass the white meat, please," Elvira Plotkin requested. Eating Christmas dinner at her house was a twenty-year tradition. Her family always accepted the invitation. There were good reasons for that. Neither wing of the family, the Wilcox's or the Hood's, owned houses large enough to contain the gathering, nor did they have the financial resources to provide the full table that their celebrity Aunt possessed. In some cases, Elvira's relatives lacked the goodwill to host a generous and joyous feast. And there was one additional reason.

"Most certainly, Auntie," Royce Hood said as he passed the plate of slabs of turkey to the wealthy widow, a widow with no children in spite of four marriages. Elvira Wilcox-Evans-Johnson-Beauregard-Plotkin married well each time. Her beauty, especially in her youth, and her notoriety as an entertainer enhanced her ability to attract wealthy men. The share-cropping farm she sprang from duplicated the birth places of those seated at the huge mahogany table. Small farm incomes didn't allow for genuine Choctaw spears, antique tree ornaments, and Chippendale side pieces to adorn their dining areas, in most cases their kitchens. Those fortunes had changed little. Fifteen bodies were seated around the polished wood. Those adult relatives represented Elvira's heirs for she deplored young children, which she described as "buggers with undeveloped minds."

At seventy-six, Elvira's measurements had changed from 38"–24"–36" to 41"–45"–47." The raven black hair was dirty gray after she'd abandoned the dye bottle ten years ago. Though her body succumbed to the ravage of age, her mind hadn't. It remained sharp, mischievous, and diabolical. She smiled at her sister's son and said, "Why thank you, nephew."

Royce stood, clanged his spoon against his burgundy filled wine glass, and with the proper amount of pomp, proposed, "A toast to you, Aunt Elvira. Christmas wouldn't be the same without you." He raised his glass and proclaimed, "Cheers!"

"Cheers!" The remaining fourteen echoed the rousing confirmation, the warmth in their voices rose from genuine affection and avarice.

"Such heartfelt expressions," Elvira smiled as she accepted their adoration. "Or what a way of inquiring about what will happen to this table, we're sitting around, after I die. No offense, Royce." She ignored his display of ruffled feathers.

Murmurs of 'no' and frowns shown round the room.

Elvira held her hand up and shook her head, "It's only natural that you should wonder what will happen to my belongings…when I croak. I believe it to be best that I enlighten you all today. My doctor tells me that I may not see Santa again. I may not decorate another Christmas tree. And as you know, that is one of the things I do that is nearest to my heart."

"Auntie E, you'll live another twenty years," Fred Wilcox suggested from his place at the farthest end of the table from Elvira.

"Twenty more years? Goodness, I hope not! Things hurt enough now," Elvira smiled. "I'm sure some of you have asked yourselves, 'how much is the old broad worth?' I'm going to end that secret. My accountant and lawyer agree that I'm worth seven million, plus a dollar here and there. Now…don't let those cash registers in your minds start ringing. This house, everything in it, and the 110 acres that surround it, will go to the Mississippi State Historical Society for a park. In my name. Call it ego, I don't care. The remaining 806 acres will be divided into nine parcels, that's about 89 acres for each family unit seated around the table. It's my version of giving everybody forty acres and a mule. According to the CPA, that's worth a little over two million for the 800 acres, and a million and a half for this 3,600 square foot antebellum mausoleum and the acreage with it."

Gwen Smithers expressed her discomfort, "Aunt Elvira, is this necessary?"

"I don't want you all jockeying for position to get what I'll leave. Back to numbers. That leaves three and a half million. Five hundred thousand is cash. Edwina my faithful housekeeper gets a hundred grand of it, and I'm going to do my best to spend the rest, and what's left goes to the SPCA. That leaves three million." Elvira removed the scarf from around her neck. "I've converted that into the jewels in this necklace you see me wearing."

Sighs and gasps came from around the table.

Aunt Elvira removed the necklace and gave it to Royce. "Would you pass it around the table, nephew?" It was a command phrased as a question. "If you want to count: there are twenty-seven diamonds, seven emeralds, and five rubies in the piece. That's the real value, not what they are held in. I will be leaving these to all of you. Or, all of you who don't cheat to find it. The first Christmas after I die, you'll all return to this house for a last supper of sorts. I'll have left you each an envelope. In each envelope is one of fifteen clues you'll need to find where I've hidden the jewels. You'll need most of those clues to get rich. Once the honest among you find them, you must divide them equally…or however. That's up to you."

Some scarcely heard the old woman's words as the necklace was passed from person to person. The glare of the jewels captured the eyes of anyone who've held it. Once seen and held, the guests' thoughts spiraled out in many directions.

Aunt Elvira placed a red velvet sack with white fur around the opening on the table in front of her. She took out the first envelope, and announced, "Buddy Wilcox." He accepted it.

The procedure repeated again and again… "Trixie Hood." Arthur Hood watched his wife eagerly take the clue.

"Fred Wilcox, one for you." Elvira threw the envelope across the table.

So it went: "Bonnie Wilcox," "Marigold Garret," "Harold Smithers," "Ben Wilcox," "Arthur Hood," "Royce Hood," "Gwen Smithers," "Nannette Hood," "Jimmy Garret," "Cindy Hood," "Hartley Wilcox," "Evelyn Wilcox." When Aunt Elvira finished, the room had become coffin quiet.

Finally, Royce broke the silence, "What if we can't find the necklace?"

"There will be a lot of happy puppies and kitties," Aunt Elvira gleefully said as she watched the shock spread over the faces around the table.

"Is that fair? One of us can ruin it for all the others. What if they refuse to cooperate…or cheat?" Royce stammered.

"Royce, you're fond of saying how will this work…it is what it is! Let me save you all from some mistakes you could make if you're thinking about retrieving this necklace and the jewels…early." Elvira took the jewels from Evelyn's hands and held the sparkling gems so they caught everyone's attention. "First, my lawyer, Hillard Higgins, will put this in a safety deposit box in Pearl River. It will stay there until one week before the first Christmas after my death. Under my instruction, my lawyer will place the jewels somewhere in this house, that day. As I said, you all will come here for Christmas dinner a week later. Edwina will have decorated the house, have the tree up, and cook a sumptuous meal. Then you will take all your clues out, combine them, and find your inheritance." Elvira smiled, "Or not."

"How did you find out?" Bonnie Wilcox asked.

"Edwina called," Evelyn Wilcox answered.

"Same here. Did you see her obituary in the *Hattiesburg American?* The picture?" Bonnie Wilcox shook her head. "They should have found one that was more reflective of her later life."

Evelyn laughed, "Aunt Elvira would have enjoyed being remembered that way."

"As a stripper on Bourbon Street? Most of the important part of her career, as a singer and actress, came after that! I thought it was disrespectful." Bonnie spoke indignantly, "I intend to ask them to print an apology to the family."

"Come on, Bonnie. How many times did she tell the whole family her tits were her ticket to the big time? Aunt Elvira didn't have one drop of prudish blood in her body." Evelyn leaned forward in the restaurant booth. "You didn't invite me to the Horny Catfish and offer to pay for a lunch because you like fried catfish or crayfish creole. Those are my favorite dishes. We've been sisters-in-law long enough for me to know you want something. Let's shovel the cow crap out of the barn. What do you want?"

Bonnie looked reticent. She glanced from side-to side, leaned close to Evelyn, and said in a low voice, "Hartley and I have been talking and we don't think it is fair. Not even a little bit."

"What's not fair?" Evelyn immediately became suspicious.

"What's happening to *our* side of the family! That's what!"

"Why do say that?"

Bonnie pounded her fist on the table. "The amount of Elvira's inheritance *they* stand to get! The Hood side of the family inheriting anything from Aunt Elvira is a joke. Their Grandma, Nancy Hood, was a whore who didn't collect for her services. Everyone in Hancock, Pearl River, Perry, Stone, and Forrest Counties knows that. The whole Hood family are a disgrace. Look at them. The Hoods are jailbirds and perverts." She slammed her fist into the table twice. "And look who'll get the most? The damned Hoods. Nine of the people sitting at Elvira's table last Christmas weren't Wilcox family members. Why should the Hoods get 60%? It isn't fair."

"I don't see it that way. Aunt Elvira saw to it that we all got what she considered a fair share. You and Harley already got eighty acres of some of the best farmland in south Mississippi. It was her money. She is the only one who can make the decision who gets what. She did it. Case closed." Evelyn leaned forward. "Getting greedy could screw things up for everybody. Did you think of that? Lawyers are expensive!"

"That won't work. We've talked to one and she said it would be nearly impossible to break the will."

"Murdering the rest of us would be suspicious," Evelyn jestingly suggested. "We have eight weeks until Christmas. Are you considering bank robbery?"

"Ha-Ha! No, I wouldn't be speaking to you if I could do that. There is that week between when the necklace is planted and the dinner. The

Hoods get it? Not if we get there first. If all the Wilcox heirs pool their clues, we should be able find that necklace. Two million divided by five is a hell of a lot more than dividing by fifteen." Bonnie's countenance reflected that she'd shared a great secret.

"Five? Why not six? There were six Wilcoxes at the table?" Evelyn asked.

"You know Fred. He's all tied up in his sense of pseudo ethics. He'd never see the practical side of all this." Bonnie nodded her head slowly. "I've talked to Ben. He's in. If you and Buddy join us, that's five clues or one third of the puzzle. We can find it for sure. Elvira told us it will be hidden a week before the big dinner. That will give us six days."

"What about Edwina?"

"We should all agree to take a small part of our share and give it to her if we need to. All she has to do is pretend we aren't there." Bonnie's eyebrows lifted. "That's only if she stays at the house. I doubt she'll do that. She's terrified of the possibility that ghosts exist. I'm sure she'll stay away until she has to be there…with others. I guarantee you she believes Elvira's spirit is patrolling the halls."

Evelyn stared at her sister-in-law. After several seconds of serious thought, she answered. "I passed eighth grade math. Four-hundred-thousand dollars is a hell of a lot more than $133,333. But I also went to Sunday school at the same age. I learned stuff there that won't allow me to participate in what you're doing," She sighed, "Easily…You can speak to Buddy. We're very married, but we make our own decisions. He might think differently. I doubt that." Evelyn held up one finger. "Let me warn you though, if Buddy doesn't agree to join you, he'll probably blow the whistle. You've asked me to come to lunch and keep what we discussed in confidence…so I will. If you're interested in what I think the chances are that Buddy will join you, I'd say elephants flying and politicians never telling another lie will happen first."

Lawyer Hillard Heyward Higgins stood in the spot at the dining room table normally occupied by Aunt Elvira in the many years before her death. "We still have seven minutes left for them to join us. Your Aunt's instructions are very explicit."

Royce Hood asked, "What happens if they don't show at all? Are there instructions for that?"

"Yes, there are," Higgins responded.

"What are they?" Royce asked.

Higgins checked his watch. "I can't divulge that for...six minutes."

Trixie Hood asked, "If they don't come, do you have the clues and can you share them with us?"

"I can tell you that in six minutes," Higgins advised.

"What happens if Bonnie, Hartley, or Ben show up after six minutes?" Gwen asked.

Higgins shook his head, "Royce already asked, but you'll know in six minutes."

Some of the gathering chattered with their neighbors. Others sat silently, stolidly waiting for that six-minute eternity to pass. A couple gazed at the extensively and profusely decorated Christmas tree sitting in front of the room's window. As the Grandfather Clock in the adjoining room struck two, Edwina pushed through the door from the kitchen to the dining room. She carried a huge turkey on a plate. "Merry Christmas from Aunt Elvira," Edwina delivered the message without the normal smile and joyful tone they expected. After several trips, huge bowls of mashed potatoes, sweet potato, green bean casserole, dressing, cranberry salad, and fried okra covered the gleaming table surface. An eerie atmosphere and accompanying quiet invaded the room.

"Huurrmm," The lawyer Higgins cleared his throat. "I will read this greeting from your aunt, and we will eat before the search begins." He removed a letter from his coat pocket and read, "Merry Christmas to all. Enjoy your meal! You have one hour to eat and to sharpen your senses for the treasure hunt. I've given Hillard my rules and he will enforce them. I've told him to use his judgment if there is a problem. Eat hearty, work together, and good hunting! Your Loving Aunt." Higgins smiled at all and said, "First change. I'll *answer your questions after we eat.* Your hour is up at three. Bon Appetite."

Never has a Christmas Dinner been eaten faster.

"Huurrmm," the attention getting device that Higgins used wasn't necessary. The Grandfather Clock's three clanks drew everyone's attention to the lawyer's imposing presence. Hillard Heyward Higgins didn't fit the visual of an officer of the court. Rather, he seemed more like someone in the World Wrestling Association. His hulking build, heavily bearded face, and ponytail belied his excellent legal skills and affirmed his black ops military background. The suit coat he wore didn't hide his shoulder holster, a fact he preferred to disclose, not hide.

A good measure of Higgins' social style was revealed by his tastes in music. His shyster brothers professed to embracing Bach and Beethoven along with a few rock musicians. Devotes of Dirty Honey and other groups back to The Grateful Dead, clandestinely stuffed their earbuds with 'group' tunes, and into heads topped by conservative haircuts. Not

Higgins. He played his music loud…on a boom box. He considered the Oak Ridge Boys' rendition of Hey Baby, 'his classic,' and on the music loop he continually listened to, Hey Baby played between every five songs. A George Jones devotee, 'He Stopped Loving Her Today,' was worked into every third loop.

"I promised to answer questions, and I will, but only the ones I postponed before dinner. Royce, Gwen, you asked what happens if someone doesn't show; they lose their claim to the jewels. They don't get anything. Trixie, you asked about the clues. If an heir died of natural causes, or didn't show up, those clues are lost to you. If an heir is murdered, I have the clues and instructions to share them…in that case only. End of questions."

Higgins slid his index finger across his throat, freezing the words on tongues of several of those seated at the table. "Here is how this is going to work. I'll call your name. You'll read your clue. I'll put it on this white board." He placed the board on the table and produced a marker. "Then when everyone adds their clue, you solve the location." He looked at the first person seated to his right. "Gwen Hood-Smithers."

"One dozen donuts, plus three for the baker," she answered. Higgins wrote that on the white board. He repeated the process with each answer.

"Harold Smithers."

"Where do you find nuts?"

"Nannette Hood."

"One little, two little, three little Indians…and so on."

"Fred Wilcox."

"How low can you go?"

"Royce Hood."

"Tennis and soccer have this in common."

"Cindy Hood."

"Pull up the bucket."

"Trixie Hood."

"What a shape...36...24...37" Snickers arose from the table. Higgins frowned, and silence returned.

"Arthur Hood."

"Look for a color not in the rainbow."

"Evelyn Wilcox."

"When is a safe, not safe?"

"Elmore Wilcox." No one answered. Higgins tried again, "Buddy Wilcox."

"Go ahead, bust your bubble," Buddy growled.

"Sorry, but get over it," Higgins suggested, then continued, "Jimmy Garret."

"Don't get too close to stay well."

"Marigold Hood-Garret."

"Pick a stairway: to heaven or hell."

Higgins propped up the white board so everyone could see the printed clues. "Who wants to start?" It remained silent. The lawyer prompted, "One of Elvira's rules: you have forty-eight hours or it's over."

Nannette shyly held her hand up. "I think I know what my clue means. It's the one about Indians. Aunt Elvira always told me to get my ducks in a row. I think this means we need to put the clues in order."

Higgins nodded, smiled, and said, "That sounds logical. Anybody disagree?"

"No's," and head shakes signaled agreement.

"I think mine might be next," Marigold volunteered. "The stairs to heaven or hell...it means we'll need to go to the second floor or the basement, to find the jewels or more clues or we might discover more clues. Aunt Elvira loved doing things for shock value."

"That makes sense," Evelyn agreed. "Why don't we copy all that's on the white board, divide into two groups, and scour both up and down to find the clues."

"Good! Two groups of six." Royce pointed to himself. "I'll lead one group—"

"And I'll take the other, to the basement," Evelyn interjected, "I used to help Aunt Elvira store her jams and preserves there."

Higgins nodded his approval as the two leaders copied the clues from the whiteboard. He said, "That surprises me. I never thought of Elvira as the homemaker type."

Within a minute, both groups left, leaving Edwina and Hillard Higgins alone in the dining room. Edwina fidgeted for several seconds before asking, "Can I clear the table, cleanup, and go home? I want to get out of here a might quicker than it will take those folks to find them jewels."

"Not curious?"

"No sir! I got my gift and I'm satisfied with it." Edwina's voice rose as if she was speaking to a spirit hiding somewhere in the huge house.

"Sure…cleanup. But before you go, I want a word with you."

Afterward, Edwina raced to clean the table and soon the sounds of clanging pots and clinking dishes came to the dining room through the closed kitchen door. Higgins removed a novel from his briefcase and had read two chapters when a scream came from somewhere in the basement. Tossing his book aside, he mumbled, "Sounds serious…but expected," and raced downstairs.

Evelyn, Buddy, Gwen, Harold, Marigold, and Jimmy were clustered in a circle, their heads bent over as they stared toward the ground. Both

Jimmy and Harold held flashlights pointed at the focus of their vision. Higgins knew what they were looking into. The basement where the group stood, housed a well. They focused on something in its depths. Higgins asked, "What's up?" though he had a strong suspicion.

"There are bodies in there!" Gwen hissed and pointed down at the well.

Higgins approached the seven-foot diameter hole in the ground very carefully. The flashlight beams swept back and forth over the three bodies twenty feet down. The nauseating stench of decaying human flesh rose to the basement floor from the bloated bodies. Two of the bodies were face-down, and the third revealed the distorted features of Bonnie Wilcox. Higgins told them, "Give me a flashlight. Then all of you return to the dining room table. I want two of you to get the other group back there. No one goes anywhere by themselves."

Higgins spoke to Elvira's remaining heirs who were all seated at the table. "I have some good news, at least some will think it is, and some bad news. I examined the area around the well. The stones on the edge were broken loose. After a more careful examination, I saw pieces of the well's edge *on top* of the bodies. When I looked at the area around the rim of the well, I found marks obviously made by a wrecking bar or crowbar. We can assume the bodies are Bonnie, Hartley, and Ben. That strongly leads me to believe they were murdered. The edge was trashed to make their deaths look like an accident." The lawyer paused for several seconds, then continued. "It also means that Elvira's wishes are that you receive the rest of the clues. Since I believe they were murdered, here they are." Higgins added the three clues to the white board.

"Time to go to the well."

"The sum of the parts equals the whole."

"March…Left…Plus…2…Right…Left…Less…1"

As Hillard Higgins placed the cap on the marker, he said, "And now the bad news. One or more of you, seated at this table, is the murderer."

Instantly, the murmured words of suspicions and fear erupted from the gathering.

Higgins held a hand up. With the other, he reached inside his suit coat, removed a Glock 9mm, and placed it on the table in front of him. "We're not in immediate danger. I will be calling the sheriff, but not until you solve the location of the jewels. We will stay together in a group-no one leaves by themselves. The reason is that when we solve that mystery, we will know who killed those three in the well." He grinned. "I have the only gun."

"How will you know who the killer is?" Fred asked.

"That is for me to know and you to find out," Higgins explained. "Now it is time to get on with the process. I will help you by informing you that two additional clues will be uncovered by using the ones you have. So, it is up to you to try to solve the mystery. Who has an idea of where to start?"

"I do," Fred volunteered. "The stuff about the well. I think the 'how low can you go,' 'time to go to the well,' and 'don't get too close to stay well,' all are connected and are the instructions that follow the stairs clue."

"I think my clue would be next. 'Pull up the bucket.'" Cindy Hood shuttered, "I won't do that."

"Because of the circumstances, *it's best no one does that.* The sheriff wouldn't want us to disturb the crime scene more than we have. Since I know all the clues, I'll tell you all what you should have found. With the bodies falling in there, who knows what's in the bucket now." Higgins waited until all eyes were riveted on him. He looked at each person to be sure he had everyone's complete attention. "What you would find in the bucket is the necklace with all the jewels removed, and a clue. That clue is written on the picture of a painting. It says, 'A safe place.' What does that mean?" No one spoke. Higgins waited a full minute and said, "If no one has an idea how to proceed, I can terminate this scavenger hunt at any time and donate the jewels to the SPCA."

Evelyn answered reluctantly, "Logically, that a painting hides the safe."

Higgins hesitated, then asked, "Who knows where the painting is?"

After many long seconds, Evelyn said, "I believe I do."

"Good," Higgins smiled and said, "Lead us to it."

All were gathered in Elvira's bedroom. After Higgins removed the painting Evelyn pointed out, he asked, "What's the next clue?"

"That's easy, it's mine." Evelyn recited, "When is a safe, not safe? The answer is when someone has the combination."

Trixie cackled excitedly, "I have the combination." She tried spinning the dial to 36-24-37. It didn't work. She tried entering them again but this time turning the dial in different directions. Her luck remained the same. "Damn!" Trixie exclaimed.

"I think one of the clues Hillard added is what we need. When I first read it, I thought it had to do with footsteps. Let me try something." Fred took Trixie's place at the safe. He spoke as he turned the knob, "March…Left…to…36…Plus…2, Right…to…24, Left…to…37… less…1." When he pulled on the handle, the door swung open. He said,

"There's a paper inside." Fred removed it and read, "*Return to go and have your dreams fed! Auntie E.* We have to return to the dining room."

Higgins held up the white board. "We have six more clues. Does anybody have any ideas?"

"I think we can throw one out," Cindy Hood said. "The one about the sum of the parts equaling the whole, I think that was to tell us the jewels were removed from the necklace so we wouldn't know what to look for."

"Good! That leaves us with five," Higgins crossed out a line on the board.

Gwen's eyes opened wide, "I know, I know! 'Where do you find nuts.' In a tree. The Christmas Tree! They're in it."

"They're hidden in the glass balls," Royce was so excited he almost slid out of his chair. "Tennis and soccer have this in common. It could only be nets and balls. There are no nets around. The jewels are in the balls."

Arthur waved his hand, "We look for color balls that aren't in the rainbow. That means the red, blue and green ornaments are out. It leaves silver and gold!"

Higgins nodded. "Two left."

"Of course. One dozen donuts, plus three for the baker. Fifteen… one for each heir." Evelyn corrected herself, "Well, not anymore."

Fred Wilcox walked to the tree and counted the gold and silver ornaments. All were five inches in diameter. He announced excitedly, "There are fifteen silver ones and only twelve gold ones."

"The only clue left is 'Go ahead, bust your bubble.' Give me a minute to collect the silver ornaments from the tree." Higgins removed his gun from the table and returned it to his holster. He stuffed his coat and pants pockets with the globes that would not fit in his hands. When he returned to the table, he placed one of the silver balls in front of Buddy. He told him, "Go ahead, Buddy, bust your bubble."

The suggestion didn't have to be repeated. Buddy covered the ornament with a place mat and brought his palm down hard on the silver ball. The muffled tinkling of broken glass resulted. Buddy quickly removed the mat. Interspersed in the shards of silver glass were a number of diamonds, and the cool deep green of an emerald shimmered before the eyes of the group.

"Each of the fifteen ornaments has the same value of jewels inside. Each of you will get one. Well all, but three. The three that would have gone to the murdered heirs will go to the dogs, so to speak. The lawyer distributed the ornaments. "Buddy, you have yours. Marigold here is yours." He moved and set the silver balls in front of each heir. "Jimmy… Arthur…Gwen… Harold…Nannette…Fred…Royce…Cindy…Trixie." He looked at Evelyn and said, "You realize why you aren't receiving one."

She dropped her head and muttered, "How did you know?"

"Actually, you told me. Neither the safe, nor the painting covering it were installed until after your Aunt Elvira died. *Only someone* who saw the clue in the bucket would know about the painting. In fact, I didn't hang the canvas over the safe until the week before today. *Only someone* who had been in this house in the past week would know about either. You were the only one who knew. I'm sure when the sheriff questions Edwina in more length, they'll get the collaborating testimony that you were here. My question is…why?"

"As Bonnie told me, dividing by five shares would amount to a lot more than fifteen. Well, one share meant I'd get it all."

Sirens sounded in the distance.

Little Annie's

Christine Clemetson

Christmas Wish

S hame prickled inside Anne Cooper's head like the drip drip drip of a faucet, always reminding her.

Never letting up.

Not even at the Christmas festival she and Jim loved.

They bustled through the crowded St. Dominic School's parking area, now closed off with orange cones.

At the fairground's entrance, the plastic Chester Ridge Christmas Festival sign slapped in the wind. Alvin and the Chipmunks squeaked out "Jingle Bells" from the loudspeaker hanging on a utility pole.

Anne gave her ticket and zipped up her coat, which now barely stretched across her pregnant belly.

Jim squeezed her hand. "If you get too cold, we'll go, okay?"

"I'll be fine."

Two years married and she still hadn't confessed.

Further in, craft vendors and games dotted the area, connected by strings of white Christmas lights. A woman dressed as a Christmas elf shouted from the reindeer booth, "Pin the tail on three reindeer and take home a stuffed Rudolph."

The guilt made it even worse.

The warm mix of funnel cake and hot chocolate simmered in the air. Anne's stomach growled. "If my indigestion behaves, I need something chocolate. Anything, really."

Jim pointed to the food trucks just beyond the games. "With a cheese-steak for sure."

"Anne!" Sylvie, another teacher in Anne's school, manned a table with a handwritten sign: Learn Your Future. "C'mon in. Maybe the tea leaves will tell you if you'll have a boy or girl, or other things."

Anne's knuckles whitened on her purse strap. "I don't know."

Jim smirked, his engineer mind most likely on high alert. "Science based?"

"Just for fun, you know," Sylvie chuckled. "It's my daughter Josephine. Cheer squad needs donations to go to the championship."

Anne's shoulders relaxed. "Well then, who can say no to that?"

"Not me for sure." Jim grinned. "But I'll check out the Kris Kringle beer tasting contest and meet you after? Unless you really want me to join you."

Anne playfully pushed him away and walked to the tent. Sylvie dropped a spoonful of olive-colored leaves into a white mug.

"Tea leaves, huh?" Anne commented, stifling her ridiculous unease.

From a carafe on the folding table, Sylvie filled the cup with steaming water. "Take a sip or two if you want." She directed Anne to the tent's open flap, outlined in Christmas lights.

Inside, Josephine waved from a small table. Her tight, high ponytail swung loosely. "Hey, Mrs. Cooper."

"So awesome you're going to the championship," Anne said. "Congratulations."

Josephine clapped. "Yay."

Next to Josephine, a woman with broad shoulders and a plaid scarf sat upright, stiff like a weathered flag waiting for the next storm.

"And this is my grammie Louisa," Josephine introduced. "She's teaching me how to read the leaves."

Louisa grunted and crooked her bony finger, gesturing for Anne to slide the cup across the table.

Excitement sparked in Josephine's eyes. "Do you want to know if it's a boy or girl?"

Safe question. "We never found out so that would be fun."

"Let's see." Josephine dumped the remaining tea water into a bucket and then examined the leaves clinging inside. She pointed in a pattern above the cup as if tracing the outline of the shapes.

"Hmm. I don't know about girl or boy, but it looks like a ladder."

Anne folded her arms. "What does it mean?"

"A vacation," Josephine exclaimed, "You're going on a vacation, Mrs. Cooper. Right, Gram?"

Louisa's forehead wrinkled in a question, and her chest rattled.

"A trip, yes, yes." She brought the cup's rim to her nose. "And—"

Or other things.

"I don't need to know anymore." Anne pushed her purse back on her shoulder and stood up. She forced a smile. "My husband is waiting."

The woman's voice deepened. "The trip…has danger."

Anne gripped the tent flap. "A trip where?"

Louisa tipped the cup toward Anne. She pointed to a cluster of leaves. "See the cross shape here, and how it groups there…" Her watery eyes opened wider, bulging, and she tsk tsked. "There will be a journey. But your child…"

Anne hugged her arms around her abdomen. "What about the baby?"

"Gram," Josephine patted Louisa's shoulder, "you shouldn't say that."

"Danger is coming. And it will be in the blood moon."

The pulse in Anne's wrists quickened. "Is something wrong with my baby?"

"Mom," Josephine called.

Sylvie strode into the tent, swishing her arms as if swatting away a fly. "This is all for fun." She ushered Anne outside. "I'm sorry you had to hear that. My mom lost a baby one time, and now in her old age, she sometimes…Well, it's nothing to do with *your* baby," she whispered.

The rest of Sylvie's explanation faded into the background as Anne excused herself.

"Hark the Herald Angels Sing" echoed from the tent next door where folks were busy decorating wreaths. Frigid air whipped from the ground, blasting the perspiration on Anne's neck.

Danger is coming.

She clutched her purse against her center. The baby kicked and moved, punching at her insides.

Where was Jim?

It can't be real.

Back at their apartment, the smell of vanilla and pine filled Anne's nose. A floor-to-ceiling tree stood in the front window, waiting for them to decorate.

The old woman's voice vibrated in her head. *Danger is coming.*

She shrugged off her coat and swished damp hair from her forehead. The words had to be meaningless.

Jim wrapped his arms around her, nuzzling her neck. The odor of beer and outside air wafted around her. "You're not still thinking about that tea leaf thing, are you?"

"I don't know. Why?"

"It was a kid with leaves probably from the grocery store."

He was right. Why had she wasted so much time obsessing over it? But her hormones had been on overdrive lately. She eyed the box of tree decorations. "Okay, then let's do the tree."

"Seriously." He squeezed her shoulder.

"I know, I know." She kissed him on the nose.

The kitchen phone rang.

Jim laughed. "Saved by the bell."

"Only calls we get on that line are sales."

"I'll check it." He pulled away and headed into the kitchen. "Last week the dentist called on that line."

"Uh huh." Anne flipped the lid off one of the tree boxes and tugged out a glass ball painted with the words: Our First Christmas. "I don't think the dentist calls at night."

"Caller ID says Clover's Point," Jim called, "we don't know anyone there, right? I'll let it go to voice mail."

The ornament slipped between Anne's fingers, crashing to the wood floor, its pieces bouncing and scattering.

Couldn't be.

She dragged in a haggard breath.

Jim sprinted to her. "You okay?"

"Yeah, yeah, fine." She stepped away to yank open the closet, grabbing the broom. "So clumsy."

Clover's Point?

"You sure? Here, you sit." Jim took the broom. "I'll pick this up."

As the bristles swished the hardwood, a woman's voice sounded through the machine.

"I hope I have this right. I'm looking for Annie. Umm. I know this is a weird message. I don't know if you know who I am, but I just found out about you." The voice hitched. "I think we may be sisters. Our mom has just passed, and I…I really would like to talk to you. Please, if this is Annie, born 1992 in Clover's Point, can you please call me back?"

The message clicked off.

Jim stopped sweeping. "That can't be for real."

Anne twisted her wedding ring, pinching the diamonds. She moved toward the phone and played the message again.

"I have—I have no idea."

He swept the glass pieces into the dustpan. "Is it a scam?"

Anne swallowed back a sob. The baby kicked on the left side. "I told you I was adopted."

"But you said your mom died at birth."

"Yes, yes, that's what I was told." She crossed the kitchen. Out the window, the neighbors across the way fiddled with tangled Christmas lights on their bushes. "But then things changed, and I couldn't handle it."

"What changed?" Jim rested the broom against the counter. "I'm not getting this."

She couldn't bring the words from her mouth. "I did an ancestry thing in college and found out…found her."

"Your birth mother's been alive up until now?"

Anne strode to the couch. "Apparently. I never told anyone."

Not even you.

Jim's face morphed from concern to disbelief. "Did you ever contact her? Or this woman that could be your sister?"

"There's more to it, Jim." The ornament's broken pieces in the garbage pail sunk into that morning's eggshells and coffee grinds.

"Then tell me."

"I c-can't."

"Your arms are trembling, babe." He went closer. "It can't be that bad that you can hardly look me in the eyes?"

Anne locked on to his gaze. "I've been lying to you."

"Okay, now you're scaring me."

"For so long, I wanted to sit you down here and tell you, but then time…" She soaked in the hurt surrounding his eyes. "I wasn't good enough for her."

"No.. no. Don't think that."

She shook her head. The air between them thickened into silence. The past reared in front of her. How could she explain the shame? That being unwanted by her birth mom meant there was something wrong with her? It had been easier to avoid it all by perpetuating the lie, even when she found out the truth.

Her throat burned.

"I just couldn't—"

"Trust me." His voice bordered on a whisper. "You didn't trust me enough."

"That's not true." Panic tingled in her throat. "I wanted to tell you. But I couldn't admit it to anyone. It was just too painful."

"It must have been awful for you." Jim's face drained of color. "But I could've helped. I would've listened."

She twisted the cross on her necklace. "I didn't mean to hurt you."

The stillness of his gaze put an ache in her chest. "I need some air. Just give me a few minutes to think about things."

Anne dragged a floral raggedy hat box out from the back of the bedroom closet and popped off the top. She lifted out the pile of papers. Insurance. Adoption. Diploma. Social Security card.

The hurtful smell of memories leached onto her.

She thumbed the rough edge of the newspaper clipping at the bottom of the box.

1992 New Year's First Babies – Twin Girls from Clover's Point

Below the article was a picture of a young woman lying in the hospital bed, holding Anne and the sister she never knew. Both babies had dark hair, or at least as far as she could tell from the grainy black-and-white picture. Their noses were no bigger than a dime.

Why had their mother given up Anne?

Anne had been ready for the answer a long time ago. But if she had pursued her birth story, it would have broken her adoptive mom's heart. So she pretended to believe the lie and focus on the family who'd been there for her.

The front door slammed and footsteps pounded down the hall.

From behind, Jim touched her shoulder. "I'm sorry, baby."

"I found this article years ago when working on a college project." Anne handed him the paper. "My sister and I were born four minutes apart."

"A twin?"

She had tied up the truth years earlier, cinched it like a garbage bag, and buried it deep inside her. Hidden from her family.

But now, she had to pull at the edges.

She needed to let her husband in. She couldn't carry it alone anymore.

"You know my birth mom gave me up for adoption. But what you don't know…is that she kept my sister."

For a moment, the explanation felt like a lie, still unbelievable to even her own ears.

"I'm so sorry." His voice scratched. He brought her close, stroking the back of her neck.

She pressed her lips together, waiting for the words to come.

"It was too hard."

She stared back at the photo. The woman smiled at the camera, but her eyes looked blank, almost sorrowful. Did she know at that moment that she'd give Anne up?

"I would've been there for you," he said.

Something inside her chest quivered. "Because of what she did, I'd always wondered how I could be good enough for someone else."

"Her choice didn't make you any less of a person. All that's happened to you is why you are so wonderful."

Her eyes burned. "It's so hard to see that when—"

"You think that would be a deal breaker with us? That I would leave you because she did?" He shook his head. "You're the best part of us, of me, of our baby, and none of this would have changed our life together."

Holding her belly, she lumbered to standing. Her birth mother must've already decided that something about Anne wasn't lovable. Why else would she have given her up? "I tried so many times to tell you."

"I can't imagine how hard it must've been to handle this all on your own."

"I've always felt something was missing, and when I saw this picture I understood. Twins have this thing I guess."

"From that message, sounds like your sister didn't know about you, either." He sat on the bed, elbows on his knees. "But there has to be more to all of this."

"That's the hole I feel. I need to know why. Things will get busy after the baby is born."

"You want to go now?"

"I do."

He slid his cell phone from his pocket and brought up the Baby Planner for Engineers app. He pointed to the slope of the green line. "From the trend, this week puts you into the baby window. You could have the baby at any time."

She stilled his hand. "I have five weeks, Jim, and Clover's Point is only a few hours away."

"Are you sure?"

"I need to know so that I can be a better mom to our baby and focus on our little family. On us."

He clicked on another option on the phone app. "This could be doable if we come back right away."

"I'll run it by Dr. Kaler at my checkup tomorrow, and we can leave Friday."

"On Christmas?"

The acrid smell of the tea leaves from earlier needled inside her nose.

You have a journey.

Danger is coming.

Anne dismissed the prediction, determined not to obsess about it. Not about a five-dollar reading at a Christmas fair that meant nothing.

Something not real.

She folded up the article and swiped a finger under her eyes. This was the last chance she had. After the baby is born, she'd be torn in all new directions. "I'll tell that woman from the message that we're coming."

Hellooooo, Bethlehem, Pennsylvania. Spend your Christmas here with KMA radio.

The baby had stirred inside Anne from the moment they'd left the driveway. Maybe he or she understood the stakes, too.

Let's start off our Christmas countdown with a little Mariah Carey's "All I want for Christmas."

Main street in Bethlehem was lined with rustic shops, lit up by twinkly lights. Shoppers filled the sidewalks. The setting sun cast a pinkness across the snow patches.

Jim turned the SUV onto Route 485.

Interrupting your 24-hour Christmas music. A prisoner broke out of Pennsylvania Point Penitentiary...

"Isn't that around here?"

"More west." Jim gestured to the fancy GPS with buttons and more buttons. "I don't think we'll go near it."

Anne shifted in her seat. "You're sure that thing is right? Seems like we've been on the road forever."

"You okay?"

"What if this is a mistake, meeting her?" The first-day-of-school-like jitters had started the night before.

"Whatever happens affects nothing. You can take or leave what she says. This is for you. Not her."

"I know," she whispered, clasping her hands across her belly.

We'll be fine, baby.

The broadcast went back to Mariah belting out what she wanted for Christmas. Anne just wanted closure.

The beep beep beep of an alarm brought her attention to the dashboard. A blinking yellow light lit the panel.

"Dammit," Jim said, "the garage said they replaced it before we left."

"Out of gas?" She swayed her head to the left. "Are we going to break down?"

"They were supposed to replace the gauge." Jim clicked a button on the GPS panel. "Last exit up ahead until a ten-mile expanse of nothingness. We better fill up to be sure."

A Quickie Mart sat at the bottom of the exit. People bustled in and out of the parking lot. At least ten cars waited at the only open gas line.

"I'll see if they have a bathroom." Bubbles of nervousness felt like they had lodged into Anne's back. "This baby needs to move."

Inside the hot mini-mart, the line for the bathroom stretched to the door. Bing Crosby's calming voice filled the tiny aisles. Blinking colored lights hung from the lottery sign.

Anne yanked off her coat and held it on her arm.

The ticker on the television above the counter ran an update on the manhunt.

Forty-six-year-old white male, last seen wearing black shirt and pants, 5' 8", goatee...

A photo of the escapee flashed on the screen.

A twinge of foreboding rose up her center. She leaned on the wire potato chip display, the bags crinkling.

A police officer at the front of the line gestured to her. "Come up here, ma'am. Take my spot."

Heat rose up Anne's neck. "That's okay."

A man in a Santa hat at the counter added, "I remember when my wife was in that state. We met every exit and every bathroom in the state of Pennsylvania."

He was right.

Anne scooted reluctantly forward, not making eye contact, her coat scraping those waiting in line. She thanked the young cop, her cheeks likely matching the color of a ripe tomato.

After she finished up in the bathroom, she stopped at the drink case and yanked out two waters.

Suspect moving north and police are tracking...

That road sounded familiar. She inhaled. What felt like a rolling pin moved inside her belly.

"You okay, miss?" a man asked.

She exhaled and nodded, steadying her legs. As quick as the sensation came, it went. She just needed fresh air.

Outside, Jim had pulled up to the pump. "You don't look good."

"Just nerves. The news said Route 202 is barricaded because of the police. Wasn't that the next highway we have to take?"

"The GPS shows a detour that will only take us out about ten minutes. You okay?"

"They're expecting us by eight, so that should be fine."

Danger is coming.

The SUV's headlights pushed through the fading light and stretch of farmland. The once tall wheat stalks were now deadened, flattened with snow.

"Look at that blood moon," Jim said, "Not even all the way out yet."

Out the windshield, the sliver of burnished red peeked above the horizon. The woman's premonition came into Anne's head. Full center, like a blinking sign.

Danger is coming in the blood moon.

"Is that something bad?" she asked.

"Just the lunar eclipse." Jim rubbed her thigh. "You still don't look good. Why don't you close your eyes?"

She rested her head back, the pangs in her abdomen growing more frequent. Ping. Kick. "The baby is doing gymnastics."

"I'm going with my gut here," he said. "Let's stop and check in somewhere. Rest tonight and get a fresh start tomorrow."

"No…No. I'm fine. We're not that far from her house." She wiped her cheek. "The baby is just restless. With all the excitement, I wasn't able to sleep last night."

He clicked on the navigation panel. "There's a hotel about two miles off the highway."

"Holly Jolly Christmas" suddenly stopped playing on the radio.

Escapee spotted south of Clover's Point…manhunt ongoing …roads blocked off…

"That settles it." Jim pushed new coordinates into the GPS. "Safer to stop and get back on the road in the morning."

He was making too much of it. Jim looked like he was ready to jump out of his skin. Anne had had this feeling of being overwhelmed a zillion times since she first got pregnant. Especially after a day of teaching fourth graders.

But he was right. With a potentially dangerous convict out there, they should get off the road. The baby squirmed in agreement. "After some sleep, we'll all feel better."

Less than ten minutes later, they pulled into Meadow Inn motel. Christmas lights outlined the sign out front. The vacancy sign was lit.

When Jim got out, cold air blasted the car. Through the large window of the office, the clerk shook his head.

Dread came up inside her. Anxiety had been Anne's worst enemy since she was sixteen.

Jim jogged back to the car. "Nothing here, most of the rooms are closed for renovations, but he said there's a place a few miles up."

She gulped from the water bottle. Something felt different now. The pains weren't letting up.

He shifted the car in reverse. "It'll get us off the main track. Thirteen minutes away."

The car sped down Meadow Road. A spasm pulsated through her spine. She clenched the door handle.

As things unfold, we'll bring you the latest. Bringing you back to around-the-clock Christmas music.

Anne pounded the dashboard. "We need to stop."

"What?"

They passed a green sign that read: "Welcome to Clover's Point."

"Stop, Jim." She dug her heels into the floor, arching back. "I'm having this baby right now."

"Now? You still have four weeks and one and a half days."

"It's now."

Jim jerked the SUV to the side of the road, the tires bobbling over the rutted grass, and jolted to a stop. Farmland for as far as they could see filled the headlights. He dialed 911 on his phone.

"My wife is having a baby. What do I do?"

Anne shut out the voices around her. She closed her eyes and inhaled. She could do this. The moon shined outside the window.

Jim clicked the cell phone to speaker, shoved it on the console, and turned on the SUV's cabin light. "She'll walk us through it, okay?"

Anne sucked in air and nodded, following the instructions. Nat King Cole's "Oh Holy Night" played through the speakers.

Emergency services have been dispatched.

Do you have something to use as a blanket?

Jim ripped off his jacket and crouched closer. "We need to slide the seat back further."

Anne grasped his sleeve, gulping. Fear filled his eyes.

The pains rolled over her abdomen, quicker now.

Jim pushed up his sleeves and quickly pumped sanitizer between his palms. "You ready, Anne?"

Air felt trapped inside her, like a balloon that wouldn't break. Pain reared up her front.

"I don't—know."

The operator's voice came on. "Sir, help ease the baby into whatever you're using as a blanket."

He knelt closer to her and positioned the jacket. "You can do this. I know you can."

Danger is coming.

"This baby's too early." She panted. "Too soon."

"Inhale," the operator instructed, "and push on the exhale."

"You're strong, Anne," Jim's voice hitched, "the strongest person I know."

Their eyes locked. Even in the dimness, she saw his fear had been replaced by the determination of a man about to be a father. She grabbed the cloth seat edges and pinched until her nails burned.

And pushed.

And breathed hard.

And pushed more.

Please let my baby be okay.

"Keep going, Anne," Jim's voice got louder, "just a little more…little more. It's a girl. We have a girl."

Jim laid the baby on Anne's chest. The warmth soaked into Anne skin but there was no movement.

Only stillness.

Emergency lights pinged off the inside of the SUV. A police officer came into the rearview mirror, slapping on plastic gloves. A second officer followed, talking on his shoulder radio.

"Please help us!" Anne held the baby, wrapped in the jacket. "Oh my God… she's not breathing."

In the background, the 911 operator instructed about checking the airway.

"I'm going to move her a little, ma'am." The first officer leaned inside, gently turned the baby, slanted her downwards on his palm, and then patted her back.

Please, let her be okay.

He patted more.

"I don't hear her." Anne's voice shook.

As the officer moved the baby slightly, a small sound came out. Like a squeak. A blip.

Was it a cry?

"Is that her?" Dizziness mobbed Anne's head, flowing downward into her limbs. She blinked hard. "She's okay?"

"Congratulations."

The officer returned the baby to Anne's chest and reported to the 911 operator.

Fresh cries vibrated off Anne's chest. She swaddled Jim's jacket around the baby, her hands shaking. "She's gonna be okay."

The officer spoke into his radio. Relief and sweat marked his face. "Hang tight, ma'am. Ambulance is three minutes out."

"You gave me your spot in line at Quickie Mart."

He grinned. "I recognized you, too. Name's Jeremy."

"How can we ever thank you?" Jim shook his hand.

"No thanks needed."

Anne nestled the bundle closer. Her daughter's tiny eyelids fluttered ever so slightly. "Hello, there."

Outside the car window, the wind stirred. The moon's glow rested on them like a soft blanket. As if it had been waiting.

"She's looks like you." Jim pressed his lips to Anne's head. "Beautiful."

"Lilly?"

"Yes," Jim gestured to the rickety fence outlining the farm. Two deer stood frozen, staring at them. "And she already has an audience."

Lilly.

This precious being lay across Anne's chest and entangled her soul. Now directing Anne's life: her decisions, her love, her worries, completing her heart with love she hadn't known existed.

The invisible thread she'd only heard about, that nothing could ever break.

She smoothed a wisp of Lilly's hair near her ear.

Her throat shuttered. How could her own mom have loved like this and then given her up? Choosing one child over the other?

The roar of approaching sirens yanked her back into the present. Swarms of red and blue lights gathered outside their SUV.

"Is that the ambulance?" she called to Jim. "What are they doing?"

Cops encircled them like pillars, facing outward, guns drawn. What felt like a rock squeezed through her esophagus.

The baby cried in small squeaks. "What is it, Jim?"

The same fear had crept back into his eyes. "That guy who escaped is close to here."

The crack of what sounded like a gun blasted in the distance. Shouts. Flashlights lit up the deadened farmland.

"No!" She angled her body to the left, putting her back to the door, and covered Lilly with her arms and torso.

Out the front windshield, a man stood in the edge of the headlight beams. Stoic like a tree. His gun glinted in the moon. He turned slowly, as if he had known she spied him, and their eyes locked. Even in the distance, she saw the darkness in them.

Her breath caught.

"You drive and follow me," Officer Jeremy said. Jim shut the passenger side door and sprinted to the driver's side. The car lurched forward.

Anne squeezed her eyes shut, her head swarming with dizziness.

Only when lights from the County General Hospital colored the dashboard did Anne exhale. What if, somehow, they and the convict crossed paths again? And he followed them to the hospital?

The feeling needled inside her head.

Nothing mattered now except keeping her baby safe.

Inside the glass incubator, Lilly's chest rose and fell in an even rhythm. Every single beautiful breath spoke to Anne.

I'm here, mom.

Even the small Santa decal on the glass smiled as if he knew this was the best Christmas wish ever granted—getting her brand-new daughter to the hospital, healthy and safe.

Getting to the hospital safely and their recovery.

The door to the NICU buzzed opened, and Jim came in. "She's here."

"Okay." A dart of pain traveled down Anne's center as she stood. She touched the glass and whispered she'd be back.

When Anne entered the small waiting room right outside the NICU, a breaking news banner streamed across the television.

Escaped prisoner captured in Clover's Point.

The convict's picture flashed onto the screen; the same man Anne spotted in the weeds.

A shiver tingled her skin. How close she had been. She pushed the thought aside and approached the woman who was also watching the program.

Anne's stomach twitched. "Maribeth?"

Her sister turned, a reflection of Anne from her soft brown eyes to the sharpness in her cheeks.

The invisible thread pulled tight.

Goosebumps charged up the length of her spine. She closed the gap and pulled Maribeth into an embrace. For the first time since being in the womb, she felt her sister's heartbeat close.

They clung to each other for everything they lost.

All of the years. The birthdays. First periods. Trying on bras. Dances. Boys.

Anne drew back. Heat rose into her cheeks. "I—I wish I had…"

"I never knew about you, either."

"She didn't tell you?" A physical pain, like a knot, formed inside Anne's chest. "How could she not have…Didn't it matter to her? Did she look for me even a little bit?"

"You did matter." Pain or possibly uncertainty washed over Maribeth's face. "It's so hard to even know where to start."

"All these years…" Anne toed the floor with her thick sock. Words wedged inside her throat.

"It wasn't until the night before she died that she told me." Her voice cracked. "She was just fifteen years old when she had us."

Anne clutched her throat. "Fifteen?"

"She lived in so much shame." Maribeth glanced at the ceiling. "Her parents were so angry with her for getting pregnant, and—"

"And what?"

"They were already struggling to pay the bills, keep food on the table. So they forced her to choose. Either she left with both of us or she kept only one."

A sob traveled up through Anne's core. "My God." How could anyone make that kind of decision? And at fifteen? "What about our father?"

"What little I know, our mother was told to cut off ties with him. It's so hard to tell you the rest…" Her words trailed off and she glanced at the television.

Anne's chest pounded. "What is it?"

"Our father is Jerome Pitts."

"The convict?"

"Mom sent a letter to him in prison to tell him she was sick. They hadn't spoken since they were teens." Maribeth's lips visibly trembled, and she nodded toward the TV screen. "He must've escaped to see her one last time."

The truth churned in Anne's center, making her feel weak. She stared at her father's mug shot in the corner of the screen. Not seeing dark in his eyes anymore but instead sorrow, and the pain that must've led him to this tragic life.

Maribeth pulled a stack of sealed envelopes from her purse, secured together with a rubber band. The letters gave off the faint scent of raspberries. "Mom wrote one on each of your birthdays."

"For me?"

Maribeth wiped away a tear. "I promised her I'd find you. And tell you her story. And that she loved you with every ounce of her being."

On the top one, the name Annie was written in cursive with a date below. January 2, 1992. A day after she was born.

Maribeth's gaze stayed on the papers, and she pushed the bundle toward Anne. "Giving you her name was a way to always be in your heart, even if she couldn't be with you."

Anne held the letters to her chest. The rest of her rehearsed speech —the blame, the accusations, all of it melted away. "You have no idea how much this means."

"Growing up, I had this feeling. I knew something else was missing."

"I did too," Anne wiped her nose, blinking, "until I found this article and picture…and I found out about you."

"I know this is all too much. You just had a baby, but I'm here for you, Annie." Maribeth looked at the ceiling with wet eyes. "If I had known all these years…"

"We found each other now. Would you like to come in now and meet your new niece?"

Maribeth nodded, and her voice broke again when she said, "And when you're feeling up to it, I want to tell you everything Mom said."

Mom.

The missing piece had clicked into place. Her mom was scared and just a child when she had to make such an awful decision.

How grateful Anne was to understand that now and grow her family in the space of a single day.

I'll be Home

Don Bruns

for Christmas

W ade Russo was in trouble, and, yes, he was drinking before noon. He needed something to calm him down. The vultures were circling. The banks were calling in overextended loans. Vendors were threatening to stop delivery of crabs, lobsters, and steaks to his twenty-eight Captain Andy's Lobster Pot restaurants. Andy, his enterprising father, had started with a beachside stand, selling crab cakes, fried clams, and cold beer. The food was good, cheap, and very popular with the locals and the tourists.

His father had done well, nose-to-the-grindstone kind of thing. Wade didn't quite have that same passion. Obviously, he didn't have the attention to detail. Didn't want to work that hard. He did have a passion for wagering. And ponies, craps, sports…

And then Andrew expanded, adding lobster rolls to the menu then oysters. Shucked them right in front of the customers. Then he added a chef's table, where select customers could sit, watch, and eat as lobsters were steamed in front of them. Live crabs were steamed in a white wine and lemon sauce, and steaks, chops, and boils were prepared with a flair just several feet from the diners. Then he added an indoor restaurant, and included T bones, New York Strips, rib eyes, and boneless loin chops to the menu. And another location and then another. And people clamored for reservations. The phone never stopped ringing. And Captain Andy was the darling of the restaurant industry.

Food and Beverage magazine had said, "The chef's table at any of the Captain Andy's Lobster Pot restaurants is worth the three-month wait. Well worth it."

And Andrew threw parties. The reservations for his legendary events were even longer than three months. But the greatest party Captain Andy threw was his Christmas party. His wife, Wade's mother, loved Christmas. Loved the tree, the presents, the candles, the carolers, and the food. For the family, she baked cookies for a week. And Andy put together the traditional Christmas feast with a flair. For Elly, Eleonor Russo, His beloved wife. And she loved it.

There was turkey with Maryland crab seafood stuffing, salmon with cranberry sauce, hot-crab and cheesy artichoke dip, and a chocolate souffle yule log that was the best desert you would ever have. Bar none.

Christmas was the heart of Captain Andy's business. Pleasing his Eleonor was what drove him. There were decorated trees throughout the restaurant, a life-sized gingerbread one-room house where one lucky couple could eat each night, with candy ornaments, a sidewalk made of one thousand candy canes in front of every house, and dozens of lights. And for the night before Christmas Eve, every restaurant got their own Santa, complete with a comely Mrs. Clause.

Eleonor was happy, everyone was happy.

And Wade was drinking bourbon before noon to get just a little numb. Maybe a lot numb. At an early age and with an inflated salary, Wade became part of the family enterprise, rapidly working his way up to line cook then manager of one of the locations. He was family so there was never any doubt.

Wade took to wearing colorful sportscoats—orange, powder blue, yellow, and unlaced deck shoes with no socks. His soft brown hair fell over his ears, a tan from boating, and he enjoyed mingling with customers who obviously adored the fashionable restauranter. A good front man. Not so good on the business side. However, Captain Andy had bookkeepers, accountants, and attorneys who watched out for the corporate entity.

The son-turned-manager hired cute, sexy Marcy as a hostess, married Marcy, then cheated on her and divorced Marcy. Or she divorced him. Either way he didn't come out so good. Marcy walked off with a million and property. He wasn't happy.

And mom and dad were not happy either. But the business was growing, and they were hiring for positions that didn't even exist a year ago. They needed more and stronger top-end management. And Wade took over five stores, then ten. Now there were twenty-eight stores. He worked the outlandish promotions, helped build the brand, fired, hired, and hooked up with some of the staff.

Then Andy died. One second he was there, the next second he wasn't. Dictating to his secretary, he died mid-sentence.

"The Christmas celebration needs more…"

Keeled over in his office, a heart-attack. His doctor suggested it might be the stress from running fifteen, twenty-some, very busy restaurants. Whatever the reason, all fingers pointed to Wade to take charge. Take charge of a business that was charging full-steam-ahead into the future. The demand was strong, the future secure, and the expectations limitless.

And Wade's mother gave him her blessing. The wonderful woman who tried to turn a blind eye to her son's philandering, gambling, and wild lifestyle.

He loved his mother deeply. Was more-sorry for her than himself when the patriarch died. More than anything, he wanted her to be proud of him, proud of his ability to take the leadership role and keep the business thriving. And of course, her entire livelihood, her future, depended on him keeping the business thriving.

And all went well, except for the fact that Wade Russo had a gambling problem. And a drinking problem. And Wade had a womanizing problem. And those three problems tended to take up a lot his time.

So he let some things slide. He didn't pay enough attention to the quality, and word filtered back through calls, complaints from regulars, and a lot of social network sites that the food wasn't quite as good. That service was slow. That the Easter party was a little off. The plastic eggs with usually wonderful gift certificates inside weren't quite that wonderful. On the surface, things seemed all right. But they weren't.

And the business started to crumble. He borrowed against the assets because he could. And then he squandered those assets. He had a bad streak with the ponies and near disastrous results with his last two trips to Ocean Resort Casino in Atlantic City. Not quite true. One result wasn't near disastrous. It *was* disastrous. Wade wagered over one-million dollars in two decisive moves. Having successfully won a one-hundred-thousand-dollar payout playing craps, he decided to bet ten times that winning.

He'd been over-served, his ego over-inflated, and when Wade decided he could turn his mini-fortune into a huge cash payout it didn't work out so well. So he doubled down.

He lost money he didn't have. A lot of money he didn't have. And nothing he did seemed to right the ship.

Wade Russo was in trouble. Handed a gold mine, he'd turned it into fool's gold. Pyrite. And right now, as the business was hitting historic highs, he was descending to historic lows. The seemingly successful organization was on quicksand, slowly sinking.

Mark, his accountant, called him that morning.

"Don't know how long we can hold some of these guys off, Wade. You owe a boatload of money, and I don't see it."

"How long?"

"I don't know. Obviously every bank, every vendor will have a different cutoff date. We're trying to get them to stretch out the payments. But, my friend, you have burned most of your bridges."

"We'll sell the house, the car, the boat, and…"

"You are smarter than that." The accountant sighed, the sound of disgust. "You don't own any of those. They are leveraged beyond what they are worth. Wade, you are flat out broke, in debt beyond a place we can pay it back."

"So what do I do?"

"You asked me a year ago. I told you. Stop with the gambling, stop with the women, stop with the…"

"Now. Now what can I do?"

There was a long silence. Heavy breathing, and Wade waited. Waited for the answer as to how he was going to save his late father's empire.

"I don't have an answer, Wade. But you are six months back on your obligation to my firm, and we need immediate payment. I loved your father, and I'm stretching this obligation because of him. Because of your mother. However, we need to receive your payment or you are on your own. I'll call your mother and explain."

"Mark, give me time. I'll figure it out."

"Get me something, Wade. You owe us a lot of money."

He took a last swallow of the Four Roses Single Barrel Bourbon, got into his, actually the bank's, Porsche Carrera GT and opened it up for two hours, pulling into the driveway of his lakefront cottage. All six-thousand square feet of it. He drove into the empty six-car garage, walked out, and closed the door, ignoring the expansive stucco covered mansion with sixty windows that looked out onto the crystal-clear lake. He walked directly to the boat house, the upper level complete with an outdoor kitchen, a lounge area, and below, *Eleonor*, a thirty-two-foot cabin cruiser with a galley, two cabins, two heads, and two Twin Crusader 270 HP gas engines. The boat could move big time. The yacht kept him calm. The water was his salvation, and the women he invited on board excited him, kept him alive and young at heart. There was no woman this time. He needed to think this through. By himself. The pressure was on, and he needed to be levelheaded with a clear view of how to survive this crisis. He was about to lose his inheritance. Within six months, maybe sooner, the banks would close on his restaurants.

He turned the key and pushed the throttle forward, the power beneath him. There was a roar, an exhilarated feel of man over water. The feel of skimming over the sea, and his problems disappeared. For a moment.

He reached for the Four Roses Bourbon directly next to the pilot's cockpit and poured himself a fresh drink and started to feel the buzz. One hand on the wheel, his drink in the other.

Don't drink and drive? He wrote the book on how to drink while driving. But he'd never had an accident, never hurt anyone. He'd only been picked up once, and the cop had been a fan of Captain Andy's so he got off with a warning. The drink tasted so good, he mixed another. The water and bourbon calmed him. He needed to find a solution. Now, he was relaxed, ready to take on the challenge.

Someone had said "Fill your life with lakes, not things." And he was reminded of the Midnight Cowboy theme song sung by Nilsson with the lyric 'skippin' over the ocean like a stone.' He was skippin' over the water.

He checked the fuel gauge. Not where it should be but enough gas to get him to point B. Literally. The stopping point, the small marina, the restaurant, Point B. And he decided that was his first goal. Point B.

And he pushed the throttle, kicking up a back-wave, a wake that would go for half a mile. He was skippin' over the water, like a stone.

Detective Evan St. Lifer got the call at two in the afternoon. And he recognized the name. That didn't happen very often. Eleonor Russo reported her son, Wade, as missing. There were thousands of people missing in the United States. In his community, there were several, but very seldom did he recognize the name of the missing victim.

"Wade Russo?"

"Yes," she said. "He visits religiously on Monday at five."

Captain Andy's Lobster Pot. Everyone knew the name. He happened to recognize the owner's name.

The frail sounding woman was breathing heavily, obviously agitated.

"He didn't show up yesterday and hasn't called as of today."

"One day doesn't necessarily mean…"

"No, detective, you don't understand. He always calls. There are no ifs or buts about it. Wade calls me. And he didn't. So I called his office. They haven't heard from him for five days."

"Does he sometimes take time off?"

"Yes. More than I think he should, but he calls in. Touches base with Ruth, his secretary."

"We'll need some more information," St. Lifer said. "Were there personal problems, problems at his workplace, any financial considerations? Is there a romantic relationship that might be the reason?"

He needed to lay it all out, get her considering what might be the reason the missing person was missing.

"I don't mean to be insensitive, but when someone disappears, there are often underlying concerns."

She paused.

"I don't interfere with the work environment. I try to keep my mouth shut and opinions to myself. Wade isn't a detail person. I'm afraid he's gotten used to everyone else doing the work. Maybe he's taken his eye off the ball. I don't know if that has anything to do with his disappearance."

"Ma'am?"

She paused again. St. Lifer dealt with it daily. Always hard to discuss family with a stranger.

"I really shouldn't mention this. It probably has nothing to do with his not calling, but his accountant, my accountant…our accountant, called me today. Apparently, our business is in some financial difficulty. I'm certain we'll take care of this but please keep this private. Detective, this can't get out. It might hurt our business."

St. Lifer nodded. She couldn't see it, but he nodded. St. Lifer understood. The secrets he uncovered while searching for missing persons… he could write a book. He'd actually considered that.

"I promise you; we are not going to divulge any private information."

"I certainly hope not. Anyway, Wade might have been responsible for spending…"

She choked up.

"Mrs. Russo, can we meet? I think sitting down face to face might help us get a clearer view of the situation."

"Of course."

St. Lifer scrolled through his phone calendar.

"Tomorrow at two p.m. We could meet here at the station?"

"Two is fine, but can you come here?"

"Of course."

She gave him the address. He knew it anyway. One of the mansions that lined River Front Parkway. Five homes that had been built on the town's water way. The first, in the early twenties, by Jason Albright, who started the national chain JA Hardware. By hometown standards, the palatial residences were like manors. There was Rosco Griffith the concrete king, George Cramer who invented a coupling for railroad cars, and Ruth McClaren, who built a bank. They'd all been sold except for the Russo home. Russo's had been a staple in the community. Philanthropists, a wing of the hospital was named after two of them, the entire city library funded by the restaurant owner. He wondered if Mrs. Russo was in danger of losing her property.

She hung up.

"Morisey," St. Lifer looked at his older partner one desk back, "any plans tomorrow at two p.m.?"

"I've got seven missing person cases, Evan. I'm always busy."

St. Lifer took a swallow of coffee from his colorful mug. A picture of a cop car, lights flashing red and blue, and the caption "I drive a company car."

"This one is interesting."

"What missing person case isn't interesting?"

"This one is the owner of Captain Andy's Lobster Pot."

"Really?"

"Really."

"That's a big deal. We eat there two or three times a year, the one over in Chesterville. Man, Christmas is so festive. Do you know they build a life-sized gingerbread house inside there? My wife loves that place. The owner is dead, right? Andy?"

"Yeah, a couple of years ago. Their kid now runs the chain. And mom is worried because he hasn't visited or called in about a week."

"So she's coming in?"

"No, we've been invited."

"Really? River Front Parkway? One of those homes? Forget about these seven missing persons. I'm there."

"It seems, and you've got to keep this to yourself, that there are possibly some financial problems."

"It's always financial problems," Morisey smiled and shook his head, "unless it's a spouse. A lover. Get rid of the financial situations and the lovers and no one would have any reason to disappear."

St. Lifer had put out an all-points bulletin even though the case was thin. If any law enforcement agency in fifty-states heard about this guy, they were to call St. Lifer. It only took minutes to make the profile. Picture from the restaurant website. Brief description of who he was. It wasn't much but a start.

She answered the door, dressed in a deep green, floor-length skirt and pristine white blouse that buttoned around the neck. A striking woman but obviously anxious, her hands clasped in front of her and her brow furrowed. Music played softly in the background, and Evan made out part of the chorus. "Thank God for kids."

She motioned to the gentleman beside her, dressed in a pearl-gray sport coat, burgundy tie, and sharply creased black trousers.

"This is David. David is our house manager."

St. Lifer glanced at Jim Morisey. The things you can afford when you had money. He didn't have a house manager and was pretty sure that Morisey didn't either.

The couple walked them down a long hallway, past a partially opened closet with overcoats and rubber boots. St. Lifer noticed a jacket style BCD, a buoyance control device used by divers. Two oxygen tanks were tucked into a corner.

"Do you dive?"

"Oh, heaven's no. David does."

They walked into a spacious living room.

"Please, Detectives, have a seat."

She led them to a gray velvet sofa, and she sat across from them in a blue check-patterned chair.

"David, would you please bring in the tea?"

He walked out of the room.

"There's really no need," St. Lifer said.

"It's a civil thing to do," she replied. "After all, you gentlemen came out here to help me find my son."

The well-dressed 'manager' walked in with a silver tray, a pot of tea, and three cups. He set the tray, pot, and cups on the coffee table.

"David is going to sit in during our interview."

"Great."

"I want this on record," she said, "David knows Wade and understands our relationship."

"David." St. Lifer smiled and put out his hand.

The man shook his head and didn't return the gesture. Instead he poured the steaming beverage into the cups and passed them out. He then sat down in a chair next to Eleonor.

"Mrs. Russo," St. Lifer blew on his tea and concentrated on Andrew's widow, "can you again elaborate on the disappearance of your son?" She closed her eyes and recited the story she'd told him.

"Wade calls on a regular basis. Two times a week, minimum. And he visits every Monday. He's an only child, and he and I have always been close. I think as adults, parents and children are often distant. In our case, there is a bond. David and I work up a meal for him. We all have dinner together and talk about the business. Sometimes, he stays over."

"It hasn't been that long since you noticed he hadn't contacted you. Possibly, he was called out of town, maybe he's working on getting finances together…"

David gave him a sharp, disapproving glare.

"I told the Detective that there were some concerns, David. If I want to find Wade, I've got to be honest with someone."

"Is the financial situation enough of a concern that he would try to get away from it?"

"I'm not comfortable talking too much about our business to an outsider. However, other than his marriage, I've never known my son to walk away from anything. In fact, he likes a challenge. Most of the time. Anyway, the accountant, Mark, is coming by later to discuss details. If this is more of an issue than I think it is, I'll call you."

Morisey said, "David, you've known the family and Wade for a long time. Any reason you can think of that he would disappear?"

The dapper dresser shook his head. He obviously wasn't going to be much help.

"We will need his address…"

"He lives two miles from here."

"You don't have a restaurant here. Why did you, your husband, and Wade decide to locate here?"

"Believe me, Detective, it's a blessing to get away from the stress."

"So where does he live?"

"On Oak Park Boulevard. It's a small unassuming house."

Unlike the one they were in now.

"David drove over there a number of times. My son isn't home, and his car is gone."

"We'll need his address, information on his car, and access to the home. Where else would he go, what…"

"His summer house. Up at Lake Charles. David called neighbors, but they are a mile or so away and haven't gotten back to us."

David called? David could talk?

"So it may be as simple as he drove to the Lake Charles home, a pretty tony area, and he's just taking a break."

"He would have called."

"Give us the information. And, only because it's standard procedure, we will need some DNA samples. Possibly a hairbrush, toothbrush, unwashed shirt…"

"Oh my God. You think…"

Morisey put his hand up.

"We don't think anything, Mrs. Russo. As Detective St. Lifer said, it's standard procedure, okay?"

There were tears in her eyes.

"David, can you please put together those things for the Detectives."

Frowning, the man stood and walked up the curving staircase, his hand on the polished walnut railing.

"The music, what is it?"

"*A Country Christmas Eve.* The Oak Ridge Boys."

"Ma'am, It's May."

"I'm well aware of what month it is, Detective St. Lifer." She wiped her eyes with the back of her hand. "In my house, it's always Christmas."

The neighbor at Lake Charles reported. *Eleonor* was missing from the boat house. One problem solved. It would appear that the son had taken the portable house out on the lake, and there were numerous stops he could make. There were twelve restaurants, two hotels, three marinas, two campgrounds, one McDonalds, and even a miniature golf course. All accessible by boat and all with docking facilities. And you could live on a well-stocked cabin cruiser for weeks.

"Is this even worth our time, Evan? The guy went for a joy ride. No crime, no foul."

Morisey turned from the coffee pot and walked to his desk.

"I've got more important cases in this stack."

"Yeah, but you got to meet David, and you had some very expensive tea."

And at that very moment, the desk phone rang.

"St. Lifer."

"We've got a call from Charles City police department, Detective."

"Put it through."

"Detective, this is officer Robin Bardot. We're on Lake Charles and noticed you're looking for Wade Russo."

"We are. You've seen him?"

"No. But we know his boat *Eleonor.* The locals know it as well."

"And?"

"This afternoon, a large piece of scorched fiberglass washed up on a beach just North of us. Printing on the side was *Eleo*. It was a fragment. A section had been broken off after that."

St. Lifer was quiet.

"Detective?"

"Yeah, yeah. What are the odds? So you're assuming there was an accident?"

"We're assuming nothing. We've got a patrol boat out and a copter overhead. We're sending two drones with live feed so hopefully we'll have more information soon. We will keep you informed when and if we find anything else."

"Thank you, Officer Bardot. Please give me your number and be sure to call at any time."

"Doesn't sound good," Morisey said.

"A piece of what has to be his boat washed up near Charles City. Sounds like an accident."

"Well, that would be the perfect escape, wouldn't it."

"It could be," St. Lifer said, "the truth. Maybe he had an accident."

"On Lake Charles?"

"It could happen."

"That's a pretty calm body of water. But maybe a whale hit the boat. A shark took a bite of it."

St. Lifer smiled.

"No, maybe does not fit. I think we need to investigate. Now, we have reason to explore this story."

And St. Lifer went home to his lonely apartment, to Cat, the cat who only tolerated him because of a shelter and food situation, to a king-sized bed that he used to share with Cara. She'd found other accommodations with another officer, someone he considered a friend. She'd left her cat as a reminder.

And after a bourbon and soda, and another, St. Lifer considered how an accident could solve a financial situation. And on his third drink, it registered. Either Wade Russo had truly died in an accident or he had decided to disappear so he wouldn't have to face the fallout. The possible collapse of his family business. And if that was the case, maybe there was life insurance. That made more sense than anything. He made a note to check on the insurance angle tomorrow. Didn't know how, but someone would know if Wade Russo had some serious life-insurance. His bet was that he did.

The next morning poured more fuel on the fire. Literally. Two other scorched pieces of fiberglass washed up on shore along with a chair cushion. Later that day, the copter saw remains of a boat and called in coordinates. A rescue craft was dispatched to what was left of the burned yacht's carcass. Divers went down, but the only things that were salvageable were some hard furniture frames, ceramic toilets, and a quartz countertop from the galley. The bottom of the lake was littered with pieces of ceramic, metal pots and pans, and assorted unburnable items.

At some distance, they saw a floating piece of fiberglass with a white cloth snagged to it. The rescue boat netted the board and the remains of a piece of someone's wardrobe. The clothing, a blood-soaked shirt, became a critical part of the investigation.

St. Lifer got the news when he walked into the office. He took off his sport coat, hung it on the back of his chair, and walked to the coffee pot.

"Evan, they're delivering part of a bloody shirt today." Morisey saw his eyebrows rise. "Never thought I'd ever say that. They want us to run a DNA test to see if it's our Wade."

Deoxynucleic acid, DNA, could make a strong case that Russo had been killed in an onboard fire or explosion.

"So no body?"

"Not yet," his partner said. "They're combing the bottom of the lake."

"What do you think?"

"I'm starting to agree. He may be dead. You know that lake is a hundred and thirty feet deep in some areas. Divers can only stay down maybe ten minutes at a time, or nitrogen builds up in their system. So it could take some time. And by the way, the cops in Charles City have kept it quiet to the press. I mean, it's a small community with only a weekly paper, but it's going to get out probably today. We need to tell Mrs. Russo."

"Morisey, we need to find out if he had some large insurance policies."

Morisey punched in a key on his cellphone and put it on speaker.

"Jed, Jim Morisey."

"Need some more insurance, my friend?"

"I've got too much already. You're a good salesman. Listen, how do I find out how much life insurance someone has? Someone who is deceased."

"Could take a little time, but you send information on the person to NAUPA."

"NAUPA?"

"National Association of Unclaimed Property Administrators. They send out a notice to all insurance companies who register with them."

"Sounds like some work."

"Jim, why not try the obvious."

"Apparently it's not. To me anyway."

"Call the beneficiary. They may already know."

St. Lifer threw up his hands. Duh.

"Let's assume," St. Lifer sipped his second cup, "that there is no body. We can't produce one. If they have a policy, a large policy that would take care of their financial problems, how long would it take for him to be declared legally dead? How long before the payout?"

"Call Judge Fare."

Fair Fare, his nickname fit him. He was a very fair judge, and almost anyone who came before him in his court respected that.

"We had a case in front of him two years ago, remember? The single mom who took off on a camping trip with a boyfriend. He came back, she never did and there was never a body."

"Boyfriend did it."

"Not a shred of proof," Morisey checked the numbers on his phone and called.

"Judge Fare's office, Janet speaking."

"Janet, is the Judge in? This is Jim Morisey."

"Detective Morisey, he's in court. Can I help you with anything?"

"A person comes up missing. How long before we get a verdict that they are legally dead if we never produce the body?"

"In this state, seven to ten years. Then we issue a death certificate."

"Wow. You know this because?"

"Because I know a lot of things, Detective. I'm a very bright person."

On the other end, she smiled. He felt it.

"Yes, you are."

"Well, Evan, that shoots holes in your theory. If he's still alive, they won't find the body. If they don't find the body, it could be ten years before a life insurance policy is paid out. If the company is really in trouble, they'd be out of business by then."

"I want to know if there's a policy."

"Pick up the phone. Call her."

"She's not going to tell me."

"Look, the press is going to be all over this boat thing. Let's drive out to her place, break the news, tell her that we are concerned, and then ask."

"It's a plan. And we need to talk to the lab. The minute that shirt shows up, we need to run the DNA."

David answered to door, impeccably dressed in a black jacket, tan slacks, and a muted yellow tie. Bing Crosby was singing "White Christmas" in the background.

"Can we talk to Mrs. Russo?"

"You should have called if you wanted an appointment."

"Look, David, we have news. She can hear it from us or on TV."

"One moment please."

He walked up the stairs.

"Jeeves has a stick up his butt," Morisey shook his head.

"Looks out for her. It's his job."

The Detectives stepped inside, and St. Lifer noticed the open closet. The dive jacket and oxygen tanks were gone.

A moment later, the lady appeared in a simple tan, ankle-length skirt and white blouse. Always looking like she walked out of a catalog.

"Mrs. Russo, we have news. Disturbing, but not conclusive."

"I'm not liking the sound of this."

"The boat apparently had an accident. Fragments have been found, but at the moment," keep the bloody garment out of the conversation until they had proof, "no body has been found."

She took a deep breath.

"So there is some hope…"

"I would suggest that until there's physical evidence, there's always hope."

"I had a feeling when he didn't call, didn't visit…"

"We should let the authorities do their job."

"I suppose," she said.

"And Mrs. Russo," he hesitated, not sure what her response would be, "do you know if your son had a life insurance policy? And if so, who was the beneficiary?"

She turned in the doorway and looked at David. Some unseen message went between them.

"I know he did. A large policy. Several as a matter of fact. And the beneficiary was the company and me. Are you satisfied?"

"Yes, ma'am. I hope and pray that your son is alive, and we will be in touch with the latest developments."

They turned, as The Beach Boys Christmas album played softly. St. Lifer smiled. It was their version of "White Christmas". She had an eclectic taste.

"She didn't show a lot of emotion," St. Lifer said. "Kind of like she expected bad news."

"It's why she called us. She knew something was wrong."

DNA tests showed that the blood belonged to Wade Russo. Thanks to St. Lifer asking for DNA samples. Everything pointed to death by…a fire on board, an accident with some collision, maybe an explosion.

A wallet with credit cards and driver's license was pulled off the lake's floor. A shoe and a gold bracelet that he wore were nearby.

"I guess we're officially off the case," Morisey said.

"No body. No death certificate."

"I agree. Everything seems too neat. But if it's insurance, the old lady might be dead before the death certificate is issued."

"Yeah," St. Lifer ran his hands through his sandy hair, "seven to ten won't save the restaurant."

The press ran with the story. Towns around the lake led with the report, networks around the country picked up on it, and many featured a photo of the good-looking Wade Russo—sport jacket, open collared shirt, flashing his teeth for the camera. And then a reporter for the Chesterville Gazette looked into the financial problems of the chain. And the possibility of suicide, or faking his death became the talking point.

Immediately the family, the business, filed for a death claim, using the DNA and possessions at the bottom of the deep lake as evidence.

And Wade Russo became a distant memory.

Until Jim Morisey got a phone call.

"Morisey? This is Judge Fare."

"Judge, good to hear from you."

"A couple of months ago, you called here and talked to Janet."

"I did," he remembered. "She said a missing person with no evidence of a body would receive a death certificate within seven to ten years."

"And, she's right. However, something she left out is this. If there is compelling evidence that the death occurred, even if you don't have a body, the death certificate can be issued within six months."

"Six months?"

"Six months. I hope this clarifies the answer to your question."

"And you called me because?"

"I was intrigued with the Wade Russo case. His business and family asked for a death certificate immediately on the discovery of a DNA sample."

"Right." Morisey was hanging on every word.

"The courts apparently agreed, if he is not found, to issue a death certificate in December. I was not aware. But that will be six months."

"And apparently, according to his mother, he had a couple of huge insurance policies."

"Death certificate means, in most cases, the insurance company pays off. Immediately."

"Thanks, Judge."

Turning to his partner, he said, "Evan, that means, depending on the settlement, the financial fiasco is solved. Work out a deal with the vendors, the banks, and show them evidence they can collect by December.

"It's off our plate, Jim."

And November came, and Morisey invited St. Lifer to their home for Thanksgiving dinner, complete with traditional turkey, stuffing, cranberry salad, and pumpkin pie.

There was talk of Christmas, maybe even visiting Captain Andy's for a holiday feast.

And Christmas Eve, he probably shouldn't have been driving, having had a couple of high balls, but he did. St. Lifer got behind the wheel of his Chevy Spark and drove over to the Russo home.

Six o'clock. He parked across the street, six months into Wade's disappearance. Six months and weeks into the meeting with Eleonor, David, and their first conversation. The radio talk show was highlighting the NFL season. Closing his eyes, he started to drift, and heard the sound of a car's engine. A Ford Fusion pulled into the driveway. A popular rental car.

He shook his head, clearing the cobwebs and watched as a man stepped out, wearing a leather jacket and a cowboy hat. As he walked to the porch, St. Lifer got out of his car.

"Wade Russo."

The man stopped and turned around.

"Do I know you?"

"No. I'm Detective Evan St. Lifer. I investigated your disappearance."

He approached Russo.

"Yeah. I have no recollection."

"None?"

"None. Now if you'll excuse me, I'm going in to see my mother. You do know it's Christmas Eve."

"The insurance companies paid off. It came to something like six-million dollars." St. Lifer sipped his coffee.

"And it is not a crime to fake your death. We know that. But if there's fraud involved…"

"But he has amnesia. Elenor and David said they were as surprised as anybody when he showed up."

"I want to know where the diving equipment went. Maybe that's nothing but…"

"We're never going to find out, Jim. He's home, the restaurant chain is solvent…"

"And I want to know why you were parked across the street on Christmas Eve."

St. Lifer smiled.

"It's always Christmas in the Russo house. And there always seems to be Christmas music. But there's only one song that expresses where everyone called family wants to be."

"You never believed he was dead."

"Insurance paid off in six months, Morisey. Six months. I'm sure there will be litigation, but…"

"So I'll be *home* for Christmas."

"And," St. Lifer said, "Christmas Eve will find me, where the love light gleams."

"Kind of sappy, don't you think?"

"Hey, I solved the case. I found our missing person."

Blessed Be the Day

Kathy Harris

# of Our Savior's Birth

One

S avannah Jackson slid her SIG Sauer P365 into her high heel boot,
tucked her Tennessee Bureau of Investigation Special Agent's ID into
the back pocket of her faded jeans, and freshened her lipstick. *Irresistible
Red*. It was the perfect color. She would need all the help she could get
tonight if she was going to catch a serial killer.

So far, the Nightshade Murders, as they were known internally
at the Bureau, hadn't garnered much attention in the Nashville press.
Politics—and a local music industry celebrity scandal—had dominated
the headlines for weeks.

As far as she was concerned, that was a good thing. She would rather
work a case without a lot of fanfare. Although, she did find it ironic that
local media chose sensationalism over covering an actual crime spree.

And a deadly one at that. There was a crazed killer in the Nashville
area, who had been poisoning young, beautiful women.

Savannah capped her lipstick tube and tossed it into her handbag.
She might be undercover, but that didn't mean she would be unrecognized.
At least one person in the crowd tonight would know her, and he
would be surprised to see her there.

In a crazy twist of fate, her ex-husband, Daniel Jackson, and his band, Straight Up, would be performing at Santa's Pub at nine o'clock. She checked her watch. Less than twenty minutes from now.

Opening the driver's side door of her white Toyota RAV4, she stepped onto the sidewalk, and scanned three hundred sixty degrees around her. Then she engaged the locks and set out at a brisk pace. Santa's was three blocks from where she had managed to find a place to park. Cars were lined up and down Bransford Avenue, the thru street that ran between Nashville's old fairgrounds and the Berry Hill community.

She engaged the locks of her SUV and set out at a brisk pace. Santa's was three blocks from where she had managed to find a place to park. Cars were lined up and down Bransford Avenue, the thru street that ran between Nashville's old fairgrounds and the Berry Hill community.

In less than a minute, the back side of the venue was in sight, and it was an interesting structure, to say the least. Rumor had it that the small karaoke club—an internationally-known dive bar—had been built from an old railroad car and a few discarded shipping containers. The building, which had the appearance of a doublewide trailer with a front porch added across the front, and adjacent privacy fencing had been painted with colorful murals of Santa Claus and other holiday art.

Although the physical appearance of Santa's Pub might be considered gaudy by some, its clientele boasted Nashville and international music celebrities, as well as tourists from all over the world. People who had read about the one-of-a-kind nightspot had added it to their bucket list of things to do.

But Savannah had decided to come here on a hunch.

Although the Nightshade Murders appeared to be random, there were some interesting commonalities. It was obvious that the killer was targeting young women who frequented nightclubs. Upon closer consideration, they were all nightclubs with live music.

Of course, clubs with live music were a dime a dozen in Nashville, especially on Lower Broadway and up and down First and Second Avenues. But none of the murders had been linked to Lower Broadway. Instead, each of the six murder victims had patronized a standalone club on the night of their demise. Those six clubs were scattered across Metropolitan Nashville, from Bellevue to East Nashville to the Gulch to Wedgewood-Houston and beyond.

And there was another common denominator in the crimes. One that Savannah hadn't realized until last night. Each of the six victims had been in a club where a celebrity—or popular —band had played. And that was what brought her to Santa's tonight.

Straight Up wasn't a typical bar band. Their music wasn't exclusively pop or country. In fact, they had charted hits in both formats. They had also garnered the attention of Christian radio in the tradition of bands like Nickelback, U2, and Coldplay.

Not many entertainers could boast such crossover airplay. And, just as Straight Up had managed to defy musical definition, they had also avoided the extravagant trappings of success. Each member of the group earned a decent living, but without the inconvenience that came with playing major arena tours. They had no eighteen wheelers, no fleet of tour busses, and no extraneous crew members. Instead, Straight Up's touring schedule took them to major nightclubs and churches, as well as to the amalgamation of the two, Christian coffee houses. Some nights, the group played small amphitheaters and performing arts centers. But a dive bar? This had to be a first for them.

Savannah stepped up her pace. There was a cool breeze out of the west tonight, but she had opted not to wear a jacket. She would soon be in a hot, smoky bar surrounded by a roomful of people who were out for a night of good music. A long night. Santa's was open until three o'clock in the morning, seven days a week, three hundred sixty-five days a year, including Christmas Day.

Although a live band was unusual for Santa's, this wasn't an ordinary night. It was Christmas Eve. And, if Savannah was right, the Nightshade killer had a fascination with word play. Targeting a victim on Christmas Eve at a nightclub that was dedicated to Christmas year-round seemed way too obvious.

Each of the six victims had died of Atropine poisoning. And Atropine wasn't your run of the mill murder weapon. Not unless you read a lot of Agatha Christie novels. The chemical, which was used medicinally for heart rhythm issues and, ironically, as an antidote for other poisons, was derived from the Atropa Belladonna plant and commonly known as Deadly Nightshade.

Ironically, the words *bella donna* in Italian translated to *beautiful woman* in English, which was appropriate in the Nightshade Murders. The victims ranged in age from twenty-five to twenty-nine. And each had been described by family and friends as attractive women with out-going, tending toward vivacious, personalities.

Although Savannah knew quite a bit about the killer's psychological profile, answers to the important questions remained. How had the victims consumed the poison? And who had administered it? She hoped to find that out before a seventh victim succumbed to the murderer's deadly spree.

Stepping from the dimly-lit sidewalk that ran alongside Bransford Avenue onto the gravel parking lot of Santa's Pub, she spotted Daniel's tour bus, which had been parked parallel to the building. As she walked by it, the front door of the bus opened and Daniel Jackson stood, looking at her from the top of the stairs.

"Hey, gorgeous." He said, galloping down the steps. "What are you doing here?"

"I could ask you the same thing." She countered.

"We're playing at the behest of Santa." He walked up beside her, took her arm, tucked it into his, leading her toward the front porch of the venue. "You can't turn the Big Guy down. Especially at Christmas."

"I suppose you're right." She stepped past him into the crowded, smoke-filled room and waited for him to catch up with her.

"Seriously, why are you here tonight?"

"Just visiting."

He stopped and looked at her, narrowing his dark brown eyes. "You're working a case, aren't you?"

"What makes you think that?"

"So, you don't deny it." He bent his six-foot frame, bringing his lips close to her ear.

Musk and vanilla. It was her favorite fragrance, and the one he had always worn.

"Don't worry, your secret is safe with me." He straightened. "Why don't you sit at the band table?"

"Oh, I don't think I—" She glanced around the room but didn't see an empty chair.

He grinned. "It might be a good idea, unless you want to park yourself next to the bar, and I don't think that's your style."

"Thank you," she said. "On both counts."

Savannah followed him to a table that was only a few feet from the stage.

"Can I get you anything?" He asked.

She shook her head. "I'm good."

"Okay. I'll check with you after the first set."

Two

Daniel had seated Savannah in the perfect place for her to watch the room and still see the show. While she vetted the crowd, he gathered his band members on stage—a small cubby with three microphones, two amps, a partial drum kit, and the mixing board—for prayer.

She spent a few minutes evaluating each person in the room, visually sweeping from left to right. Several patrons were still searching for seats. Others had found a place to stand near the back. But, for the most part, everyone was seated and ready to watch the show, and no one appeared to be particularly uncomfortable or acting suspiciously.

In her final, pre-show sweep of the room, she saw a scruffy looking man with a dark beard, who was standing near the bar. He raised his can of beer to salute her and nodded. She looked away and kept him in her peripheral vision.

"Excuse me." A blonde woman, who was about Savannah's age, hurried up to the table. "Are you using this seat?" she asked, gesturing to the chair next to Savannah. It was piled high with band merchandise, t-shirts, ballcaps, and CDs.

"Hmm, I don't know..." Savannah said, looking around for Daniel but not seeing him.

"We can move the merch, Kayla," Daniel said, appearing from behind them and scooping the items into his arms.

"You're too sweet." The blonde practically cooed, but Daniel ignored her. Instead, he winked at Savannah.

"It's no problem," he said. "I was just about to take it to the bar."

The petite blonde ignored the brushoff, settled into her seat, and turned to Savannah. "Hi! I'm Kayla." She stuck out her hand.

"Nice to meet you. I'm Savannah." Savannah shook the woman's hand and hoped to avoid an extended conversation.

"Oh... same here." Kayla said. "How do you know the band?"

Apparently, they were about to play a game of Twenty Questions. Savannah considered her response. There was no reason not to tell the truth. "I was married to Daniel."

"The lead singer?"

"Yes." Savannah glanced at her watch and then back to the blonde. "For about five minutes."

"Ha!" Kayla's face brightened. "I like you."

Great.

"Do you have children?"

Alex, Straight Up's long-time drummer, who had also been Daniel's best friend for years, kicked off the opening beat, and Savannah breathed a sigh of relief. She had been saved by the band. She repositioned herself so she could continue to monitor the scruffy looking man at the bar. He didn't move until the second song, and then he started walking toward her.

"Excuse me, miss. Would you care to dance?"

When Savannah turned to respond, she saw that he was talking to Kayla. The blonde fluttered her eyelashes. "I suppose just one."

"I'm Earl," he said, taking Kayla by the hand and leading her to the small dance floor directly in front of the stage. They were soon joined by three other couples.

Savannah used the opportunity to continue her surveillance. Nothing appeared to be out of the ordinary. For the most part, it was a typical Straight Up crowd, at least the secular side of them, mixed with a few of what looked to be Santa's regulars and out-of-towners. Patrons at some of tables were drinking cans of beer, while others were sipping on bottled water. Savannah frowned. She had just discovered a potential flaw in the theory that had brought her here tonight.

Spiking a canned beverage or a bottle of water, the only drinks served at Santa's, would be an almost impossible task. Certainly not as easy as dumping a vial into a mixed beverage or a soft drink in a glass. It took a considerable amount of Atropine to kill someone. A drop or two wasn't enough.

After the music stopped, Earl escorted Kayla back to the table. "Thank you, miss," he said, helping her with her chair. Then he turned to Savannah. "May I buy you a drink?" he asked, noticing that she didn't have one.

"Oh, no. I'm fine. But thank you. I'm still deciding what I want."

The band kicked off the next song, and Earl put his hand on the back of Savannah's chair, leaning into her. "In that case, would you like to join me on the dance floor?"

"No, but thank you again," she said. "I was, unfortunately, born with two left feet." She did her best to smile.

Earl glanced down at her. "They look fine to me."

Savannah could feel the heat rise to her face. "I meant that figuratively."

Earl grinned. "And I meant what I said as a compliment."

"Thanks, Earl. Isn't that your name?"

His smile widened. "Close enough."

"I really appreciate the offer, but I'm here to see a friend tonight." She gestured to the band. "I'm a friend of the lead singer."

He stiffened. "Forgive me, ma'am," he said. "I didn't realize you were here with someone. But, then again, you're a beautiful woman, and I understand." He turned quickly and walked away.

Kayla swiveled toward Savannah. "You didn't tell me you were here *with* Daniel. I thought you were divorced."

Savannah dodged what appeared to be invisible daggers heading in her direction. "I am… We are." She said, wondering why she felt the need to explain herself to a woman she had only just met. "I was…" She lowered her voice. "I was fudging a bit with Earl, trying to get rid of him."

Kayla didn't seem to be convinced. "You are a beautiful woman. I can see why all of the men in the room are interested in you." Another round of daggers flew.

"I'm not sure what that—"

"Ladies, are you enjoying yourselves tonight?" It was one of Santa's helpers. "Can I get you anything?"

Kayla relaxed. "I would love to have another beer."

The man turned to Savannah. "And you, miss? The lead singer of the band asked me to get you whatever you wanted." He pointed to Daniel on stage. "What would you like?"

Savannah shot a glance at Kayla, who was staring at her, and then looked back to the man. "A bottle of water would be fine."

"Of course," he said. "I'll be right back."

Three

After the second set, Daniel pulled up an empty chair from another table and took a seat across from Savannah. Kayla excused herself to go to the bathroom.

"It's really good to see you, Vanna. How have you been?"

"I'm great," she said. "Work has been busy. And I—"

"No, I mean, *really*." He studied her. "How are you doing without… us?"

She startled. Why was he asking her such a thing?

"Daniel, it has been a year."

"It seems like longer, doesn't it?"

She sat back in her chair. Was this going where she thought it was going, because if it was, she couldn't give him the response he needed.

She collected her thoughts, sorting through the emotions of the past year. "I'm here on business, remember?"

He nodded. "I guess I had hoped otherwise."

"I don't know what to say. I mean if you're—"

The scruffy man with the beard re-appeared. "Do the two of you lovebirds mind if I join you?"

"Of course not, Carl. Have you met my ex-wife?"

"Carl?" Savannah hesitated. "I thought your name was Earl."

"Loud music." He laughed. "Pleased to meet you again, ma'am." He turned to Daniel. "You didn't tell me she was this pretty."

"How do the two of you know each other?" Savannah asked. "I have a feeling it's an interesting story."

"You always were perceptive." Daniel looked to Carl and then back to her.

"This one is yours." The older man laughed and took a drink from his bottle of water. He had changed names *and* beverages. "In fact, I want to hear your version, Dan."

Daniel laughed nervously and looked around.

Savannah folded her arms. The spotlight was now on Daniel Jackson.

"I met Carl here a little over a year ago," he said.

"Here?"

"Yes," he said. "Here, at the Pub."

"You were here when we were married?"

He looked away and then back to her. "You and I were going through tough times. Band rehearsals ran late one night, but I still wasn't ready to go home. So, I decided to check this place out. I'd always heard about it, but I'd never been here."

"That's the night we met," Carl said.

Daniel nodded.

"Carl encouraged me... He told me a few things about his life that related to what I was going through. He gave me the incentive to try to work things out with you." Daniel hesitated. "Of course, we know how that ended."

Savannah nodded.

"He's a good man," Carl said, getting up from his chair. The one Kayla had previously occupied. "It's nice to finally meet you, Savannah," he said. "I've heard a lot of good things about you."

"Thank you," Savannah said before turning back to Daniel. "We gave it our best shot."

"Did we?" he asked. "You were wrapped up in your work, and I was wrapped up in mine. I think we were busy, and we just moved on not realizing that we were leaving the best part of our lives behind."

Savannah pushed back from the table. "Daniel, I'm not ready to go there right now. I have an important case, and I need to focus on—" She stopped mid-sentence, realizing that she was confirming everything he had just said.

He stood. "I understand. Your job has always been important to you." He replaced the chair he had borrowed. "Look... I need to get busy. It's my job to greet the other customers." With that, he turned and walked away.

What had just happened? Coming here tonight had no doubt been a mistake. An even bigger one than she had expected. She had not only miscalculated the location of the next Nightshade Murder, but she had given Daniel the wrong impression. *Had he really been thinking she was here to put their marriage back together?* That idea was too much to take in.

"I brought you another bottle of water," Kayla said, retaking her seat beside Savannah.

"Thank you," Savannah tried to smile, but she needed to get away. "Do you mind watching my seat while I step outside for a few minutes? I need a breath of fresh air."

"Of course! Take your time." The blonde laughed and lightly tapped her beer can to Savannah's water bottle. "Here's to us… and all of the crazies in this place."

"Thanks," Savannah stood, pushing her chair out of the way. "I'll be right back."

She made her way through the crowd and out to the front porch. White Christmas lights hanging from the eaves of the roof illuminated the stairs to the gravel lot.

She walked beyond the tour bus and into the quiet darkness, which had come early tonight. It always came early in December. She brushed her shoulders with her hands. It was colder now. Much colder than when she had arrived.

Or, maybe she just felt more alone. Or less certain about the decisions she had made in her life.

She had wanted to work for the Tennessee Bureau of Investigation since she was in nineth grade when her American Government teacher had arranged for their class to tour the Arzo Carson TBI State Office Building. It had become her home away from home. And, now that she was divorced, she spent more time there than at home.

Everyone at the Bureau worked hard, and few complained about it. They knew they were making a difference in the world. Fighting crime and saving lives she always said, half joking. But she knew it was true. And that truth was what motivated her. At least when she did her job well.

She had hoped that tonight would put her one step closer to solving the Nightshade case. But, if it didn't—and it looked like it wouldn't—she would get up tomorrow morning and start over again. What else did she have to do on Christmas Eve? Most people were spending the holidays with their families, but her family lived out of state. She would see them in a few weeks. After this case was resolved.

From the back side of the parking lot, she heard Alex's kickoff drumbeat. She would go back inside for one last set. After that, she would call it a night.

Picking her way across the gravel lot, she climbed the stairs to the porch and opened the door to the noisy bar, which looked to be filled to capacity. Santa certainly had no shortage of business.

But, then again, it was his time of year.

She stifled a laugh at her own private joke, reminded herself that she would get through this, and sent up a silent prayer for wisdom and protection. It was all a good cop really needed. That, a decent sense of humor, and the inner strength to come to terms with the depravity of man.

Remembering the young women whose lives had been cut short because of the killer she was hoping to find, Savannah worked her way toward her table, bumping into several people, including Kayla, who was evidently going to the bar for another round.

As Savannah took her seat, her stomach growled. Supper tonight had been a bag of chips. She took a long drink from the bottle of water that Kayla had given her. Maybe it would help stave off the restlessness that came with hunger.

She would go home soon and fix a bowl of cereal, like she did most nights. She hadn't cooked much since Daniel left. Come to think of it, she hadn't cooked much when he was there. She had always been too busy with work.

In a few minutes, Kayla retook her seat but didn't engage in conversation. For that, Savannah was grateful.

The band was well into the last half of the third set when Savannah found it difficult to sit upright. Her head hurt, and her vision was off. She turned to Kayla, who was smiling and clapping to the music.

Savannah tried to focus on the show. She heard Daniel introduce the next song.

"As the clock strikes midnight," he told the crowd. "Let's celebrate the real reason for the season. Blessed be today. It is the day of our Savior's birth."

Savannah's heart seemed to be racing. She had always loved this song. Maybe it would bring her the peace she needed tonight. *If she could only…*

"Are you okay?" Kayla reached out to her, putting her arm around Savannah's shoulders, staring intently into her face.

"I'm—I'm…"

"You're okay," Kayla reassured her.

"No. I'm…"

"Vanna!" Daniel had jumped from the stage and was shaking her. He pushed Kayla away. "Someone, call 9-1-1."

"I'm—I'm…"

"I've got you, baby," he said, pulling her closer to him. "I've got you. Hold on to me… I'm here."

Four

Savannah awoke in the hospital. There was no indication of the time or where she was, except for the tick, tick, tick of the medical apparatus beside her. She attempted to bring the room into focus, but when she couldn't, her heart began to race again.

"Relax, honey." A woman in a white uniform moved to her side. "You're okay." The woman patted Savannah on the arm.

"What happened?"

"Why don't I let you husband and the police officer tell you about it?"

Husband? *Did she mean Daniel?* And what police officer?

The nurse opened the door, and Daniel walked into the room. Carl was beside him.

"How are you feeling?" Daniel asked.

"I don't really know. What happened?"

"You were given a drug called Atropine, but you're going to be—"

"What?" Savannah did her best to sit up, but Daniel gently pushed her back toward the bed. "Who…?"

"Do you want to tell her, Carl?"

"Savannah," Carl said. "I was at the show tonight because of my friendship with Daniel. But I'm also a Metro Police Officer and have been for thirty years. I knew about the Nightshade case. What I didn't know was that you were the lead investigator."

Savannah nodded.

"Just like any officer of the law, I'm always looking for something that seems off. And the more I watched Kayla Mason, the more I knew something was wrong."

He turned to Daniel.

"When I asked Dan about Kayla during the break, he told me she was a regular at his shows in town, and that she had a reputation for wanting to get close, too close, to band members."

He turned back to Daniel. "Why don't you take it from here, Dan?"

Daniel lightly touched Savannah's arm. "At some point during the evening, Kayla injected you with the Atropine. Most likely it was when you walked past her in the crowd on your way back to the table."

He paused. "When I saw you struggling, I rushed from the stage to help you. In doing so, I pushed Kayla away, knocking a syringe from her hand."

Savannah gasped.

"Carl was right there in a matter of seconds, and he saw it happen. We later found more syringes in her handbag."

"So Kayla is the Nightshade Murderer?" Savannah asked.

Carl nodded. "She's an ER nurse, which is probably why she had access to the drug. My guess is that she was using it to kill women she considered to be competition in her quest to snag a well-known musician for a husband."

"Do you really think so?" Savannah couldn't hide her surprise.

"It's funny, isn't it?" Daniel laughed. "If she only knew it wasn't the perfect life that she thinks it is."

"It's not that bad." Savannah reached for his hand. "I had the best one of all, and I didn't appreciate him as much as I should have."

Carl cleared his throat. "Why don't I leave the two of you alone? I need to call my wife. She's probably wondering why I'm not home yet."

"What time is it?" Savannah asked.

"It's seven o'clock on Christmas morning." Daniel squeezed her hand. "And I'm feeling blessed to be spending it with you."

"No. I'm the one who is blessed," she said. "Blessed Be the Day." She wiped a tear from her eye.

She would be spending Christmas with family after all.

Murder All the Way

Kelly Irvin

(Jingle Bells)

Christmas was the best time of year.

Correction, Christmas *used* to be the best time of year.

Janelle Moore stuck her hand over one ear while she held her cellphone to the other in an attempt to hear her executive chef over the dulcet tones of Michael Bublé crooning "A White Christmas." The static-filled connection in the rustic cabin her husband had rented on Eagle Canyon Mountain threatened to fade out. Plus, Rob kept turning up the stereo's volume—his passive-aggressive way of telling her to get off the phone. She needed to straighten out a snafu involving her catering business. Thousands of dollars in food would go to waste if she'd booked the reservation on the wrong date. A rookie mistake and not one she would make. Owning a catering company had turned the Christmas holiday season into stressful, nonstop work.

"Come on, Janelle, we agreed." With a venomous scowl that contorted his Ken-doll face, Rob held out his hand and wiggled his fingers. "No work and no electronics for the next forty-eight hours. And especially no calls to your boyfriend. This is supposed to be a romantic holiday getaway."

Anger spiked Janelle's blood pressure. Rob was one to talk. "Hang on a second, Kevin. I'll be right back." She held the phone against her chest and shot Rob her own scowl. "Kevin is my executive chef. He's not and has never been my boyfriend."

Kevin was a good guy. And good looking. A good looking, happily married guy. Besides, Janelle drew the line at cheating. Her marriage vows meant something. Rob was the one who seemed to think "until death do us part" contained wiggle room.

"Give it up or I'm getting in the Tahoe and going home."

"Where I'm sure Daphne will be waiting with open arms to comfort you."

"Look, if you're not going to try, we might as well call this off now." Rob put both hands up in mock surrender. "Dr. Crawley said this could help. Why did you agree to come up here if you didn't plan to even try?"

He was right. Their marriage counselor had urged them to completely unplug so they could focus on each other in a last-ditch effort to save an ailing twelve-year-old marriage that had been on life support for the last three. But she hadn't specified it had to be during the busiest time in any caterer's business—the Christmas season. Janelle had thirteen years of her life and all her—their—money tied up in her Boulder, Colorado, business Festive Eats. Janelle held up one finger. "I do want to try. Just let me wrap this up. One more minute."

Rob shook his head. He snatched the phone from her hand. "Kevin, Janelle is on vacation—with me, not you. Get your own side show. Whatever the crisis du jour is, deal with it."

He disconnected and stuck the phone in the back pocket of his tan slacks.

"You're nuts. You're jealous for no reason." Arms flailing, Janelle tried to dodge him. She took a stab at his hind-end. "I need to—"

"Nope. You do realize this is our last chance." Rob thwarted her end run with an agile bob and weave. The scowl melted into a sardonic grin. "I always was faster than you."

"Give me my phone. One call and I'm done." She marched over to the stereo and silenced Mr. Bublé. After four hours of Christmas music in the Tahoe, she'd had enough for one day. "Totally done."

Rob followed her. He put both hands on her shoulders and forced her to turn around. His scent of Polo drifted over her. She used to love how he smelled. When did she stop noticing? "Just answer one question for me. Which is more important: our marriage or some stranger's Christmas party?"

When he put it that way, what could Janelle say? "Our marriage, of course, but it's not just a Christmas party. It's our livelihood."

Especially since the real estate market had cratered. Rob had been a successful real estate agent when they married, but the last few years had been hard, and his commissions had fallen off. Festive Eats, the business she'd started a year before meeting her future husband, had survived, just barely, but now everyone wanted a party—the bigger the better.

"The real estate market is picking up. I may even get a year-end bonus." Rob moved closer still. He cupped her face. His hands ran down her arms then moved to her waist. He pulled her against his solid body. An unfamiliar, almost forgotten, thrill raced up Janelle's spine. The frosty air in the rental cabin warmed. Rob was closing in on forty, but he maintained his twenty-something physique with squash, tennis, and golf. He still had a full head of blond curly hair and those sky-blue eyes. He slid his hands down her back. "I've heard that pumpkin spice scent can be considered an aphrodisiac. For the right person. Or people."

He was trying. Definitely harder than she was.

"Aroma is certainly critical to the success of any dish. Chefs know that." She leaned her head against his broad chest. His heartbeat sounded in her ear, steady, and strong. When was the last time they had been this close? She couldn't remember. "Maybe we should forget about unpacking and check out the bedroom."

Rob drew back. Smiling, he shook his head. "I like the way you think but not yet. I have a surprise coming. You'll want to put on more clothes for it, not take them off."

"A surprise! I love surprises."

"I know you do." He tapped his watch. "It should arrive any minute. You might want to look out the window."

Rob, of all people, knew how much Janelle delighted in surprises. When they were first married and his career flourishing, he gave her surprise birthday parties, trips to Hawaii and Cancun, and a new car for Christmas. That tradition too had disappeared in recent years, along with the funds needed to make them happen. Her contributions to this weekend consisted of packing the ingredients for her famous eggnog and three kinds of Christmas candy, including Rob's favorite triple-chocolate peppermint fudge.

Shame welled in Janelle. She'd done nothing else except work, up until the last second of the last minute—even then he'd had to pry her phone from her hand. Of course her hard work had paid for the cabin. Rob had used her business credit card to book it.

It didn't matter. He was trying. "Thank you for this. I'm sorry I was so distracted. I'll do better."

She kissed his chin and ran to the window.

The big, heavy, wet snow that had accompanied them on the four-hour drive up a steep, winding road with the occasional hairpin curve had abated. The porch light cast a swath of light on the Tahoe, and an empty road covered with at least a foot of snow. "I don't see anything."

The faint sound of bells jingling carried on the wind. "What's that?"

Rob moved to stand next to her. "Be patient."

A whinny mingled with the bells' jingle. A sleigh, painted a bright red and drawn by a gorgeous dappled gray horse, whished over the snow toward the cabin. The horse, a regal Standardbred, wore red straps adorned with silver bells. A pickup truck pulled in next to the sleigh and parked.

"A one-horse open sleigh." Janelle clapped. She not only loved surprises, she loved horses. She dreamed of owning one—or several. "It's beautiful. The horse is so beautiful. Amazing. I love it. How did you get a horse-drawn sleigh up here?"

"The caretaker for the rental cabins runs a side business renting out his sleigh and horse to visitors. I was afraid you would see the sign when we turned onto the road up here, passing the cabin."

She'd been too busy talking Kevin down from a ledge regarding a demanding unreasonable client who wanted to completely change her menu at the last minute. "How long do we have them?"

"For as long as we can take the cold. Then we'll drop it off at his cabin. He'll bring us back up here." Rob nudged her toward the bedroom. "Put on a sweater, your coat, scarf, hat, gloves, everything. It's colder than the Artic out there. I'll tip the driver and send him on his way."

This was so great. Rob still cared. He still loved her. He wanted to please her. Maybe Dr. Crawley was right. Maybe they could make this work. Janelle dashed into the bedroom. She paused. Roomy king-sized bed. Beautiful Log Cabin patterned quilt. Lots of fluffy pillows. A fireplace. They could build a fire later. In more ways than one. She donned two more layers of clothes. Five minutes later, she traipsed—skipped, truth be told—back into the living room.

Rob and Daphne stood on the welcome mat engaged in a full-body embrace complete with lip lock.

Janelle dropped her scarf. Her mittens followed. A pain so visceral she tasted blood sliced through her body, head to toe. "What are you doing here? And why do you have your tongue down my husband's throat?"

The two parted only slightly. Daphne's dimpled cheeks were red. So were her kiss-bruised lips. Her dark blue eyes sparkled. She tugged her crocheted cap from her head, allowing her long, black hair to fall down around her shoulders. In every way the opposite of Janelle with her Nordic looks and blonde hair. Smiling, Daphne slipped her hand into her coat pocket. Out came a small pistol. "Surprise."

Rob chortled. "Yes, surprise, surprise. You love surprises."

Run. Scream. Hide. Fight back.

Janelle's body refused to cooperate. Her feet, clad in fleece-lined boots, suddenly weighed ninety pounds. Blocks of ice encased her arms and hands. Her mouth opened, but her voice escaped in a silent swoosh of air.

"Come along, my friend." Daphne motioned with the gun in one hand and crooked her finger with the other one. "You were so looking forward to a sleigh ride. We wouldn't want to disappoint you."

Pull yourself together.

Janelle swallowed acrid bile in the back of her throat. She sucked in a breath. Daphne was a hot-shot Realtor with model good looks and the morals of an alley cat—which made her even better at her job. She chuckled gleefully while filleting colleagues like a fish in a fight over contract terms.

You're no pushover, either. You kept a business going against all odds. You employ forty people. You support your husband.

"I'm not going anywhere with you."

Daphne smiled. Her brilliant white teeth gleamed against her tanning-bed bronzed skin. "Not with me, Hon, with Rob. You trust Rob, don't you? He arranged this wonderful romantic getaway for you . . . and me. A two-for-one. He's such a generous man." She moved away from Rob slowly as if regretfully. "Rob, your wife looks a little peaked. Maybe you should help her out the door. A ride in the crisp fresh mountain air will perk her up."

"Rob, what are you doing? Why are you doing this?" Janelle held her ground even as Rob advanced on her. The solicitous look on his face mocked her. "If you don't love me anymore, divorce me."

"Colorado is an equitable property state. You'll get the business you started with money you inherited from your dad. I'll get nothing." He loomed over her. "Besides, I know you. You'll refuse to accept that you failed. You won't believe I could love someone else more than you. You'll follow me around like a puppy dog begging me to take you back. You'll stalk me. You'll send me a hundred texts a day, call a thousand times. You'll make me exotic meals and insist on delivering them personally."

Rob's ego was exceeded only by his hubris. "I would not—"

"Shut up." He grabbed her arm and propelled her toward the door. "And then there's the matter of the life insurance policy."

Not long after their marriage, they'd agreed to take out substantial insurance policies on each other so that if something happened to one of them, the other wouldn't have to worry about finances. A million dollars. Both ways. So long ago Janelle hadn't thought about it in years. "If you shoot me, you'll never collect."

"Shooting you is a last resort, true." Rob shoved her through the door. Daphne came out behind them. "But we'll make it work. Don't you worry about that."

He sounded almost cheerful. Somehow erasing Janelle from the world would make him happy. Had being married to her been that awful? Blood pounded in her ears. Her heartbeat careened out of control. Despite temperatures in the single digits, sweat trickled down her temples and tickled her cheeks. "Don't do this, Rob. If it's about money, I promise we can make a fair and equitable division, just like the law says."

"Like I believe anything you say. You're having an affair with Kevin and won't admit it."

Paranoid and delusional?

He shoved Janelle down the porch steps. She slipped, teetered, and fell to her knees. Gasping, arms flailing, she face-planted in two feet of snow. She inhaled a mouth full. Her lips froze. Sweat turned to ice. Her hat fell away. The wet stuff stuck to her coat and scarf.

"Get up, get up." Rob pulled her to her feet. He dragged her toward the sleigh. "Time to go dashing through the snow."

Janelle sucked in air and planted her feet. Time to get her bearings. The sleigh's white lights twinkled, grimly merry. A snowmobile was parked next to it—Daphne's mode of transportation? The horse stamped his feet and whinnied. His breath billowed in white clouds against the dark night sky. How could an animal so light, bright, and beautiful be a tool in such a dark plan? "So what *is* the plan? You might as well tell me."

"You'll see." Daphne giggled, a sound most unbecoming to a woman her age. "It's all part of the surprise. Rob's good at planning surprises as you well know."

Janelle jerked hard, trying to free herself from Rob's grip. His hand slipped. She lurched toward the sleigh. *Think. Think. Run, run.*

"No you don't." Rob slammed her against the sleigh. "In you go."

He pushed her into the seat headfirst. "Daphne, keep an eye on her."

"With pleasure."

Janelle struggled to right herself. The cold penetrated her wet gloves. Her hands went numb. Shivering set in. She wrapped her arms around her middle. The only way to get out of this alive was to stay calm. In the movies they always kept the killer talking, lulling them into relaxing, then breaking lose.

They made fictional escapes look so easy.

Rob slid into the seat next to her. "Sit tight. It'll all be over soon." His snide chuckle matched his smirk. "Daphne, give me the gun. Stay close."

Daphne complied. "Do you know where you're going?"

"I've got just the spot picked out. Steep, curve, isolated, desolate. Perfect for an awful, tragic sleigh accident."

"Sweet." Daphne trotted toward the snowmobile. "Lead the way."

Janelle's teeth chattered so hard it was difficult to talk. She clenched her jaw for a second and drew a breath. "How could you know a spot? You've never been here before."

"It just goes to show how little attention you pay to me." Barking a bitter laugh, he tucked a thick, soft, fleece blanket over their knees. "I wouldn't want you to catch a chill. That real estate conference I told you I was attending? I actually came here. I learned event planning from you. Never leave anything to chance. Attend to every little detail and the big picture will take care of itself. Isn't that what you always say? I've left nothing to chance."

"You're not a killer." Her husband was about to commit premeditated murder. Janelle cast about frantically for words to convince this stranger who'd once been her friend, then boyfriend, and finally husband to not murder her. The idea boggled the mind. "You always told me you were a lover, not a fighter. You said you loved me. You can't kill me."

"Sure I can." He snapped the reins. The horse pranced, tossed his regal head, and took off. They turned in a wide arc and headed out on the snow-covered road that would take them higher up the mountain. "Watch me."

The faster they traveled the more the bells jingled, a merry sound that carried on the icy cold air that nipped at Janelle's cheeks and nose. She couldn't stop shivering. Her teeth chattered. Her hands shook. Slowly, she swiveled and craned her neck. Daphne followed on the snowmobile. The craft skimmed over the snow much the same way the sleigh did but with a great deal less charm.

The tree-lined road shrank in width. The horse slowed. Rob snapped the reins again and again. The horse whinnied and shook his head. He didn't like this plan either.

She glanced back again. Daphne still followed.

"Stop fidgeting. You're worse than a little kid."

A little kid. Another sore spot rubbed raw over the years. Janelle wanted kids. At least two. Rob insisted he did too. But not yet. Just not yet. He kept putting it off. Putting her off. *You have a baby—your business is your baby. You don't have time for kids. You're always working.* They hadn't talked about babies in a very long time. Keep the killer talking, that's what they always say. This topic was as good as any. "How would you know? You were an only child and you never wanted any of your own."

"Not with you, no."

"Why? Why do you hate me so much?"

"Because you cheated on me."

"I didn't. I never did. You cheated on me. Obviously. You think because you're doing it, I must be too? Everyone must be?"

"You're a liar. I saw you hugging Kevin. You were all over each other."

"When?"

"It was a few months ago. I stopped by to pick up some marketing materials like the good husband I am. Always spreading the word about your business. You were standing in the middle of the office hugging."

When had she ever hugged Kevin? Janelle closed her eyes and thought back. "He'd just told me that Bethany is pregnant. They've been trying forever. They went through invitro twice. This time it took. I was thrilled for him, for them."

"Sure. Whatever."

"You're an idiot. And a hypocrite."

She had nothing to lose. The higher they climbed, the fewer her options. She could stay in the sleigh and try to fight it out when they arrived at their—her—final destination. How fast were they going? The wind whistled in her ears. The tips were frozen. Every breath of cold air hurt. Fast. They were going fast. But not as fast as a car. Maybe fifteen miles an hour. A person could survive falling from a car. Surely a sleigh was less life threatening.

She had to get help. Not just for herself but for the incredible creature that pulled the sleigh. She couldn't let these two self-centered, egotistical, narcistic people destroy such a noble steed.

Jump. Just jump. It couldn't hurt any worse than whatever Rob and Daphne had planned for her and the horse. If she jumped, they'd have no reason to drive the sleigh off the road. The horse would live.

According to everything she'd read, freezing to death was like falling asleep.

God, help me. Please help me.

Do it.

It was easy after all. Janelle simply leaned away from Rob. She grabbed the sleigh's side and thrust her body forward. She fell headfirst in a dive that gave him no time to react.

The free fall lasted only a few seconds. She slammed face-first in a deep drift of snow. It softened the blow. It also buried her. Flailing, she struggled to fight her way out. No traction. No air. *Come on. Come on.*

The snowmobile's engine revved. The horse's whinny sounded more like a scream. They were turning around. They were coming back.

Get up. Get up. Get up.

Thrashing her way through the drifts, Janelle scrambled toward the thick stands of blue spruce, bristlecone, fir, and pine trees. The deeper into the woods, the harder it would be to follow. And the darker it would be. With only the half-moon to light the way, she dodged trees, in and out, in and out. The frigid wind tore at her body, stealing her breath. Branches smashed into her numb face. Drops of blood dripped into her mouth, hot and salty.

God help me.

She stumbled, fell, picked herself up. Fell again. The ache in her feet had subsided. They were numb.

That's not helpful, God.

An opening, a clearing. This was bad. She was a sitting duck in the open. No, a cabin. A cabin. Help. She could get help.

That's better, God.

A quick glance back. The snowmobile's engine rumbled. Daphne would be here any second. Janelle eyeballed the cabin. It looked much like the one she'd just left. No cars parked in front of it. The drive hadn't been cleared. No lights on.

Not so good. She heaved a breath and dashed across the open space. If she survived, she would go back to the gym. And start jogging again. *I promise, God.* He'd probably be more impressed if she promised to go back to church after a twenty-year hiatus. *Whatever you want, Big Guy.*

She pounded on the door. No answer. "Hello, hello! I need help. Please, open up, please!"

No answer. The curtains were pulled back in the front windows. Janelle peered in. Darkness. No sign of movement. *Come on, God, seriously.*

She raced back to the door. Maybe they had a land line. She turned the knob. It opened. Folks up here probably figured there was no one around to break in. Or they would be back soon. Maybe they went down the mountain for dinner. Maybe they'd be back in time. Maybe not.

Inside it was pitch black. She didn't dare turn on a light. Janelle felt her way along the wall, waiting for her eyes to adjust. She felt around on the kitchen counter then peered at the coffee and end tables in the living room. No phone.

The sound of the snowmobile's engine broke the silence. Janelle edged up to the windows, peek through the curtains. The snowmobile zipped into the clearing. Daphne slowed and leaned into a turn until she came to a stop near the porch.

Sleigh bells jingled; a once sweet, merry sound turned sickening. Janelle peered through the window. The sleigh entered the clearing. "Did you find her? Where is she?" Rob shouted. He spewed a steady stream of obscenities. "I can't believe the moron jumped."

"I can't believe you let her jump. What's wrong with you?" Daphne screamed. "You had the gun. You had the upper hand. I told you we should've zip-tied her."

"Zip ties doesn't say accident. They say murder."

"You could've taken them off at the kill spot."

"I didn't plan to stop. I planned to jump at the last minute."

"You were afraid you'd lose your nerve." Daphne snorted. "You still have feelings for her, don't you?"

More obscenities. Rob would never run out of them. "You're nuts. I can't stand her..."

"Yeah, right."

Maybe if they kept arguing they would break up right there on the spot. Or they'd forget about Janelle and kill each other. A person could hope.

"We're not getting anywhere. I'm freezing." Rob hopped from the sleigh. "Maybe she's hiding inside."

"It's probably locked."

"I'll check."

"Give me the gun. I'll check." Her self-satisfied laugh echoed in the quiet winter night. Not a sound of another living thing broke the peaceful silence. No one to help. "If she's in there, she's not going anywhere. I'll kill her if I have to."

"You can't kill her. We'll never get the insurance money then."

"No, but we get the business. I'd be a better business manager than your wife any day."

I won't give you the satisfaction of dying, and you're never getting your hands on Festive Eats.

Their footsteps sounded on the porch loud, mocking.

There had to be another way out. Blood pounding in her ears, Janelle felt her way through the living room. She strained to see. No back door here. Bedroom? Probably the master bedroom. If it had the same floorplan as their rental, it would be to the left. Had there been a backdoor in their bedroom? She had no time for wrong moves. She closed her eyes and envisioned it.

Yes. Next to the fireplace.

She veered left and careened into the bedroom. The front door squeaked. Footsteps sounded on the pine floor. *Go, go, go.*

A back door beckoned. Janelle careened toward it, flipped the lock, and plunged into the backyard. She shut the door behind her. It might buy her a few seconds if they thought she was hiding.

She summoned every bit of her remaining strength. Her boots sank into the snow drifts. Her heart screamed for mercy. Her legs were so heavy. *Don't give up now.* She chanted *go, go, go,* over and over again.

She raced around the cabin to the snowmobile. *Thank you, Daddy.* Her father had taken the family to Yellowstone National Park her senior year in high school, the perfect time to go because most tourists flocked there in summer. She'd learn to drive a snowmobile that winter break.

Think, think!

She fumbled with the kill switch. Her frozen fingers were all thumbs. *Come on, come on. Pull up the kill switch. Turn the key. Pull the cord. Throttle on the right. Brake lever on the left.* Janelle squeezed the throttle. The engine revved. The craft shot forward.

The front door flew open. Daphne emerged, Rob right behind her. The inevitable stream of obscenities rained down on Janelle. She leaned into the turn and pulled away.

Down the mountain. Anywhere there were people.

Janelle crouched low, hugging the machine's body. Icy wind burned her face. Snowflakes hit her eyes. She'd always loved snowfall at night. Not tonight.

The narrow road curved to the left, then the right, tightening against a straight drop into a canyon. She leaned into each turn. The snowmobile lurched over deep ruts. Finally she hit the paved road that would take her down the mountain. She opened the throttle wide. "Show me what you can do," she whispered.

The speedometer needle rose steadily. Forty, fifty, sixty, seventy. The road narrowed, the sheer rock drop-off to her left plunging thousands of feet. Heart in her throat, she hugged the mountainside like it was her best friend.

The terrain in Yellowstone had been flat. Fleeting memories floated to the top. *Keep your body center mass. Stay seated.* The last thing she needed now was to flip the machine.

One hairpin curve after another forced her to slow and slow some more. Her heart threatened to escape her chest. Her stomach tied itself in knots. Despite the fierce cold, sweat tickled the skin between her shoulder blades. She hazarded a glance back. Nothing but darkness. How fast could a horse-drawn sleigh go? Fifteen, twenty miles an hour? No match for a snow mobile. She was home free. She would make it. She would live. She would tell her story to law enforcement. Rob and Daphne would be arrested and charged with attempted murder.

And Janelle would get a divorce and never have to see either of them again.

The engine sputtered. The craft slowed, slowed some more. Janelle squeezed the throttle harder until it was wide open.

The engine died. The snowmobile glided to a stop in the middle of the road.

"No, no, no, no!" Janelle turned it off. She ran through the sequence to restart it. Nothing. She peered at the dashboard. Out of gas. Who was the moron now? Who rented a snowmobile without a full tank of gas?

She felt anger and fear so fierce they made her teeth hurt. She hopped down and started to run. From now on, she would cook only healthy foods. No more heavy sauces. No more fancy desserts. She'd lose the twenty pounds she gained.

Her chest hurt. Her feet and hands didn't hurt anymore. They were numb blocks of ice.

She needed to rest. Just for a minute or two. If she could just sit down on the side of the road for a few seconds, she'd get her second wind. She slowed, stopped, and bent over, her hands on her knees. Every breath tortured her lungs, burned her nostrils, and sent pain shooting through her teeth.

Think beach, think ocean, think Cancun in August.

Keep moving. No time to stop. Don't give Rob the satisfaction. No, don't give Daphne the satisfaction.

One step, two steps, three steps, four. It was downhill after all. She could lay down and roll the rest of the way.

Think hot cocoa with marshmallows. Think Earl Gray tea with lemon and honey.

Bells. Were those bells jingling in the distance? Janelle picked up her feet and pushed forward. She tripped. On her hands and knees, she crawled forward.

A light. Was that a light? Or a figment of her delirious brain?

No. A cabin off the road. A spotlight shone on a sign. "Eagle Canyon Mountain Retreat Office" and below it, "Rent Your Sleigh Here!"

The caretaker.

A fresh rush of adrenaline raced through Janelle like a flash fire. She hoisted herself to her feet. Blinded by snow that had turned thick and heavy, she dragged her body toward it. Lights. Heat. Warmth.

Bells jingling. Jingle. Jingle. Jingle.

She threw herself up the steps and across the porch. The sweet sound of people singing "O Come All Ye Faithful" floated on the notes of a piano. Laughter mingled with it.

"Help, help, I need help." She pounded on the door. "Please help me."

The music stopped and with it the song. The door flew open. Light and warmth poured out. A tree trunk of a man in a flannel shirt and overalls filled the space. Behind him a dozen people of all ages and sizes stared. Janelle stretched out one hand toward the man. "Help me, please."

"You look plumb frozen. Come in, come in." The man took Janelle's arm and gently tugged her over the threshold. "Who are you? What are you doing out there?"

He stuck his head out the door and looked around. "How did you get here?"

No time for long-winded introductions. "They're after me. They're coming. They're going to kill me."

It sounded crazy. Delusional. They would never believe her.

"Lilith, get her a blanket and some of that hot cocoa." The man motioned to a woman as petite as he was larger than life. "Sit down by the fire."

"There's no time. They're coming. They're in your sleigh and they're coming."

"The sleigh . . . my sleigh . . . my Prince?" Realization dawned in the man's face. "Mr. Moore who rented my horse and sleigh is trying to kill you?"

"Please, you have to call the police. They were going to drive the sleigh off the mountain with me in it."

A murmur ran through the people who'd gathered around, like children at a macabre story hour. Lilith returned with a blanket and a lethal looking shotgun. "I called the sheriff's office, Gene. Daryl and Carl are on duty tonight. They're on their way."

Lilith was the brains in the outfit, no doubt about it. Scowling, Gene accepted the shotgun. "They were planning to kill Prince?"

Janelle pulled the blanket around her shoulders. It did little to stop her body's uncontrollable shivering. If only it were Kevlar. "Yes, your beautiful, gorgeous, sweet horse. And destroy your sleigh. And kill me."

Bells jingled. "They're here." Janelle dropped the blanket and jumped up on trembling legs. "Give me that shotgun."

"Sorry, ma'am. No one handles this weapon here but me."

"Daphne has a gun, and she's much more likely to use it than Rob."

"So do I." Lilith pulled a pistol from her apron pocket. It matched her in size. The fire in her eyes suggested size had nothing to do with how deadly one can be. "When you live in isolated areas like this and rent to strangers, you learn to protect yourself. Don't you worry none, we've got this."

Janelle ran to the window and pulled back the drapes. Rob had stopped the sleigh several yards from the cabin, just beyond the light cast by the porch light. He and Daphne seemed to be arguing.

The first notes of "Hark the Herald Angels Sing" trilled. Gene snatched his phone from the solid oak coffee table.

Now? Now he was taking a phone call?

"Eagle Canyon Mountain Retreat. This is Gene. How can I help you?"

He paused, grimaced, hit a button, and held the phone out flat on the palm of his hand. With his other hand, he put one finger to his lips. "So Mr. Moore, you're looking for your wife. How did you manage to misplace her in the two hours since you arrived?"

"I didn't misplace her. We had a little tiff, and she went for a walk." Rob's disembodied voice blared on the phone's speaker. "I just need to know if you've seen her."

"Where are you? I'll come out and help you look for her."

Rustling and angry whispered words. "That's awfully kind of you, Gene, but not necessary. I'm sure she'll show up."

"It's three degrees out and snowing heavily. She may have frozen to death by now, sir. You need to call the sheriff's department. They'll round up search and rescue."

"She's probably back at the cabin by now. Sorry to have bothered you."

"No bother at all. What about my horse and my sleigh? Are you planning to return them now? You're in your SUV, right?"

"Actually, we're—I'm close by in the sleigh. I can turn in the sleigh if you wouldn't mind taking me and my . . . friend . . . back to the cabin. We can get my Tahoe and go searching if my wife hasn't shown up."

His Tahoe. Janelle bought it with proceeds from Festive Eats. She made the payments. She used it to haul food to events. He'd already written her off.

"I'll meet you out front. How far away are you?"

"We'll be there in two or three minutes."

"See you then."

Gene disconnected. He pumped his fist like a teenager. "We've got them."

"You can't go out there. Daphne has no conscience whatsoever. If she thinks you're a threat, she'll shoot you."

"The sheriff's deputies are on their way." Gene grabbed a puffy down jacket from a coat rack next to the door. He shrugged it on. "But I'm not leaving Prince with the likes of them for one more minute than necessary."

Janelle turned to Lilith. "Give me your gun. Please, please. This is my fight. I involved you and your family in it. Let me back up your husband."

Lilith nodded. She held out the weapon. "Gene has another rifle in the back. I'll be right behind you."

"So will I." A man who bore a striking resemblance to Gene stepped away from the cluster of folks watching the conversation with the avid expressions of theater-goers at a Broadway production. "I'm Gene's son, Mike. I never go anywhere without my side piece."

Janelle took Lilith's offering. It felt heavy and more substantial than it appeared. Lilith spun around and disappeared into the back again.

"Mr. Moore has no idea who he's messing with." Gene sounded almost cheerful. "He'll get his just desserts."

"They're moving up by the porch." A teenage boy, yet another much younger carbon copy of Gene, let the drapes drop. "Looks like they're arguing about something."

No doubt.

"Stay away from the window, Junior. LeeAnn, take the kids in the back bedroom. Stay back there until the deputies arrive. LeeAnn, a hugely pregnant woman with a curly headed toddler on one hip, rounded up the rest of the children and did as Gene directed.

Gene tugged on gloves, picked up his shotgun, and headed for the door. "Mrs. Moore, do me a favor. Wait a minute before showing your face. I want that element of surprise."

"Understood." Janelle grasped the pistol tightly. She wasn't a fan of guns—until this very moment. "But I've got your back."

A big genial smile fixed on his grizzled face; Gene tromped out the door. Mike tucked his gun back in his coat pocket and followed. The desire to follow vibrated in every bone, muscle, and sinew in her body. Janelle huddled with the door open a crack.

"Why the rifle, Gene?" Rob spoke first. "That's a funny way to greet a customer."

"No worries. I just wanted to make sure it was you. A guy can't be too careful these days." Gene sounded as chipper as a guy with a new sports car. "If you'll get down off the sleigh, I'll get my son here to drive it into the shed out back."

Janelle peered through the crack. Gene patted Prince. He ran his hands down the horse's long neck and smoothed his mane as if making sure he was uninjured. "Good boy, you done good, Prince."

The horse tossed his head and neighed. "Yeah, I bet you're hungry. You need a good rub down and a nice supper."

Rob hopped from the sleigh. Daphne took her time following. Their faces were bright red. She stamped her feet and clasped her hands around her middle. Good. They were frozen too. "We need to get going. Now."

"Sure," Gene spun around and lifted the shotgun level with Rob's face, "just as soon as you hand over the gun."

"What gun?" Rob sputtered. "Are you out of your mind?"

"The one you threatened to shoot me with." Janelle burst through the door. She sped down the steps, halted next to Gene, and pointed Lilith's pistol at Daphne. "Drop it on the ground now, or I'll shoot you. You know I will."

Her eyes filled with venom; Daphne bared her teeth in a vicious grin. "I don't believe you. You don't have the guts."

"Don't believe her? Believe me." Gene's son stepped up. His gun was much bigger than Lilith's. "I was a Ranger in Afghanistan. A sharpshooter. I don't miss."

Daphne's face crumpled. She pulled the gun from her pocket, puny in comparison to the son's, and pitched it into the snow. "I told you this wouldn't work. I told you we should've poison—"

"Shut up, you idiot." Rob's voice shook with indignation. "Janelle, honey, I didn't mean it. Forgive me, please. It was all Daphne's idea. She mesmerized me. We'll start again. Don't throw away twelve years of marriage. Honey, look at me—"

"You jerk. You thought the whole thing up." Daphne smacked him on the arm. "Shut your mouth, you imbecile—"

"You're the one who needs to shut up." Pistol leveled at them; Janelle inched closer. "Hand me my phone. And yours."

"Why mine?" Rob assumed the whiny tone of a tired toddler. "I need it to call a lawyer."

"You'll get your call." She grabbed the phones and tucked them in her coat pocket. Text messages would prove her story and premeditation. "You'll have plenty of time to think up a defense in jail."

"Back away from them, Mrs. Moore." Gene's voice softened to the tone a person would use to calm a flighty horse. "I've got them covered."

Sirens screamed. Lights flashed red and blue in a crazy pattern against the dark night sky. Two sheriff's department massive pickup trucks roared into the yard. One came to a stop after a wonky half-circle slide across the driveway. The other slammed to a halt just short of the sleigh. Still, Janelle didn't—couldn't—move.

This was it. Her time was leaking away. Last chance. Janelle hauled back and swung with every bit of anger, betrayal, hurt, and loss in her half-frozen body. She punched Rob's Ken-doll face right in the kisser.

It seemed only fair.

Sputtering, he staggered, flailed, and landed flat on his back.

"How's that for a surprise?"

With that, Janelle spun around and left a big chunk of her life slowly disappearing under a heavy blanket of snow. Whatever happened next it would not involve Rob. She stopped and petted Prince. "Merry Christmas," she whispered. His ears flicked. His head bobbed.

He understood everything. "I'm buying myself a horse for Christmas, Prince, one that looks just like you. Happy New Year!"

It would indeed be a happy new year.

Ordinary

Delores Topliff

Days

One

W. Thomas Dunn signed his name with a flourish on the final exam of his last MBA class for the University of Washington. He'd finished early, so the rest of this December day was his.

His advisor, Lamar Penrod, accepted the exam with a handshake.

"Tom, I know this is strong work even before reading it. Congratulations on your degree. Where are you off to now?"

Tom stretched the kinks out of his back. "I'm just hoping for an ordinary day. Grab a coffee until my girlfriend gets off work early. Then we have plans."

"Sounds good. Does Callie still work for Underground Seattle Tours?"

"Yes. She loves the people. Gets good tips, too."

"Nice." Penrod nodded. "My daughter wants to work for them, but it's a rough part of town. I know of several recent arrests. Are you okay with Callie being there?"

Tom's head jerked up. "Yes, but it's hush-hush. How did you hear about that?"

"It's a dad thing." Penrod shrugged. "My friend works security. I know they just rescued a missing girl plus found drug paraphernalia in distant areas."

Tom leveled a glance. "They're adding more lights and surveillance cameras. That will help."

"Good. I'm careful where I let my daughter go. I know Callie's great. I'll sign up for her tour and get a feel for the place."

"Good. Tell me later what you think. Here's my phone number."

Tom scribbled his number on the card he gave Penrod. Five minutes later, he had almost reached the coffee shop when his phone buzzed. He didn't recognize the number or caller ID, Masterson Mortuary.

A man's voice asked, "Thomas Dunn?"

"Yes?"

"This is funeral director, Brett Masterson. The body of your uncle, Walter Thomas Dunn, has been brought to us for burial. We're performing the final plans he requested and paid for. He told us to notify you as next of kin."

Tom gasped. "Wait. There's some horrible mistake!" He stood dead still as pedestrians moved around him. "My uncle, Tommy Dunn, died in UN peacekeeping action five years ago. Tom says, "Since my parents are deceased, I arranged his funeral and burial in this city."

A sigh crossed the line. "He told us about that and said you'd find this confusing. He gave us your name, address, and phone number for contact now. If there's a mistake and you believe you are not the right person, that can be cleared up if you'll pay a short visit here."

Tom's head whirled. "How did you get this number? It's unlisted. I only share it with close family members."

"I told you. From your uncle."

"This sounds as weird as *The Twilight Zone*. Discussing a mistaken identity with a funeral home is not on my list of things to do today."

"I understand." Tom heard the caller rustling papers. "Your uncle said there were reasons you could not know his true circumstances. You will understand more as you work through his final arrangements."

Tom's voice rose. "Wait. How can you hold a funeral for someone already legally buried? You have the wrong person and shouldn't be talking to me at all."

"If you don't think you're the Walter Thomas Dunn named, just come in and sign off on the paperwork. That will also remove you from the financial benefits attached and release us to find the true correct next of kin to carry out Mr. Dunn's wishes."

"This is so bizarre." Tom stared at his phone. "Maybe I'm misunderstanding. Are you perhaps saying Gunn or Lund?"

"No. Dunn—D-U-N-N."

Tom leaned against the brick wall of the coffee shop behind him, appreciating its coolness. Could he be asleep and dreaming? If so, he classed this a nightmare. No, he was awake, all right. Tom says, "If Mom were alive, they'd laugh together at this confusion because she had helped him handle Uncle Tommy's funeral."

The funeral director's smooth voice continued, "Please stop at your earliest convenience to resolve this."

"You're not on my schedule today, but it's worth coming in just to have this over with."

"Good. Here's our address . . ."

The funeral director greeted Tom at the door, eying him carefully.

"You strongly resemble your uncle. Thank you for coming. Let me show you his final instructions."

Mr. Masterson extended signed papers.

"Please confirm that this is your correct name, phone number, and legal address."

Tom's jaw dropped, dumbfounded. Everything matched. He tapped the sheets of stiff paper with his fingernail.

"It's my information all right, but how did you get it? I've only occupied this apartment for two months and just bought my new phone. That's my street address, but my mail goes to a post office box, which you also show listed here. I keep my contact information confidential and only gave it to my university advisor minutes ago. How did you get it?"

"I already told you. I'm sure you're confused and this is hard to process. You'll understand more soon. If you doubt your connection to the deceased, shouldn't you at least view his body?"

Tom hesitated. "I suppose. This has to be the strangest experience of my life."

He studied the facility. The building looked familiar, and memories rolled back. Had Uncle Tommy's funeral been right here in this same building with a younger version of this director officiating? He thought so.

Tom massaged his temples. He disliked viewing dead bodies. Seeing Dad motionless after the car accident was too much for him as a four-year-old. Uncle Tommy had stepped in as a father figure for the next seventeen years whenever he'd visited Seattle. They'd built great memories but he'd left another hole when he died.

There had been other deaths when Tom volunteered with Mt. Rainier Search and Rescue. Thankfully, their team brought home far more people alive than dead.

Other than the graveside service honoring a military friend, Tom had avoided funerals and funeral homes since Uncle Tommy's passing and then Mom's. He'd known enough heartache to last a lifetime.

If there was any chance this man was another distant relative, why wasn't his own and Mom's name on the paperwork since they'd handled

Uncle Tommy's funeral? Nothing on this paperwork indicated this man had already been buried.

"I was named for my Uncle Tommy and remember him well," Tom confided to the funeral director. "He was my father's only brother and made a big difference after we lost Dad."

"He thought the world of you," the funeral director said. "I'm glad you remember him."

Tom shivered involuntarily. "You knew him? What can you tell me?"

The director paused. "Not more than you know. I'm bound by client confidentiality, but he was a man to be very proud of."

Tom waited for Mr. Masterson to say more, but he only thumbed additional papers.

"I'm missing an item," the director said. "I'll go to my office to get it. Please proceed to the chapel in the end room where your uncle is resting." The man gestured.

"He can't be my uncle," Tom said so quietly he didn't expect to be heard.

But Brett Masterson smiled as he padded away.

Tom stepped forward, wondering why funeral homes usually looked alike. His feet sank into thick, soundless carpet. Dim lighting and slow music from recessed speakers created an atmosphere making it easy to release tears. The building smelled of bouquets, disinfectant, and his own nervous sweat. He tugged at his shirt collar to loosen it and shivered although the room temperature was probably set at normal. Everything today seemed chilling.

Each alcove area held banks of magnificent flowers—stark white lilies, sweet pink and red roses, aromatic blue-gray eucalyptus sprays, twining green vines, and armfuls of spicy carnations. Yet an underlying cloying smell reminded him of expensive bouquets standing too long in stagnant vase water that needed changing.

Mr. Masterson's shoes barely marked the thick carpet as he returned. In subdued light, he led the way to an expensive mahogany casket with gleaming bronze handles. He stepped to the head of the coffin and opened the lid's heavy top half while leaving the lower half closed.

Steeling himself, Tom lowered his eyes to view the distinguished man cocooned in white satin. And shuddered. The man in the casket resembled Uncle Tommy as he'd been five years ago at his funeral— except this man had aged an additional five years. His features mirrored Uncle Tommy's—one eyebrow sliced by a childhood fall from a tree plus a small dark mole at the left of his mouth like one Tom also displayed. It was like seeing himself lying there. Or a lookalike from Madame Tussaud's Wax Museum.

Tom's brain spun. He reached out to steady himself against the coffin.

"Uncle Tommy," he whispered. "Where have you been? What happened during the five years in between? Why didn't I know?"

"You do recognize him!" Mr. Masterson said.

It was a statement, not a question.

"He has my uncle's features, but he's wearing a uniform I'm not familiar with."

Tom leaned closer to see better, relieved to only notice a mild antiseptic smell. Stitching over the uniform's upper left chest read *Interpol Incident Response Team*.

"International Police? That's incredible! My uncle served with local law enforcement and then did undercover work around the country before joining UN Security Forces action. I wish I knew where he went after Seattle and what paths he took."

"You will know most of it before this is over."

Tom studied the director. "I understand he couldn't be in town much, but why didn't he stay in touch?"

"Please consider that perhaps he wanted to but couldn't."

Maybe his uncle needed to maintain alternate roles and identities. He had hinted of such things. *He probably faced cloak and dagger stuff. What had Dad known? Was Dad's car wreck death really an accident? Or was he involved in covert events, too?*

Interpol fought international crimes. Online sites emphasized drug sales, securities fraud, and money laundering. Recent incidents added international hacking that captured data worth fortunes in cryptocurrency ransom. Much came from Russia or Eastern Europe.

Dad and Uncle Tommy's grandparents had immigrated from Prussia, now part of Poland. Both Dad and uncle had tracked down distant relatives—even talked once of meeting them. Tom should have paid closer attention but had been cramming for exams and tuned out their talk as background noise. That's where much white collar hacking now took place. He wanted his natural family to stay clear of that.

He tossed his head to clear away frightening thoughts before lifting his iPhone to photograph the man in the casket. He didn't notice the red light in the upper wall take his picture by flashing twice.

He turned to Mr. Masterson. "Any chance I could get a glass of water and an aspirin or two?"

"Sure. Those are requested often here." The man accessed sealed packets from a sideboard where two hallway corridors intersected and grabbed a paper cup from a neat stack next to a fountain.

"Who brought my uncle in? May I see the paperwork?"

"Of course." Mr. Masterson's face stretched into a wide smile. "Your uncle said in light of his circumstances, you might prefer a private celebration of life rather than the usual standard viewing and public funeral. He left you that choice."

Tom startled. "Thank you. It would be horribly awkward to write a second obituary and bury the same man twice. Relatives and I have come to the cemetery each Memorial Day and tidied grass around his plot. We also visited other times and left flowers."

Tom raised his eyes. "Wait a minute. Is anyone buried in his coffin?"

"You'll find out later today."

Thoughts spinning, Tom was interrupted by his phone blaring.

"Sorry. I should take this call."

He stepped down the hall. "Callie? You're finished? Good. You won't believe where I am. Please come to Masterson Funeral home on East Pike. I'm okay, but they have the body of my Uncle Tommy here—

The one I buried five years ago. Except he's been alive all this time and only died now. Apparently in Seattle. I don't know all the answers but plan to find out."

Mr. Masterson appeared beside Tom and cleared his throat. "If you're ready, follow me."

Tom entered the director's office.

"Here are some of his last effects. His watch and key to a bank safety deposit box. Please look these over and sign the release form. The police precinct will give you his remaining effects."

Next, Tom found the digital phone chip. Only one inch square but big enough to hold a thousand pictures.

"Here is his death certificate and funeral instructions. After you view the photos on the digital chip, your uncle wanted you to visit the police precinct listed here. Their chief detective has your uncle's wallet, passports, and police department file. Following that, the bank president named will explain the details of your uncle's estate and the foundation he created before his death. This accounting report lists the amounts involved."

"The foundation he created?"

"Yes, which he generously endowed."

Tom read the list of numbers on the stiff paper and gulped. There were so many printed zeroes on this card from Seattle's biggest bank, it stole his breath. Surely, this was another mistake.

"Once you've completed each step, you'll receive the last information."

A final challenge, Tom thought.

When Callie arrived, he introduced her.

"Pleasure," the director said.

"I'm glad you're here. Tom exhaled a deep breath. "Come see my uncle. Help me make sense of this."

She slipped her hand into his. When they reached the coffin holding W. Thomas Dunn, she looked back and forth from Tom to the older man several times.

"Incredible. And unnerving. This has to be really hard for you. How are you holding up? He looks like you probably will in thirty more years. Pretty handsome."

"It's uncanny. That's how much older he was to me." A quiver traveled Tom's spine.

"So, he's been alive until now?"

"It seems that way. Maybe nearby part of the time. Will you help me figure this out?"

"You know I will." She stood on tiptoe to kiss his cheek.

"Thanks. Before going to the police precinct, let's find a photography shop to see what's on this photo chip."

"There's one down the street."

After entering the store, the clerk found a camera able to read the integrated circuit. Several pictures were of Uncle Tommy. Many were of Tom himself. Of high school and college graduations taken long-range. One showed him with Callie. Another was a photo with Mom that she had added to their family album. Had she given Uncle Tommy this copy? Or had he given it to her? How much did Mom know?

Others showed Uncle Tommy with strangers. Tom recognized several as crooks in photos displayed in Underground Seattle scenes. Many had foreign appearance and clothing. By some trick of hair and clothing, Uncle Tommy fit into each group.

Years ago, he had told Tom that some crooks called him, "Tommy Gun" for his accurate, rapid-fire shooting like the firing pattern of the Thompson submachine guns preferred by Chicago mobsters.

"Can you print these photos?" Tom asked the clerk.

"Certainly, sir."

Tom reviewed the instructions on the paper in his hand. "Our next stop is the police precinct."

Callie frowned. "I'm starved. Can we please eat something first?"

He slipped his arm around her. "Sorry. With classes over, I wanted us to enjoy today. I didn't plan on this surprise. Can we buy from a food truck now and I'll do better later?"

"Fine. Anything works."

They found Mexican tacos and then easily located the precinct.

"We also called him Tommy Gun." The chief police detective smiled and handed over Uncle Tommy's wallet. It held over five hundred dollars in cash denominations plus other currencies in side pockets. Tom also found numerous credit cards, IDs, and Tom's name, address, and phone number on one card written in his uncle's familiar handwriting.

Last came four well-used passports from different nations issued in other names. Each photo showed Uncle Tommy with slight changes in facial appearance or hair style. Entry stamps proved he had traveled widely throughout Europe, Central Asia, and sometimes Central and South America.

During the five years they'd believed Uncle Tommy dead, he'd been chasing international criminals and shutting them down—like a white paper and internet crime Sherlock Holmes.

"You must be enormously proud," the detective said. "He arrested many of this nation's worst bad guys and did things for Interpol few people can ever know about. He should have been dead a hundred times but always got his target. He even choreographed his final shootout."

Tom's forehead puckered. "Tell us about that."

"More details are in his funeral instructions. For now, I'll print out his career highlights and have his service medals sent to you."

"Thank you." Tom swallowed the lump in his throat. "I knew he did major stuff here in his early days in Seattle but had no idea that his heroics reached so far internationally."

The chief detective nodded. "At times, he made James Bond look like a schoolboy. To protect you and your mom, he kept his career quiet. That's also why he never had a family of his own."

"I wondered." The lump in Tom's throat grew bigger.

The detective handed Tom the police evidence record containing grainy black and white photos.

"Callie, come look at these."

She scooted closer. "Incredible. What a heritage."

"But he lost his life. Do you think it was worth it?"

"Considering all he accomplished, I do. Just think how many disasters he prevented!"

"That's right," the detective said. "You're catching on. Well, here are the last instructions. See you at the funeral—if you decide to hold one."

"That's the thing," Tom said. "I'm not sure. If there's an observance, it has to be small—just people who worked with him and knew him well. Can you make a list?"

The man grinned. "Easy. Here's a copy of the list he made. He pictured you and this group sitting in a good steak house sharing stories and enjoying each other."

Tom scanned the names. "What an incredible group. I'd love that."

"Fabulous," Callie said.

Tom counted on his fingers. "So, no newspaper coverage because there's already been an obituary. The tombstone stays the same."

"Right."

He raised his eyes. "Is anyone buried in that coffin?"

The detective leaned over and whispered.

"Rocks?" Tom said. "They buried his weight in dirt and rocks? That's what we brought flowers to every year?"

"No. To the memory of a man you loved and honored. He watched sometimes and took more long-range photos than you've seen."

Tom cratered.

"That hurts." His voice ached. "I would love to have seen him. I would have kept my mouth shut."

"That wasn't the problem. He wouldn't put you at risk. Your mom knew a little."

"She did?" Tom's jaw tensed as his eyes met Callie's. "Why didn't she tell me?"

"To keep you safe. You're from a family of heroes," the detective said. "Be proud. Tommy had to *die* five years back to trick his enemies. His death now was on his terms."

Tom pushed a hand through his hair. "What do you mean?"

"Exactly that. Here's his death report."

Tom and Callie leaned forward as the detective read aloud.

"A bullet through the heart from an international crime figure in the Underground Seattle tour area at the same instant Tommy got him. He rescued the girl, but your uncle left off his bulletproof vest on purpose. He wanted to be shot. Read the pathology. He had an inoperable brain tumor with only weeks to live. When he fired the bullet that got his enemy, it gave him a clear shot. Tommy's *accidental* death doubles the funds going into his foundation."

The detective slapped his desk. "I admired the man. He figured everything out."

"Mercy killing by enemy fire?" Tom shook his head.

"Heroic!" Callie's eyes shone. "I wish I'd met him. Tom, I think you're a lot like him."

"I hope so." Tom turned to the detective. "I seriously want to honor him."

"You will. What do you see ahead for your life now?"

"This morning, I thought I knew my path, but after today—"

"You're carrying a legacy." The detective slapped Tom's shoulder with a beefy hand. "I know you'll do him proud. See you at the funeral."

"Or the steak house," Tom said. "Do you know his favorite place?"

"Yeah. It's written in there. There's still more of your uncle's story for you to hear. Check your sheet."

Tom read. "Meet the President of Seattle's biggest bank."

"Right. I called him. He's expecting you."

"This is like a progressive dinner," Callie said. "An appetizer at the first place, then salads and the main dish here—"

"Great analogy." The detective chuckled. "You're in for a treat because dessert is next."

The couple stood and shook the president's hand while leaving. Dazed, Tom found a bench in the grassy park across the street.

"Let's sit a minute. My legs are rubber."

"Mine, too." Callie picked clover blossoms from the grass at her feet and braided them.

"The stuff we're hearing sounds like spy novels. I wish I could have been in his life these last five years."

"But it sounds like he knew what he was doing. What do you think we'll hear at the bank?"

"Callie, after everything else today, nothing will surprise me."

Two

They entered the city's biggest branch, a fortress of marble, sleek metal, and gleaming wood, where impeccably dressed employees looked like they were trained on Madison Avenue.

Tom and Callie checked their own clothing in dismay.

"We're already here. Let's give it a try." Tom introduced himself to a lead manager.

"Good. Mr. Thornquist is expecting you. Follow me."

The woman introduced them to a middle-aged, surprisingly fit bank president. Professional award plaques and photos of projects in foreign countries lined his walls.

"Please sit down. I'm so pleased to meet you and Callie. Your uncle told me so much about you."

"He did?" Tom and Callie exchanged glances.

"Yes. Once we planned his foundation, he invited me to go with him establishing the first projects—not any crime fighting ventures—just several humanitarian centers. Those results got me hooked with no turning back. I was privileged to call him friend and assist with the foundation's growth ever since.

Tom leaned forward. "Tell us about it."

"With pleasure." He opened a thick folder and photo album. "There are also videos and spreadsheets you can download. It's the W. Thomas Dunn Home Base Foundation. He hopes you'll maintain that name since it's yours, too."

Tom smiled.

"He explained he and your dad came from a disadvantaged background but that help and encouragement from caring individuals made the difference. Look at how well they both turned out."

"So he was passing help on," Tom said.

"Yes. Home Base nurtures individuals and families with the resources or training to get established, thrive, and nurture others."

"Excellent." Callie said, "Where and how is that done?"

The president waved a hand to the photos on the wall. "He started in the U.S., but now his projects stretch around the world. The more he donated, the more his investments prospered so he kept expanding. It was incredible. You'll be amazed at the assets you have to work with."

"That I have to work with?" Tom asked.

"Yes, if you accept his challenge. He said your MBA equips you perfectly to guide the foundation and some of your training may qualify you to uncover hackers and end international white-collar crime, too, if you're game."

Tom's eyes brightened. "I'd love that!"

"When you're both ready, I'm to escort you on a trip visiting a few of his projects around the world."

"Really?" Tom looked at Callie.

"How soon do you think that can be?" the president asked.

"Uh, we have a few things to decide but hopefully not long."

She squeezed Tom's hand. "Not long at all."

"Good. Instead of you returning to the funeral home, I'm privileged to present your uncle's final challenge now."

He handed Tom a sealed envelope and letter opener.

Tom's hands shook. He struggled to read aloud.

> Dear Tommy,
>
> I can call you that now. If you're reading this, I've gone to my eternal reward and you're learning about the years I lived after you buried me.
>
> It hurt me not to stay in closer contact with you after your dad's death and then your mom's. As my photos showed, I've followed your accomplishments and attended many activities from a distance.

Tom stopped and wiped his eyes.

"He was in my life and I didn't know it? That's almost harder to take than losing him earlier."

"What did he die of the first time?" Callie asked

"I thought it was cancer. Or some sudden thing like a heart attack. His doctor handled it."

Tom scanned more lines. "Next, he explains why the foundation is important and why he hopes I'll be involved."

She laid her cheek against his. "Will you?"

"That depends. So far, I'm interested if you are. What do you think?"

"I definitely want to hear more. Please read it all."

Congratulations, Tom and Callie. You're invited to lead Home Base plus consider joining the brand new Interpol unit just being formed. We've faced danger and spilled blood, but the next phase is where your MBA and computer tools could penetrate and bring down enemy systems. This is your opportunity to take your place in our family's heritage and make this world a better place. I believe you're well-prepared but am proud of you whatever you decide.

With all the love and affection a heart can hold, I salute you and wish you God's blessings always. Your loving Uncle Tommy.

"That's amazing." Callie took Tom's hand. "If it's what you want, you'll do just great."

Smiles wreathed Mr. Thornquist's face. "I know you two have things to discuss."

Tom nodded. "I can't believe how much has happened since this morning. I thought my final exam defined my future. I planned to apply for your Director of Financial Analysis opening in this very bank."

"I would have hired you. It's still yours if you want it."

"But my uncle's challenge is so much bigger. Callie and I need to talk."

"Of course."

Tom tugged her to her feet.

"Thank you, Mr. Thornquist. You'll hear from us soon."

"I'm counting on it."

"Callie, let's take my car. At least, there's one thing I can still control. I wanted today to be nice, to show you what ordinary days could look like after grad school. That would have included a good lunch, not a food truck."

"I wouldn't change anything, Tom."

"I thought I'd charted my future, but now? I can't guarantee the steps ahead, but I do know I want you at my side."

A smile lit her eyes. "I'm not going anywhere."

"You'd better not." He pulled her left hand to his heart.

"Feel those heartbeats? I want to put a ring on your finger but wanted to do it right, even rent a sailboat on Lake Washington. But after all we've experienced today, I need to do this now. Callie, I love you. I want our lives joined forever. Please marry me."

Her eyes glistened. "I thought you'd never ask."

Even before his lips met hers, she flung her arms around his neck and pulled him into a tight hug and tingling kiss.

"Wow. That feels like a yes. And changing your name to Mrs. W. Thomas Dunn matters more than any degree I'll ever earn."

"That's right." They kissed again.

He fished a stick of gum from his shirt pocket and removed its aluminum foil wrapper. He rolled it into a ring he slid on her finger.

"Callie, this is a ridiculous token until we go to a jeweler and choose something you love."

"For now, it's perfect!" She lifted her hand and turned it this way and that, admiring his symbol of promise.

"Our rings and marriage will last forever."

"And continue your family's legacy. I can't wait."

Tom chuckled. "Somehow, I think Uncle Tommy knows. But at least there's still one more thing I can control in this crazy day."

"What's that?"

"This." He pulled two cardboard rectangle tickets from his front shirt pocket. "And we're dressed right for this."

She checked her Underground Seattle tour guide clothes. The red top, blue shorts, and white tennis shoes had stayed fairly clean through today's scavenger hunt. Tom wore casual clothes.

"Where to?" she asked.

"The State Fair in Puyallup. I know you love the Oak Ridge Boys. Uncle Tommy did, too. I snagged these tickets for tonight's live Christmas concert."

"Wonderful! How did you do that?"

"Planned ahead to officially celebrate one thing today. We may be a little late, but we'll arrive for most of it."

They ran into the arena, holding hands, and squeezed along the right row to their seats. After lengthy introductions, they missed only half of the opening song.

When that ended, the emcee announced, "Ladies and gentlemen, as requested by a Seattle man who just finished graduate school, our next song is *Ordinary Days*."

The gentleman smiled at the audience. "Ready?"

"Yes!" everyone roared.

"All right then. Joel, Duane, William, and band, take it away!"

A baton flashed and the powerful music and words rolled on.

Callie leaned her head on Tom's shoulder.

"Thanks, love. That song is perfect, and my answer will always be yes."

Tom tightened his arms around her. "If we accept my uncle's challenge, our days won't ever be ordinary again."

"I'm okay with that. Frankly, ordinary can be boring."

He laughed and threaded his fingers with hers, turning the aluminum foil band on her finger.

"We'll go to a jewelry store tomorrow—"

"Right after we give Mr. Thornquist our answer. And start planning a brand new year together."

"You're sure?"

"Totally. You and I were both made for this. I'll accept challenges and excitement with you every day, forever, above anything else this world offers."

They kissed again as *Ordinary Days* finished and the band swung into a still livelier song, *The Warmest Night of the Year.*

Uncle Luther

Vanessa M. Knight

Made the Stuffing

One

Jenny had to move, but her feet were leaded to the ground. She had to help, but she was stuck, stuck gawking at the blue covering her grandma's lips.

Shallow bursts of air begged to enter Grandma's lungs in short gasps. Her wrinkled skin sallowed, invoking that blueish hue as Jenny's body finally jumped to attention.

One foot in front of the other, she ran to her grandma's cupboard and threw open the door looking for an epinephrine injector. No pen.

"EpiPen! Does anyone have an EpiPen?" Aunt Mary kneeled at grandma's side, her tinsel covered hands hovered over grandma's chest. Her nurse training probably kept her calm while the rest of the family stood in shock, not being able to offer up the life-saving device.

Except for Jenny. Jenny knew she had to act. Grandma was tough-as-nails, but her allergy to nuts was her kryptonite. Her obsession with eating said nuts was what ensured the family always kept an EpiPen on hand.

Jenny opened another cabinet and pulled out the elf-made store-bought cookies and the spray cheese. No pen. This was where her grandma usually kept it. She was sure of it. She emptied the shelf faster than it took to eat grandma's famous chocolate chip cookies—heck—faster than it took to say the words "grandma's famous chocolate chip cookies."

Still no pen. Where could it have gone?

Grandma's purse.

Jenny ran across the single-story home and whipped open the bedroom door, looking for the knitted purse Jenny had made Grandma for her last birthday. The purse was nowhere to be found, but Grandma's red and green leather purse sat on her bed.

Grandma must have gone back to her old purse. Part of Jenny's chest pinged, just a little, as she'd spent months on that darn thing. And Grandma had just tossed it aside for her old leathery one. She dumped the contents on the bed.

Bright red lipstick that always seemed to smear on grandma's front teeth, crumpled notepad pages lined with Christmas tasks, and plastic baggies fell onto the holiday quilt. Sifting through her grandma's treasures, white boxes toppled from the wad of tissues.

EpiPen boxes. Her grandma must have started keeping a stash. Jenny grabbed one of the boxes and ran to her Aunt Mary's side. "I have it!"

Mary grabbed the box, pulling the EpiPen out. She yanked the tab and pressed the top to Grandma's thigh. With a click and hiss, the injection must have been successful. Grandma's lips pulled in a large puff of air.

"Mom." Mary tossed the pen to the side and wrapped her mother in a hug. "Don't do that to me."

"I didn't do nothing." Grandma huffed. "Get off me so I can breathe."

"Stop eating nuts! Why is that so hard, Mom?" Uncle Eddie looked up from his string of Christmas lights. He was normally clueless, and his current focus was on the glowing strand in his hand. He slowly switched the bulbs so duplicate colors wouldn't sit next to each other.

"I didn't do any such thing." Grandma rolled to her side and began to stand.

"Not yet, Ma."

Grandma shook off her daughter's hand. "I've been dealing with this since before you were born. I'm fine." She stood to her full height of four-foot nothing and glared at her five-foot daughter. "Is that a problem?"

"No, Ma'am." Mary shook her hanging head.

"Now, I didn't eat no nuts." Grandma swayed on her feet. Mary caught her arm and helped her to the couch.

"If you didn't eat nuts, what did you eat?" Jenny had been with Grandma on a few occasions where Grandma had found a peanut butter square that was calling her name. And sometimes Jenny had to use the EpiPen depending on how much nut butter was used.

"Mom, please just relax." Aunt Mary placed her hand on Grandma's wrist as she talked.

"I just ate some of that stuffing on the counter."

Jenny looked over the living area where her family was hovering. "Who brought the stuffing?"

"Uncle Luther."

Uncle Luther stood in the corner.

"What was in the stuffing?"

"Not nuts." Luther glared at his sister.

Jenny went into the kitchen and grabbed the pan. She tilted it from side to side. Brown from the bread. Light green of celery. Orange from carrots. It was hard to see anything with all the ingredients and herbs mixed together.

With a tilt of the pan, she saw it—little chunks of light brown pieces scattered on top. She grabbed one and bit it, and the familiar oily, salty taste hit her tongue. "There's nuts in this."

"Why did you put nuts in the stuffing? Are you trying to kill us?" Mary's eyes narrowed into her mother-hen-glare. Grandma wasn't the only one in the family allergic to nuts.

"I didn't put nuts in the stuffing." Luther stomped up to the counter separating the kitchen from the living room. He grabbed the pan of stuffing and sniffed before dumping the evidence into the trash.

"Then who did?"

Everyone looked around the room like a defunct game of Clue. Was it Colonel Mustard Greens in the conservatory? No, it was the stuffing in the kitchen with nuts.

Jenny's dad craned his neck as he leaned back in his recliner. The excitement of the room had worn off, so he was probably trying to see the football game on the large screen. "I think we're overlooking the most obvious culprit."

Dad grabbed the beer from the side table and groaned as someone did something on the television. Jenny wasn't a huge football fan and with Grandma sick, she couldn't care less who was winning or fumbling.

"It's obviously a reindeer. The suminabitch has been trying to run Grandma over for years. He finally got smart and switched to nuts." Her dad guffed out a short faw. Grandpa snorted a laugh that lasted longer than Grandma's allergic reaction.

"Not funny." Mary patted Grandma's hand as the old woman glared at her husband for laughing.

"Maybe it was you, Dad." Luther crossed his arms over his chest. "Maybe you put nuts in the stuffing to kill Mom."

"Pshaw. If I wanted to kill your mother, I wouldn't fail." Grandpa returned his wife's glare but then ambled over to the couch and placed a kiss on her cheek. The man might be ornery, but he knew he couldn't live without his wife of fifty-five years.

"Well, someone put nuts in the stuffing." Luther moved forward. "It wasn't me. So why? And did they contaminate any other food?"

Those would be the questions they needed to figure out before anyone else started eating.

"We should probably start with who's allergic to nuts. They wouldn't have contaminated the stuffing." Luther raised his hand. "I'm allergic, Mom."

"I'm allergic, too." Jenny's mom raised her ladle-holding hand. Her apron bunched, the snowman on the front appearing to wink. "Not that it matters, this is ridiculous. It was probably a mistake."

"So you made the mistake?" Mary grinned at her sister with an air of superiority. Although, that was always how Mary looked at her homemaker sister.

Jenny's father snorted. Jenny's mother almost knocked herself out with the ladle as she covered her heart with her fist. "I did no such thing."

An ear-plitting sound came from the kitchen, followed by the faint smell of smoke. "My turkey!" Mom ran from the room.

Dad sighed and grabbed his cell phone. "Do you think McDonald's is still open?"

"Dad." Jenny took the phone from his hands. "Mom's been working on that turkey since four this morning. We're not having fast food."

"We're not having stuffing. And from the smell of it, we won't have turkey either." Dad snatched the phone back. "McDonald's doesn't make mistakes, and they don't hold grudges. Who wants me to order up a couple Big Macs?"

A few me's were shouted out.

"Stop it." Grandma shook her head and leaned back as her eyes closed. "We worked hard on this meal. Put that thing down."

Jenny's father sighed as he set the phone on the side table. His beer replaced the phone in his hand, and he leaned back—his attention back on the screen.

"Maybe we should get you to a hospital." Mary rested a hand on her mother's head.

"Pshaw. Why go to the hospital when I have a nurse right here."

"Fine," Mary sighed, "But I want you to lie down for a few minutes."

"No…"

"Either you listen to me and lie down, or we go to the hospital and they make you. Choose."

"Fine." Grandma stood up, her husband reaching out to help. She shooed his hand away and looked over at Mary. "This is why you're not my favorite."

"Mom!"

"Grandma!" Jenny didn't need to be a rocket scientist to know that Mary was not the favorite, no matter how hard her aunt had tried.

"What? She knows I'm just playing." Grandma ambled toward her bedroom, Mary following behind. "Hurry up. I'm not lying down all night."

Mary and her mother disappeared into the room and closed the door with a click. Grandpa sat in his chair and focused on the football game.

"Okay, so which one of you tried to kill my mother?" Luther looked directly at his brother Eddie.

"No one would try to kill your momma." Grandpa's eyes closed.

"I don't know." Jenny's cousin Sarah sat on the couch, one of her red cowboy boots hung over her boyfriend's waist as her knee rested on his inappropriate places.

Not that Jenny was looking at those inappropriate places. She hadn't even looked at his inappropriate places when they had been dating. Well… she'd looked. But he wasn't hers to look at anymore.

"Grandma has a lot of enemies."

What? Why were they talking about Grandma's enemies again. Oh yeah. The nut covered stuffing.

"Who is her enemy?" Jenny loved her grandma. How could anyone not? She was full of stories and fun. And she was the only one who ever listened to Jenny.

"The women down at her church group. Her doctor. Grandpa." Sarah sighed.

"Grandpa is not her enemy." Jenny could sigh, too. See. "Humph."

"The TV always says the easiest answer is always *the* answer." Sarah leaned against her stolen boyfriend. Did Jenny mention that Sarah had snatched her boyfriend from Jenny while he and Jenny were still dating? Buried the lead. Although the whole Grandma thing was really the lead here.

"Luther brought the stuffing. BAM!" Sarah lifted her hands and snapped them down in true BAM fashion.

"What BAM?" Luther shook his head. "You're as bad as your mother. Always blaming everyone else for your problems."

"My mother does not." Sarah wasn't exactly wrong. Aunt Mary didn't blame everyone for her problems, just Jenny's mom… and Grandma…

"She probably put nuts in the stuffing."

"Why would she do that?" Sarah sat forward with daggers shooting from her eyes. "My mom was the only one saving Grandma. You sat there like a scared rabbit chewing on your nails. Probably worried everyone would find out you did it."

Luther glared back. "Why would I hurt mom? I have nothing to gain."

"Who has something to gain?" Jenny crossed her arms.

"Well, since Mom just updated her will and left everything to Jenny…"

Wait what?

Luther leveled a glare at her. "…I'd say Jenny is the prime suspect."

Two

They were all staring at her like she was some nut-wielding murderer. What kind of person would kill for money? Not Jenny. And the fact that they thought she would was… was insane.

Like her grandma would leave her everything. Another thing that was pure insanity. The old woman had three children and five grandchildren. "That can't be true."

"What can't be true? That you're a killer or that you're getting all the money?" Sarah snorted.

"Both."

"Why does she get all the money?" Uncle Eddie twisted a bulb, and it glowed red along his broad chin.

"Did you know about this, honey?" Jenny's dad seemed to have forgotten all about the game on the TV and was staring at his daughter. Like everyone else.

She fought the urge to check her nose for boogers. "I don't know about anything. This can't be true."

"Of course it's true. You've been sucking up to Grandma for years. You knew exactly what you were doing," Sarah snarled as she ran her hand up and down her boyfriend's chest.

"I didn't…"

"Sarah…" Jenny's dad tried to talk.

"What? I'm just saying what everyone is thinking." Sarah's fingers went lower as her face somehow gloated. How does one even do that?

But that wasn't Jenny's biggest concern. Her family was all looking at her. Was everyone thinking that? It felt mean. And crazy. Jenny wouldn't hurt anyone.

"She doesn't even need the money." Sarah's mouth kept running.

Wait. "I don't?" Not that the money was hers, but anyone could use an influx of cash.

"I have school and a wedding to pay for."

A wedding. They were getting married. Fantastic. But the school thing… Jenny was on her fourth year. The government loans had opened up because she'd stuck with it, but she was still working two jobs to get through. "So do I."

"Yes, but not everyone has someone else footing the bill." Sarah said.

Someone else? "You mean the scholarship I won that covers a third of my tuition?"

Sarah smirked. "Must be nice."

"Yes. It is nice. I wrote a ten-page paper on the influences in my life. Then I got to miss our family trip to Florida so I could sit through two interviews, where I was asked why I thought we needed another physical therapist in the world."

"To be fair, do we really need another therapist in the world?" Luther shook his head.

"A physical therapist is integral to the healing process when someone injures themselves." Why did Jenny constantly have to defend her major choice?

"Or people could just stop whining." Sarah's hand roamed over the stubble on her boyfriend's face. He smirked—probably— but Jenny couldn't take her eyes off the hand.

Jenny's hand had been there once upon a time... and then it wasn't.

Sarah's hand slid down his chest, and Jenny's eyes followed. A smirk rested on Sarah's lips as she brought her hand back to her boyfriend's pecs. "See something you like?"

Jenny gulped. Gulped. Because she had liked him. A lot. She'd thought they'd be together forever, but apparently forever translated to until he slept with her cousin. "No." She tried to lie. Although, she did have a hard time liking someone who could cheat on her—who could like someone like Sarah. But he'd been Jenny's first serious boyfriend. Her first everything—so far.

"You know my eyes are up here." Sarah lifted her hand and pointed at her evil-twinkling eyes.

Jenny's gaze had somehow landed back on Sarah's hand and the boy beneath those fingers. And her cousin had called her out on it. That lack of luck rearing its head.

Heat crept up Jenny's neck. Everyone was watching her drool over her ex. It was bad enough everyone knowing she couldn't hold onto him. But now they had to know she was still in love with him... or at least in drool with him. What? You can drool over the outside and not want what's on the inside. Look at chocolate covered cherries.

Jenny focused her eyes away from her duplicitous cousin and her cousin's boy-toy.

"We have bigger things to deal with."

"Like your killing grandma."

"Like your insistence to point the finger at me. I didn't put nuts in the stuffing. I actually ran around and found the EpiPen. What did you do?" This whole conversation was making Jenny's head hurt.

"She did nothing." Uncle Eddie twisted a lightbulb in place. The string haloed red, blue, and green on his face. "Mom was dying on the ground, and Sarah was sucking face with the Jezebel."

"Uncle Eddie!"

"What?" Eddie's focus never left the bulbs.

"Why don't you focus on something else besides my lips." Sarah's lips were now snarling.

"I wasn't looking at your lips. Damn string started with the wrong color." Eddie grabbed another string and plugged it into the end of the first.

"Then how did you know what I was doing?"

"I can hear the spit swapping between your mouths." He swore under his breath as he twisted off a red light bulb that sat next to another red bulb. "Cows chewing cud make less slurping noises. I was afraid your boyfriend was going to suck your head down his throat, and we'd have to pry it out with the jaws of life."

"Uncle Eddie!" Sarah snarled.

"What? I'm just saying what everyone is thinking." He switched another bulb as Jenny held back a laugh. She couldn't help it. Her uncle had just used the same B.S. line that Sarah had used on Jenny. Somehow it didn't hurt as much when it wasn't aimed at her.

"It doesn't give me a motive for trying to kill grandma." Sarah glared at Jenny.

Are we still on this? Why was she glaring at Jenny? Jenny didn't say it.

"No, but I have a feeling if Jenny were going to kill someone it would be the one who cheated on her. And since he's not allergic to nuts, we should just keep looking." Uncle Eddie's tongue wedged between his lips as he twisted another bulb.

Jenny wasn't sure if she should thank him or gasp in offense. "Thanks." She chose thanking since he was currently the only one defending her against murder charges.

"If it's not Jenny, and I know it's not me, then who is it?" Sarah crossed her arms over her ample chest—one of the reasons her boyfriend said he'd fallen in love with Sarah.

"Maybe it was your boyfriend."

"What would he have to gain?" Sarah looked as excited about the conversation as Jenny was feeling. "My boyfriend has been with me the whole time. When would he have done anything?"

Jenny hated to agree with her cousin, but no one had anything to gain by hurting grandma. Well, except for Jenny and the reindeer. And Jenny knew she didn't do it. She couldn't bring herself to admit that reindeers actually existed, so that left them at square one.

"How is Mom doing?" Jenny's mom walked out of the kitchen, wiping her hands on her apron. Jenny didn't have the answer, so she turned to look if anyone else might.

Mary came out of the bedroom and leaned against the wall, sifting through the red and green bag at her hip. "She's resting but fine." She pulled a tube from inside. A red box spilled out and hit the floor boards with a thud.

The EpiPens. "Is that grandma's purse?"

"She gave it to me when you made her that knitted bag."

Her grandma was using the knitted bag. Which meant… "Aunt Mary, why do you have so many EpiPens?"

Mary didn't look up from the inside of her purse, but her hands stilled. "I'm a nurse. And my family is allergic to a bunch of things."

"Like nuts." Jenny's mind raced through the contents of that purse. The baggie. The pens.

"Why were you looking in my purse?"

Her aunt's protesting—she was lucky she wasn't a wooden boy or her nose would be growing.

"I thought it was grandma's purse." Jenny reached out her hand. "What's in the purse?"

"It's a purse. What do you think?" Mary angled the bag behind her back.

"I think there's an empty baggie that had nuts inside. I think there's multiple EpiPens. What I can't figure out is why."

"Jenny, what are you saying? You better have proof…" Jenny's mom's eyes squinted as she looked at Jenny. Like it was Jenny's fault that this conversation had to take place.

"Shut it, Sandy." Uncle Eddie looked over to Mary. "She was the only one who was in the kitchen when the tree lights flickered."

"Like you would notice. You've had your face in those lights all night."

Eddie looked up. "I can multi-task. I can twist a bulb and watch you sneak into the kitchen."

"Why would my mom have nuts?" Sarah untangled her tentacles from her boyfriend and stood up. "We're forgetting who has the motive."

"You're forgetting who has the nuts."

Sarah's cowboy boots tapped a dirge on the tiled floor. "Can you prove it?"

Jenny stepped forward in her flats. She might lose a kicking contest but Jenny had a lot of pent up betrayal to unleash if her cousin got any closer. "Check her purse."

Three

"This is ridiculous. Sandy, control your daughter." Mary slammed her lipstick back in the bag before snapping it closed. That was one way to say she wasn't going to let anyone check her purse for lethal nut remnants.

Her spine steeled as Jenny's mom glared. "Open your purse, Mary."

Mary pressed the bag closer as Uncle Luther snuck to her side and pulled the bag from her hands.

"Hey!" Mary lunged at her brother but stopped when he dumped the contents in the middle of the floor. A wallet, tissues, and the lipstick spilled out. But that wasn't what stopped everyone in the room.

Everyone gasped and stared at the red boxes that fell to the ground. Four EpiPens.

"Why do you need so many pens?" Uncle Luther dropped the bag and picked up a box. "This one hasn't been opened."

"I carry them around for Mom." Mary held out her hand. "I'm a nurse. I know how those allergies can mess with a person. What I don't see is nuts. Give me my purse back."

Jenny grabbed the bag from the floor and looked inside. Dread balled, pulling at the center of her chest as she saw plastic shining from the corner. She tipped over the bag and spread the opening by pinching the sides with her fingers. The plastic bag drifted to the ground. Light brown fragments lined the edges.

"Mary?" Jenny's mom cried.

"Those sure look like nuts." Luther hovered over the pile of purse guts. His attention moved to his sister Mary as he shook his head. "Yep, there are two nuts in the room right now."

"Why?" Jenny's mom leaned over, her butt waving in the air as she inspected the bag. Her nut allergy was extra sensitive and just touching the bag would cause all kinds of issues. "Why would you hurt Mom?"

"I didn't..." Mary started.

"You did. The bag is right here."

"It's not like that..."

"What's it like? You tried to kill mom." Eddie leaned away from the lights and lifted the bag. He sniffed the inside. "Yep, nuts."

"I wasn't trying to hurt mom." Mary's eyes lined with tears.

"Who were you trying to hurt?"

"I didn't mean it like that..."

"How did you mean it?"

Questions flew from Uncle Eddie's mouth in rapid succession. Mary's head spun back and forth as her words were cut off again and again. "Enough!"

Mary kneeled on the ground, snatching her purse and propping it open on the floor. She grabbed a handful from the pile and shoved it inside. "I wasn't trying to hurt Mom. I was trying to hurt you."

Mary cleaned off the floor and stood with her purse hanging open. Tissues and boxes peaked up from the top, but she didn't seem to care. She grabbed the bag, pulling it close to her chest, and glared at Jenny's mom.

"Me?" Jenny's mom stepped back. Her eyes rounded as a tear slid down her cheek. "You wanted to kill me?"

"Oh, don't be dramatic." Mary rolled her eyes. "I wasn't trying to kill you. Why do you think I have all these pens? I would have saved you before you died. I was trying to teach you a lesson."

"And is the lesson that her sister should be committed?" Luther inched back, probably realizing he shouldn't provoke the crazy lady who wielded nuts as a weapon.

"It was my year to bring the stuffing. You knew that. But then you asked Luther instead."

"Because you wanted to bring a grain-free stuffing." Jenny's mom sighed. "How do you make stuffing without grain?"

"It has mushrooms and carrots in it. It's healthy. It won best side dish at my church potluck. Everyone would have loved it." Mary pulled her bag to her hip.

"Wait. Stuffing without bread. Is that even stuffing?" Eddie was back to his spot on the floor fiddling with the light strand.

"Shut up, Eddie." Mary glared at everyone in the room, before honing her death-stare on her sister. "You have everything—the husband, the house, and the kids. You couldn't give me one day. You knew I was excited about sharing the dish I created. You knew Mom would love it, and you wouldn't be the favorite anymore."

"I didn't…"

"Don't give me that. I wanted to bring one thing this year, and it was my turn. I wanted Mom to see that I wasn't a complete screw-up."

"You're not a screw-up."

"Of course, I'm the family screw-up. My husband's not here because we're separated." Mary dropped to the couch. "I'm getting another divorce."

"Oh, honey."

Mary wiped away the tears in her eyes. "I just wanted one day before I have to listen to Mom yell at my poor choice in men or hear her tell me I should be more like you."

Jenny's mom dropped next to her sister. "Being me isn't all that great. My kids don't need me. My husband needs me too much, and all I want to do is get out of the house. But I can't afford to take classes or go to a gym. And no one will hire a high school graduate with no experience or work history."

"But you're still married."

"If I could afford a divorce, I'd be on husband number three, too." Jenny's mom laughed. Hopefully she was joking. Jenny had no desire to do multiple holiday parties with both her parents. She could barely handle this one.

"When are we eating?" Grandma's bedroom door flew open, and she drifted over to her husband. "I'm witherin' away here." Grandma poked at Grandpa, who had fallen asleep at some point.

His eyes opened as a snore ripped from his mouth. "Is it time to eat yet?"

"Yeah, Dad. We're going to eat." Jenny's mom nodded toward the dining room, where tables and chairs had been setup for the entire family. "Everyone sit, and I'll bring in the food."

Grandma helped her husband stand, and they led each other to the table. The room emptied, chairs scraping the floor as everyone followed them, leaving Jenny, her mom, and Mary behind.

Mary's head drooped as she stood up. "I should probably go so you can get dinner started."

"Stay. You should be with family right now." Jenny's mom angled up and adjusted her apron. She wrapped her sister in a hug. "Just stay out of the kitchen."

Back to

Danielle M Haas

Tennessee

Christmas Cookies Mysteries

One

Paxton Sterling swallowed her growing frustration with her little sister and pulled into a parking space at the rest stop ten minutes from home. Light snowflakes fell from the sky and dusted the trees surrounding the lone building that housed restrooms and vending machines for weary travelers. She avoided places like this at all costs, especially as the sun started to sink behind the Smokey Mountains and only one other vehicle sat in the parking lot. "You seriously can't wait until we get home?"

Her mother's busy schedule had forced Paxton to take a day off work to drive to Ohio, pick Izzy up from college, and bring her back to Tennessee before their close-knit family could begin their annual holiday festivities.

A favor that went unappreciated by Izzy.

Seven hours and three stops later, Paxton was anxious to get home. The last thing she wanted was to make one more stop so Izzy could use the bathroom…again.

Rolling her eyes, Izzy smacked her gum and flipped her long blonde hair over her shoulder. "No way. That second coffee went right through me. I won't be long. We'll be home in plenty of time for you to see Gavin." She jammed a pair of gray mittens on her hands.

Stepping outside, Izzy pulled her purse strap high on her shoulder then flounced up the cracked sidewalk toward the shabby brown building.

Keeping her gaze fixed on Izzy, Paxton hunched over the steering wheel and tried to ignore the pain pumping from her bruised heart to the rest of her extremities. She'd loved Gavin for most of her life, standing by his side when he went off to college hours away while she stayed in Pine Valley to support her grieving mother after her father's death.

But his decision to jump ship on the engineering career he'd barely started and join the police academy without consulting her had been a bitter pill she couldn't swallow.

A familiar frustration had her tightening her grip on the wheel. They planned to spend the rest of their lives together. How could Gavin make such a huge, life-altering decision without consulting her? A decision he *knew* she couldn't support.

Not after growing up and watching her mother worry and fret over her father every day when he went into work.

Not after her father had been killed in the line of duty, leaving her to carry the weight of her splintered family that her mother was too weak to shoulder and her sister too young to handle.

Her phone vibrated in the cup holder beside her, casting an earie glow in her darkening car. A quick glance at the screen showed Gavin calling. She'd planned to meet him at the Chill N' Grill after she finally got Izzy home. They hadn't spoken since their blow up a few nights before, when she'd stormed out of his apartment, vowing to never return.

But was that really what she wanted?

Sighing, she checked the clock on the dashboard. Izzy had been inside long enough. Her sister probably had plans and wanted to make herself picture-perfect before getting home so she could dash away to her friends, leaving their mother with barely a kiss on the cheek and a quick hello.

A tap on the window jolted Paxton back to the present. She peered outside, and the sight of a police officer released the ball of anxiety in her gut. Pressing the button, she lowered the window enough to speak to the woman standing beside the car. "Hello, officer. Can I help you?"

The woman—Officer Whipple from her nametag—leaned closer. "There's no loitering in this parking lot. I need you to move along."

Frowning, Paxton tried to look past the officer for her cruiser, but only the rusted van she first spied when pulling into the lot was visible. "I'm not loitering. My sister is inside." She dipped her chin toward the building. "I'm just waiting for her to use the bathroom. Then we'll be on our way."

Officer Whipple cast her gaze toward the ancient structure before turning narrowed eyes her way. "I just made my rounds and didn't see anyone inside. I don't know what your plans are, but I don't want trouble tonight. You need to get home."

The anxiety from earlier came back with a vengeance. She raised her hands, as if the truth were sprawled across her palms. "I promise. She's inside. She just takes forever. I'll run in and grab her then be on my way."

Cutting the engine, she swiped her phone and placed it, along with her keys, in her jacket pocket and jumped out of the car. She forced a tight smile toward the cop then braced herself against the biting wind as she jogged to the entrance. When she found Izzy, she'd kill her.

The hum of fluorescent lights vibrated off the dirty linoleum floor. A vending machine was shoved against a wall, two entries to bathrooms on either side. Finding the woman's sign, Paxton stormed ahead. The hairs on the back of her neck stiffened, standing on ends. She hated rest stops. Hated the off-the-beaten-path hideaways, out of sight from the cars whizzing by, covered by a canopy of trees. They gave her the creeps. And now here she was, alone and irritated, looking for her sister.

Rounding the corner, she found thee closed bathroom stalls. "Izzy?"

Nothing but the sound of water dripping from the single sink returned her call.

Paxton swallowed hard, refusing to give into the dread crawling up her skin. "Come on, Izzy. We need to go."

Nothing.

Stepping up to the first stall, she pushed against the gray door and it swung open. No one was inside. She went to the next, her heart racing. She pushed open the door.

No one inside.

Sweat dotted Paxton's hairline, and she wiped her brow, moving away the unwanted moisture as well as a strand of her light brown hair. "Izzy?" Her voice shook, mirroring the quiver of her racing pulse. She wet her dry lips and pushed open the last stall door. Izzy's purse swung from a hook on the door, but she was nowhere to be found.

Paxton stumbled backward, raw fear scraping against her throat. Izzy was missing.

Two

The sound of dripping water echoed in Paxton's ears, the sound louder than it was seconds before. She sucked in deep breaths full of the stale air that lingered in the small bathroom. Panic wouldn't solve the problem, wouldn't help her find Izzy.

The walls seemed to close in on her as her mind spun. Blood pumped furiously through her veins, and fear clogged her throat. She charged out of the bathroom. The building wasn't big. There couldn't be many places Izzy could be. "Izzy!" A map of Tennessee sprawled along one wall, pictures of the Governor and other political figures rested on another. Large glass windows showcased the now-dark parking lot, save the strategically placed lamp posts with dim halos of light that barely touched the pavement.

Steeling her resolve, she burst into the men's bathroom. One stall was flanked by foul-smelling urinals. Not wanting to touch anything, she kicked in the door just to find it empty. Deflated, she fought the tears pushing against the backs of her eyes. She ran to the lobby, searching for another room Izzy could have ventured into. Two more doors. One with a glowing red Exit sign above it that led to the back of the building.

She ran to the only other option that made sense, but the locked knob refused to budge. With her phone still cradled in her palm, she raised her fists to her temples, pushing the heels of her hands against her skull. This couldn't be happening. Her sister couldn't be missing. They were only ten minutes away from their small and safe town of Pine Valley. Things like this didn't happen here. Not even in the creepy rest stops on the outskirts of town.

Her phone buzzed, gaining her focus. This time, Gavin's wide grin on her screen brought her comfort instead of dread. She answered, greedy to hear Gavin's deep husky voice.

"Hey. Are you almost home? We really need to talk." He spoke with a low, lazy drawl that would have curled her toes if fear hadn't tightened every muscle in her body.

"Gavin! I can't find Izzy! I don't know what to do."

"What do you mean? Where are you?"

She pushed her wild waves off her face, keeping her fingers entangled in her hair at the top of her head as she spun in a wide circle. "We stopped at the rest stop right before our exit off the highway. She came inside, and now she's nowhere. This officer thought I was loitering and…. Oh! The officer." With the phone pressed to her ear, she ran back outside. Her feet pounded against the sidewalk as she followed the path to her car, scanning the parking lot with each step. "I don't see her."

"Izzy?"

"No. The officer. She was just here." Paxton pivoted toward where the van had been parked moments before, but the parking lot was empty. She squeezed her eyes shut. "I don't understand. Izzy didn't just disappear. This officer didn't vanish. Where are they?"

"I'll head your way. Should be there in ten minutes. We'll find her. In the meantime, get in your car and lock the doors. Call the police then keep your phone with you."

The cold air barreled into her, and her teeth chattered. "Okay. Please hurry." She wanted to keep him on the line but needed to call the authorities. Alert them to her sister's disappearance. Pressing the unlock button on her key fob, she scrambled into her car.

Before she could punch in the number, headlights flooded her rearview mirror, growing until the car slid to a stop behind Paxton's car, boxing her into her space. She squinted through the glare to make out the person behind the wheel. The lights shut off. The sleek SUV wasn't a police vehicle, but there was no mistaking who was in the driver's seat.

Officer Whipple strode to her door and circled her finger in the air, indicating Paxton should roll down the window. "I thought I told you to move along."

An uneasiness slithered down her spine. She could have sworn that SUV hadn't been in the parking lot the first time the officer spoke with her. "My sister isn't inside. I need to find her."

"And you think you'll find her by sitting in your car?" The officer tilted her head to the side, her green eyes hardening.

"Please. Can you take a look around? She could be hurt. Or something bad might have happened."

"How about I take a look around the perimeter while you head home? Give me your number, and I'll call if I find something."

She bounced her gaze from the officer to the rearview mirror. *Come on, Gavin. Hurry up. I need you.*

"I won't warn you again."

Paxton mentally flipped through her options. No way was she leaving here without Izzy. She needed to stall until Gavin got here and could help. She scrunched her nose, trying to look as apologetic as possible. "Okay. That sounds fair. But can I go to the bathroom first? I don't know when I'll get to stop again."

Officer Whipple sighed, then swept her hand to the side, a sign for her to go ahead and step out of the car. "Hurry."

She cast a few glances over her shoulder as she entered the travel center again. She checked her phone. Five minutes had passed since she hung up with Gavin. All she had to do was stall long enough for him to arrive.

Shifting, she faced the door that led to the exit off the back of the building. The only place she didn't check. Chances were low that Izzy would have left through the back exit, but she couldn't leave without knowing she'd checked every single inch of this place. Paxton could just take one little look.

She took a step toward the back door and all the lights shut off, engulfing her in darkness.

Three

Darkness squeezed around Paxton through every nook and cranny. She blinked, trying her hardest to adjust to the lack of light. Someone had cut the power. Someone who was still inside the building with her. Wedging herself against the wall, she scanned the long shadows for any sign of movement as she inched closer to the still-glowing red Exit sign. The idea of roaming around the back of the building made her chest tighten, but that exit was closer than the front doors.

Holding her breath, she slithered to the short hallway and pushed out the door. She darted her gaze around her, noting the pressed indents on the frozen grass that led to the tree line. A part of her yearned to follow the trail, but she resisted the urge.

The sound of a twig snapping sounded nearby. Paxton needed to get back to the parking lot, back to the tiny halos of lamplight and Officer Whipple and hopefully Gavin. Staying close to the building, she sprinted around the corner. A tall, dark figure stepped into her path and strong arms wrapped around her, locking her in place.

A scream ripped from her throat, and she thrashed to the side. "Get off me!"

"Paxton. Stop. It's me. You weren't in your car, and the front door was stuck so I came around back."

Gavin's deep baritone halted her frantic attempt at escape. She buried her head in his chest, inhaling the familiar scent of leather and pine. "Thank God. I went inside and someone shut off the lights. I don't understand what's going on."

He smoothed a palm over her thin jacket, the friction and adrenaline keeping the chilly air from clinging to her bones. "Everything will be okay. We'll figure it out."

She pulled back and forced a smile. Moonlight spilled over his face, showing off his strong jawline. The cerulean color of his eyes was hidden under the bill of his baseball hat, but she felt the heat of his gaze on her body. His words soothed her. This was a man she'd trusted with her heart for the past eight years. If he was with her, there was nothing they couldn't accomplish. They'd find Izzy and put this whole terrible ordeal behind them. "Did you see Officer Whipple in the parking lot?"

"No one was out front. Your car was the only one in the lot."

She frowned. "Maybe she's patrolling the area, searching for Izzy."

Gavin slid his hand down her arm to lock his fingers with hers. "Pax, I called the captain. He's never heard of an Officer Whipple. She might be new, and he's making calls to find out for sure, but she might be claiming to be something she's not. He's sending a patrolman this way in case." He tugged her forward. "Let's sit in my truck and wait. It's not safe standing here. Especially if someone is inside."

Nodding, she followed along beside him. Her feet hit the sidewalk and bright headlights turned into the lot. Finally. More help. Gavin and this officer—one she knew was legit—were here and they could find Izzy.

The vehicle shot toward them, its speed climbing and jumped over the edge of the sidewalk.

"Run!" Gavin shouted.

Paxton stumbled, her feet racing forward as Gavin hauled her away from the maniac behind the wheel. The engine roared behind her. The muscles in her thigh's screamed and her lungs burned, but she kept pushing, her hand locked in Gavin's tight grip.

At the tree line, Gavin tugged her in front of him, shielding her with his body. "Keep running," he yelled.

She didn't need to be told twice. The rustle of dead foliage shuffled at her feet, and she pushed past the prickly pine leaves from the crowded trees. Ragged breaths tore through her until silence hung heavy in the air. Panting, she leaned forward, bracing her forearms on her knees. "What in the world is going on?" she whispered.

Gavin pulled her against him, ducking low behind a full evergreen. "I don't know. But whoever was driving might come after us. The police should be here soon."

A light swung along the ground, just past their feet. Alarm blasted through her brain. She gripped Gavin's hand. "We have to keep moving."

Nodding, he led her into the thick forest. Her ears stayed tuned to every sound, every unnatural beat in the night air. Wind whipped through the branches. Patches of the star-strewn sky broke through the tall maze of trees, casting a dim glow. Was Izzy out here? Was she cold and scared? The hard earth gave way to a narrow strip of gravel. "Is this a new trail?" She whispered, afraid whoever followed them could hear her.

"That looks like a cabin of some sort," Gavin said, pointing in front of him.

Realization dawned on her. "We're at that old summer camp we went to as kids. It's been closed for a while now. That's one of the bunk houses. The lake should be close."

Gavin grabbed his phone and turned on the flashlight. "I don't hear anyone. Let's regroup in there to get out of the cold, and I'll call the station and see how close the officer is. Fill them in on what happened."

She followed him off the path and hurried to the battered cabin. Boot prints marred the snow on the crooked steps and the rusted door hung off the splintered frame. A sense of nostalgia swept over her despite the desperate fear clinging to her psyche. Memories of summers spent at camp, sneaking away to steal kisses in the woods with Gavin. Holding hands and cuddling beside a campfire.

And now, after she'd told him things were over, he was still here. Still showing up to be exactly what she needed. Maybe she'd been too harsh when she'd ended things. Not paid enough attention to what Gavin needed.

With his fingers pressed to the small of her back, Gavin ushered her through the doorway and swept his phone flashlight inside.

The narrow beam landed on Izzy slumped on the floor in the corner of the wide-open room, reflecting the blood caked on the side of her head and the tears in her eyes.

Paxton ran to her, throwing her arms around her. "What happened? Can you walk? We need to go! Now!"

A silent sob shook Izzy's shoulders. "We can't go. I can't leave them behind." She flicked a finger to the opposite side of the room.

Paxton turned, following the motion. Two teenage girls huddled together in the corner. And even in the dark, from a distance, fear shone bright in their eyes.

Four

The relief at finding Izzy evaporated, replaced by a ball of confusion that clogged Paxton's windpipe, stealing her ability to speak. She blinked, unsure if what she saw was really there. No amount of opening and closing her eyes made the nightmare before her disappear. Two girls— younger than Izzy with their dirt-smeared faces and ratty clothes— trembled as they slid as far against the opposite wall as possible. Wrists bound, feet secured to the wooden floorboards with a thick chain.

Mind racing, Paxton crouched in front of Izzy and caught her cheek in her palm. The nasty gash on her forehead was deep. "What happened? Who did this to you?"

Tears flowed down Izzy cheeks. "A man was in the bathroom. He hit me with a tool of some kind, grabbed me, then brought me here."

"I don't have a signal to call for help," Gavin said on a growl. "We have to get out of here. Whoever did this has to be close. He wouldn't just bring you all here then disappear."

"I can't leave them," Izzy said again, steel in her small voice.

"Of course not," Paxton said. "But we need to get help. The man could come back any time."

"And if he does and I'm not here, and they are, he'll take them somewhere else and then what? They're lost again? Stashed somewhere no one will find them?" Defiance set Izzy's jaw.

Paxton nodded. "Okay. You're right. Let's figure this out." Standing, she crossed over to the girls and offered a smile. "I'm Izzy's sister. We're going to help you." She lowered to the ground, feeling the thick chain keeping the girls in place. Disgust coated her gut, and she caught Gavin's gaze for a brief second over her shoulder.

He tightened his fist at his side and blew out a long breath before hurrying to Izzy and helping her to her feet.

"What are your names?" Paxton asked the girls.

One girl dipped her chin and squeezed her eyes shut. The other licked her cracked lips but locked her gaze with Paxton. "I'm Gina. This is Riley. We need to hurry. He's never gone long."

Swallowing the bile sliding up her throat, Paxton skimmed her fingers over the chain tethering the girls to the floor like animals. "Do you know who he is?"

Gina shook her head.

"How long have you been here?" Gavin asked.

Fear flooded Gina's eyes when she glanced at Gavin then quickly back to Paxton. "About a week. Riley, a couple days longer. He said we had to move soon. He's been really mad."

The girls couldn't be from the area, or Paxton would have heard about their disappearance. "The chain's bolted to the ground. We need a way to detach it from the wood."

Gavin shone the light over every inch of the cabin. "Nothing here, Izzy," he said, staying by her to support her weight as she swayed. "You said a man hit you with a tool. Did he take it with him?"

She shrugged. "I…I don't know. I mean, I guess."

Paxton twisted her lips to the side. "Why would he have a tool? That's a random weapon for a kidnapper."

"Buzz around town is the woman who now owns this land is turning it into some kind of retreat. Rehabbing all the cabins, building a fancy lodge. Maybe construction started, and that's why he mentioned needing to move," Gavin said.

"There might be something nearby we can use to get these two free," Paxton said, hope rising.

"Give me a minute." Gavin ran out the door.

The sight of him leaving stole her breath, but she couldn't let it cripple her. "Izzy, come help." Paxton grabbed a handful of the heavy metal and tugged. Decay chipped away at the ancient floorboards. The wood groaned and the structure shifted with each yank.

Izzy tighten her fists behind Paxton's and pulled.

Heavy footsteps pounded up the front stoop, and a knot of tension at the back of her neck loosened. With Gavin's help, they could bust through the wood. "The chain won't budge, but we might break the board it's chained to. Come help." She tossed the words over her shoulder, not wanting to stop the mounting pressure against the old floor.

"Good thing I don't need those old chains anymore."

The unfamiliar voice was like a bucket of cold water over her head. Paxton turned toward the door. A short man with a round middle and dark shaggy hair stood in the doorway. A gun pointed at her head. "To your feet. Now."

She raised her palms and stood.

"I don't like taking two girls traveling together. Too much attention comes of it. But you just couldn't leave it alone. Couldn't be scared off. Both of you. In the corner." He jerked his gun to the spot Izzy had been when she'd arrived.

She gripped Izzy's hand and led her to where the man instructed.

Keeping his gun trained on her, he stormed inside. "Don't try anything stupid." He fiddled with the thick cuffs around Gina and Riley's ankles and sprung them loose. "Everyone outside."

Adrenaline pumped through Paxton's body, making her teeth chatter. No way she was going anywhere with this jerk. She had to stall. Gavin couldn't be far. "What do you want from us?"

The man sneered, crossing the room to grab a fistful of her hair. "Keep your mouth shut and move. Cause any trouble, and one of these other girls will pay the price. Got it?"

A shadow shifted outside. Paxton moved as if the unbearable pain ripping at her scalp was too much, which positioned the man's back to the door.

Officer Whipple ran inside and rammed the butt of her flashlight against the man's head. His grip loosened and he fell to the ground. She kneeled on his back and secured his wrists with zip ties then shined her light in Paxton's face. "Are you all right?"

Adrenaline leaked from her like air from a punctured balloon, and her limbs trembled. "We're fine."

"Can you all walk? Backup is at the travel center."

Gina helped Riley to her feet. "We can make it."

"You all go first," Officer Whipple said. "I'll take up the rear. Make sure no one else is coming."

Paxton led the way out of the cabin and pulled in a deep breath of fresh, mountain air. She looped an arm around Izzy's waist to help her down the stairs. A rustle in the trees caught her attention.

Gavin sprinted her way. His phone in his hand.

Footsteps shuffled behind her as the girls came outside, Officer Whipple behind them.

"Gavin!" Paxton called. "We're okay. Help came. Officer Whipple found us."

"She's a fraud," Gavin screamed, running forward at full speed. "No Officer Whipple exists in the state of Tennessee."

Paxton glanced behind her as Officer Whipple aimed a gun at Gavin and fired.

Five

A gut-wrenching scream ripped from Paxton's mouth and combined with the panicked cries of the girls behind her. Gavin fell face-first on the ground. Paxton lunged forward, but a hard hand yanked her backward.

"Keep moving." The woman pushed the barrel of the gun into her back.

Izzy clung to her hand.

Paxton lifted her chin and swallowed a sob. She couldn't just let Gavin die, alone and scared, but what choice did she have? Not only did she need to get Izzy and the other girls out of this mess, but she had a gun pointed at her. She had to keep walking, no matter how much it broke her heart to walk away from the only man she ever loved.

She kept her gaze glued to him. Maybe the police would arrive and find him in time to save him. Her body yearned to get closer, to cover him with her jacket, to press a kiss to his forehead, but she couldn't chance it. With Izzy at her side, Gina and Riley now in front of her, she said a small prayer as her soul cried out, and she stepped passed Gavin's motionless body.

Nausea swam in her stomach. This was what she'd wanted to avoid by ending her relationship with Gavin before he graduated the police academy—losing him in a violent and tragic way. Instead, she'd spent the last few weeks being angry and bitter, unwilling to see her best friend's perspective. Unwilling to see past her own fears to view the bigger picture of what Gavin needed to do for his life's purpose.

A flash of movement caught the corner of her eye, but she forced herself not to react. She held her breath as she took one…two…three steps deeper into the woods.

Gavin sprung to his feet and charged the woman impersonating a police officer. He wrapped around her like a lineman on the football field, lifting her off her feet and then driving her into the ground.

A loud grunt leaked from her throat. The impact against the dirt and earth caused her to throw out her arms, and she released the gun.

Paxton scooped up the gun with shaking hands. "I got it, Gavin. I got the gun."

Pushing to his knees, he wrestled the cursing woman's arms behind her back and slapped on a pair of handcuffs he'd tucked in his coat pocket.

Pride exploded inside Paxton, and tears leaked from the corners of her eyes. Gavin jumped to his feet and engulfed her, folding her into his arms. She might have brought Izzy back to Tennessee for the holidays, but this was where home was to Paxton. Safe and loved by Gavin's side.

Colorful lights twinkled from the heavily decorated tree in Paxton's mother's living room. Hours had passed since she and Izzy had given their statements, and they'd been allowed to leave. The police had swarmed the area, taking both kidnappers—the man and woman working together before the woman decided to cut him out and make a run for it—into custody. Riley and Gina's parents had shown up, delighted to see their daughters. She'd stayed by Gavin's side at the hospital, where relief had washed over her to learn that the bullet had only grazed his side. He'd heal quickly, and she'd stand by him as he graduated the police academy, brimming with pride at what a wonderful officer he'd make.

Now, Paxton sat on the floor of her childhood home, her mother sandwiched between her and her sister. Exhaustion weighed her down, but she didn't want to miss this moment. This perfect place in time where the tree was lit and Bing Crosby crooned in the background.

A moment to appreciate all that she had in her life. All of her blessings.

A moment to reflect on all that was yet to come.

But most of all, a moment to feel the love all around her, to let a sense of peace and joy ebb through her as she sat with her family and enjoyed finally being home—together in Tennessee.

The Warmest Night

Kaye D. Schmitz

of the Year

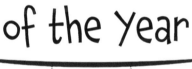

T he huge policeman yanked my hands behind my back, shackled them tight, and charged me with murder.

"Murder?" I asked, incredulity clear in my voice. "Me?"

"Trust me, pal, I don't kid about murder."

"But I'm innocent," I insisted. "Ask the waitress. I've been here the whole time."

"I *did* ask the waitress. She said you left earlier—thought you skipped out on your check after ordering food to go."

"Okay, that's true, I did go outside, but it was only because I—" The huge man jerked my arms up until I thought they would separate from my shoulders. He towered over my six-foot frame, his arms straining against the seams of his shirt.

"And…I caught you red-handed with the murder weapon."

"Well, that's true, too, but only because—" He had positioned himself in front of me and leaned in, his nose so close to mine, I could almost feel the whiskers from his orange mustache brushing my upper lip.

"I can't believe you're trying to lie your way out of this," he shouted. "I have you dead to rights. What's your name anyhow?"

"Reynolds. Max Reynolds."

He held up a huge pipe wrench in front of my face, tufts of gray hair embedded in the bloodied end of it.

"And whose name is taped to the handle of this wrench?" He gave my bound arms another painful tug.

"Mine," I choked out.

"I can't hear you," he yelled.

"It's my name. Max Reynolds."

"And where did I find this wrench?"

"You took it out of my hand, but you have to understand—"

"The only thing I understand, pal, is that you just killed my best friend and if I have any say about it, you'll fry for it."

It looked bad. Really bad. And I was innocent, of course, but at that moment, the big policeman wasn't buying it. So I simply stood still, clamped my mouth shut, and let him do his thing.

As if the damning evidence weren't bad enough, time was also my enemy. It was Friday, December 22, and if I went to jail before midnight, fewer than four hours away, no judge in the world would release me on bond—even if bond were set—until after Christmas. Which would ruin all of my sweet Jenny's carefully laid plans.

We'd had a rough go of it the past three months, and I hated leaving her and the kids in Jacksonville, FL, every Sunday morning to make the sixteen-hour drive to San Antonio, TX. But that's where the work was. And when you had four little mouths to feed, you went wherever the local union sent you. Plus, I was one of the lucky ones. As a journeyman welder, my night shift paid time and a half and supplied two apprentices who hovered on "stand-by" to bring me lengths of pipe and fresh welding rods. The work was steady and the conditions pretty good, so as out-of-town jobs go, I really couldn't complain.

Until recently, that is. Most of us in my welders and pipefitters' union, United Brotherhood, Local 462, had joined as young men right out of welding school. We'd been together for years. But the higher-ups made a deal to merge with another union, Local 330, back in October. And since then, all hell had broken loose.

Those guys in 330, all from a younger generation, had attitudes. Bad ones. They never appreciated what they had and made no bones complaining about it. They delighted in pushing every hot button our supervisor possessed. Plus, the idiots had pressed our team to strike for higher wages, even though the holidays were approaching and work was scarce.

With no wife or children to support, they didn't understand why us family men resisted their arguments. We were happy to simply put our heads down and do our jobs. But the tactics those young punks used to stir up trouble had escalated during the past two weeks, and resistance to their efforts was met with vandalism or worse. And unfortunately, I had the tie-breaker vote on whether to strike. After I voted "no," resentment among the more youthful 330 workers escalated, and my feeble attempts at peace-keeping were interpreted as confrontation.

The end of my work week couldn't have come soon enough. At eight o'clock this morning, I clocked out for a week's vacation and didn't have to be back on the job until eight o'clock the evening of January 2 in the new decade of 1990. But before I could leave, I found an issue with my toolbox. I turned the matter over to my supervisor and got the hell out of there. Normally, I would have been more upset about what happened, but I had promised Jenny I would be home in time to drive the family to her parents' house in Fayetteville, NC, for Christmas—our first family vacation in a couple of years. Jenny planned to have the car packed and the kids in pajamas so we could get on the road right away. She wanted to be there in time to help her mom with the family party on Saturday, December 23. I vowed to move heaven and earth rather than disappoint her.

With my hands behind my back and a murder charge ringing in my ears, however, disappointing Jenny was shaping up to be the least of my worries.

After I had left the construction site, I gathered the Christmas presents I'd put together for Jenny and the kids and checked out of the boarding house where I rented by the week. I tried to call Jenny to let her know I was about to get on the road, but the phone just rang without the answering machine picking up. It was an old one we had gotten from her mom, and it only worked half the time. I fervently wished this had been one of those times. Regardless, I smiled to myself because I had a brand new answering machine wrapped up for Jenny among her Christmas gifts.

I hit Interstate-10 later than I'd hoped but figured I could make up the time with one less stop along the monotonous road that rolled out between me and my family. I'd covered ten hours of it and had found it to be a harder drive than normal. For one thing, it had been snowing almost all day, but I also had to deal with some hotrod in a silver pickup who wedged me in several times and once even forced me onto the shoulder. I hoped he'd be in another state by the time I went back out there.

"I need to call my wife," I told the officer when he hauled me out to the main part of the diner. In the three months I'd been making this trip, I had learned all the places that offered the easiest exits to get me back on the road in record time and this one, on the outskirts of Mobile, was one of them. From this stop, only about six hours separated me from Jenny, so I knew I would get home in plenty of time to transfer my few things into our Ford Bronco with all-wheel drive—ten years newer than the old Dodge van I drove to San Antonio—and hit the road again. North, this time.

My mind continued to churn nonstop. I had to get this cleared up. Jenny and I did have a backup plan, but I really, really didn't want to have to use it. We had agreed that if I didn't get home by four in the morning, she and the kids would load up the Bronco and go without me. Then I would follow in my van as soon as I could.

"Later," he grunted. He threw me into a chair and with a second set of cuffs, chained me to a table. It was bolted to the floor. I checked.

I was rooted in place while the policeman wore a hole in the floor, going in and out of the diner—and shooting me venomous looks with every pass—so I let my mind revisit my time here at the truck stop, to try and remember anything that would help me figure out how I got into this mess. And more importantly, how I could get out of it.

Ironic how quickly life can change. I remembered how happy I was walking through the diner's door, smiling at the tinkling of the little bell attached to it and drinking in the aroma of fresh coffee and chicken soup. Tinsel garlands adorned every surface, and the star atop the Christmas tree next to the sandwich counter blinked to the rhythm of "O Little Town of Bethlehem," which wafted from a music box at the tree's base. The atmosphere was so charged with Christmas, it was impossible not to get caught up in the excitement.

My game plan included calling Jenny first to let her know where I was, then ordering a sandwich and coffee to go, and finally using the restroom while my order was being put together.

I had noticed the old-fashioned telephone booth when I first walked in, the tinsel garland that decorated it dipping down in front of its glass door. I started toward it, but before I reached it, a big man lumbered in, his green work jacket touting the words "Watkins Towing." He swatted the garland out of his path and dialed his number. The garland fell down again and kept the glass door from closing completely.

My earlier happiness gave way to irritation as his deep voice reached me through the open door. I stood there, waiting my turn. I wasn't trying to listen to his conversation, but his anguish was evident, and I caught a glimpse of his tortured expression through the phone booth's glass walls. Despair swam in his dark eyes, and his black brows furrowed over his nose. He reached up a calloused hand to cover his forehead then spoke again, his voice tight.

"Please, Jerry," he said, "I need help. My company folded. They can't pay me. I don't even have gas money to get home."

He had turned his face away from me, and I realized I was openly staring. I watched as his huge shoulders hunched, apparently listening to the voice on the other end and then sagged with the answer. Even from behind, I thought he looked as if he had lost everything.

"Sure. I understand," he said. "Thanks anyway."

He replaced the receiver, dropped his head to his hands, and started to cry. Quietly. In such obvious desperation it got me in the gut. I really felt for the guy. But when I realized I was still standing there staring, I coughed. He straightened up, took a deep ragged breath, and walked away.

His sorrow was palpable and seemed to fill the air in the booth. I dialed Jenny but after twelve rings with no answer, I hung up. I hadn't spoken to her all day and really wished she had gotten that darned answering machine fixed. I determined that I would try calling her one more time before I left the diner.

More anxious than ever to get home, I hurried to the counter and saw the big man sitting at the opposite end—his head down.

"What'll ya have, Mister?" the waitress asked. The name tag on her uniform read "Sarah." Molly was normally the waitress when I stopped here, but then I didn't usually arrive this late.

"A tuna sandwich and coffee to go," I said. "I'll pick it up after I use the restroom." I hesitated for a minute, then continued, "and miss," I added, surprising myself and nodding toward the big man at the end of the counter, "take him his favorite—on me."

"Sure thing, Mister," she said smiling. "Oh, but wait a minute," she added. "Jonas just went in to clean the men's room, so how's about a cup of coffee while you're waiting?"

"Sure," I said. "Thanks."

Sarah slid the coffee in front of me. I really wanted to get back on the road, but there was no way I would start out again in this snow and risk making another stop for the restroom. And I didn't relish the thought of going behind a tree as cold as it was. The entire Southeast writhed under the largest snowstorm in decades, and I still faced six hours of driving in it. The heaviest accumulation wasn't predicted until Saturday afternoon, so Jenny had done all the calculations and figured we'd make it to her parents' house before the really bad stuff set in. She even offered to drive the first shift.

I resigned myself to waiting until the men's room was cleaned and raised my coffee to my lips. From my peripheral vision, I could tell that Sarah stood in front of the distraught man, talking to him in a low voice.

"…your favorite coconut cream pie," the waitress told him. "From the man at the other end of the counter." I guess I expected him to acknowledge me in some way, although that certainly hadn't been my intention in sending him something, but he simply put his head in his hands. His broken words reached me and touched my heart even more. "…no one… nice to me…so long."

Sarah rubbed his shoulder, and I saw her take a folded bill out of her apron pocket and put it in front of him. "This won't go very far," she said, "but maybe you can at least get some gas with it." The big man's shoulders shook and he sounded as if he were choking on his sobs.

I didn't know what to do. His situation seemed so distressing. I tried to think of a way to help.

Then it came to me. For more than a month, chicken noodle soup had been my staple dinner meal so I could save money on food and put aside some extra cash for our trip. I had a fifty-dollar bill tucked into my ash tray in the van. But I considered myself a whole lot luckier than the poor soul at the other end of the counter. Without spending a lot of time thinking about it, I went to get it. Even though I had planned to surprise Jenny with it, I knew she would understand.

I didn't interrupt to tell the waitress I would be right back because I thought she needed to spend time with him. I pulled my jacket around me and waded through the deepening snow to my blue van. The guy on the last radio program I listened to said we were in the middle of the coldest night since 1965. It sure looked like it, with the snow accumulating around my work boots and falling on my bare head.

I found the fifty right where I'd left it, put it in my pocket and tried to figure out how I could slip it to the big fellow without making him feel bad. Preoccupied with that thought, I almost stepped into the path of a light-colored pickup driving too fast through the parking lot. I heard shouting and saw a policeman step out of his car and hail the pickup down.

Good. There's no sense in driving that fast with people walking to their cars.

I re-entered the cozy diner and headed back to my seat at the counter. The waitress had disappeared, but the forlorn man still sat. A rack of magazines hugged the wall to his right and sparked an idea. I sauntered over and picked up one of the magazines—rental properties in Mobile.

I thumbed through it and casually dropped the fifty to the floor. After a few minutes, I replaced the magazine and started back to my seat but touched the big man on the shoulder first.

"Excuse me, sir," I said and pointed to the floor. "I believe you dropped that."

He looked down then up at me, his eyes boring into mine. After a second, his eyes registered understanding, and tears filled them. "I don't think that's mine," he said softly.

"I'm certain it is," I answered firmly. "You'd better get it before someone steals it."

His eyes didn't leave mine for another full minute. And then he whispered, "God bless you, mister," and leaned over to retrieve the money. I nodded and went toward the other end of the counter just as I saw a man come from the hallway with a bucket, mops, and a cleaning cart.

At last. I could go to the restroom, down the hall to the left. The diner had pretty much emptied by this time, and I figured the restroom would be empty, too. So I wasn't prepared when the door burst into my shin before I could even grab the handle. White hot pain accompanied my surprise, and a man about my height bowled me down and fell on top of me.

"What the he—" I said, clearly seeing the panic in his eyes and the blood smeared on his cheek. He lifted himself and looked over his shoulder. Behind him, the open window delivered a shiver of icy air into the room.

He rolled off me, stood, and shoved a paper bag into my chest. Then he took off. In seconds, I heard the slam of a door from the other end of the hallway and I was alone. It all happened so fast, I almost wondered if I'd dreamed it, but the ache in my shin assured me he was real. Plus, a heavy object in the paper bag weighted down my chest. I raised myself from the floor, and a heavy wrench fell from the bag onto my toe. It hurt like hell.

Without thinking, I grabbed it and went to the window. Winter wind whistled from the night air into my work shirt and made me shudder. I pulled my jacket closer and with the wrench still in my hand, bent out the window to see if I could tell what had happened. A dim light illuminated figures below, one lying on the ground, one crouching over it, and another taking off around the corner.

"Halt! Freeze!" the crouching form from below commanded. "Drop your weapon and raise your hands."

"What are you talking about? What weapon?" I asked. "What the heck's going on? And who are you?"

"Deputy Johnson," the voice said. "And you're my main suspect for murder."

I jerked back from the window, but footsteps sounded in the hallway and reached me before I could wrap my head around what had happened. Strong arms grabbed me from behind, wrestled the wrench from my hands, then pulled them roughly behind me and slapped on cuffs.

"Sheriff Aubrey Winston," he said. "You're under arrest for murder."

He pushed me out of the men's room and as we rounded the corner from the hallway, I saw Sarah, the waitress, staring at me, her eyes huge. But the chair occupied by the big man at the other end of the counter was empty.

"Sarah," I said to her, "please tell the sheriff about the man who ran from the men's room and knocked me down. It was right at the door. I'm sure you saw it. He even knocked into my shin. I probably have a bruise. Look, sheriff, look at this bruise," I said, hiking up my pant leg.

"I—I'm so sorry," Sarah stammered. "But I didn't see anybody. I thought you had left. Without your food."

"Sheriff," I tried again. "I'm begging you to listen to me. Some guy ran into me on his way out of the bathroom. And the bathroom window was open. It doesn't even make sense that I would have hit somebody and then gone into the bathroom and looked out the window with the wrench still in my hand. Why would I have done that?"

"You tell me. Why *did* you have the wrench in your hand?"

"I told you—a guy knocked me down and fell on top of me. When he got up, he shoved a paper bag into my chest and this wrench fell out of it. The bag is probably still in the hallway."

Sarah left the counter, poked her head around the corner and came back. The sheriff looked at her, but she shook her head.

"Okay," I said, "the guy with the mops and bucket probably picked it up. What was his name?" I addressed the waitress with the question.

"Jonas," she said. "I'll find him." Thank God she acted like she really wanted to help.

"That still doesn't explain why the wrench had your name taped on it," the sheriff said.

"That's certainly harder to explain," I replied. "The only thing I can tell you is that my tool bin was vandalized at my job site in San Antonio."

I had discovered it at eight o'clock that morning when my shift ended. I had gathered my tools to pack up, but when I got to my bin, the shattered lock told me everything I needed to know. The lid hung open with tools scattered everywhere, many of the compartments empty where tools should have been. A number of my wrenches were missing.

I was so focused on getting on the road and reaching my family, I simply turned the matter over to my supervisor and the union representatives. I figured they had a week to investigate the matter and get my tools back before I needed them again. And if not, my union dues would cover the cost of new ones.

I offered to call my supervisor so he could verify my story to the sheriff.

"San Antonio?" the sheriff asked. "That's ten hours west of here. Look, pal, I'm willing to give you the benefit of the doubt, but why would one of your missing tools turn up this far away?"

I had no answer for that. None of it made sense. I couldn't figure out why one of my missing tools would have turned up here, either. As I sat cuffed to the table, trying to figure out what to do next, the sheriff came back in, uncuffed me and stood me beside the sandwich counter. I wasn't sure what was going to happen next, but I knew I needed a miracle.

And then I got one.

"Sheriff." The voice was deep and slow, and I whipped my head around to see the big man who had been at the other end of the counter. His dark hair was disheveled and his green jacket with "Watkins Towing" on the back hung askew on his large frame. Beside him stood a scrawny little guy who wriggled nonstop to try and escape the heavy arm tight around his neck. The deputy I had seen from the restroom window stood on the other side of the smaller man.

"I think you're gonna want to talk to this guy in connection with your dead deputy," the big man said.

"Who are you and why do you think that?" the sheriff asked him.

"The name's Samuel Hastings, and I was in here earlier." He pointed at me. "I saw this man when he went into the men's room and a few seconds later, this one," he added, tightening his grip on the neck of the man he held, "came running from that direction and kept going straight down the hall. I figure he must've hightailed it through the kitchen and out the back door. I heard it slam."

He was right. He held the man who knocked me down. But before I could say anything, the sheriff said, "How'd you find him?"

"Well," the big man said slowly, "I was down on my luck when suddenly an angel dropped good fortune into my lap, so I was able to buy gas to get home. I pulled my truck over to the gas pumps and as I stood there, this one jumped out of my truck and started to run. I chased him down and saw blood all over him and thought he needed medical attention, but—"

"I caught up to them," the deputy said, "and told this gentleman that he held the man I'd been looking for. Jim stopped him from roaring through the parking lot in his silver pickup and was writing up a citation, so I came in to get coffee. When I went back out, this one had gotten out of his truck when Jim approached him. This fella swung something, and Jim went down. When I got there, he had disappeared, and I didn't see him again until he leaned out the restroom window with the wrench still in his hand."

"But that was me," I said. "This guy knocked me down and shoved a bag with the wrench at my chest, then took off."

"Here it is," Sarah said, holding a bloodied paper bag. "Jonas had it in his garbage bin."

"What I want to know is," I said, addressing the squirming man, "how you happened to have one of my wrenches."

"Yeah," Sheriff Winston said, "I'd like to know that, too."

The scrawny man stopped squirming and hung his head.

"Come on, son," the sheriff said. "We have an eyewitness who saw what you did. You might as well tell us the truth."

The little man took a deep breath and looked at me. "It was all planned to get you in trouble. Nobody was supposed to die. That was an accident." His eyes left mine and sought the sheriff. "You have to believe me on that. I didn't mean to kill anybody." He hung his head again. "Some of the guys in Local 330 wanted to shake you up," he said, his gaze returning to my face, "when you voted against striking. They have me take care of things for them from time to time, and this time they paid me real good to follow you and create a problem that you would get blamed for. Handed me this wrench in San Antonio this morning. I kept up with you on the highway all day."

It finally made sense. My vandalized toolbox, the missing wrenches, and being followed for ten hours by a silver pickup. All to set me up and get me in trouble. My supervisor would definitely hear from me, and I would request a joint union administration meeting when I returned to San Antonio next week. We needed to have a serious discussion about Local 330.

Sheriff Winston looked at me. "I'm really sorry, Mr. Reynolds. If you'll turn around, I'll remove the cuffs." After he freed me, he reached out to shake my hand. "If you want to press charges against this fellow, I'll be glad to testify."

"I will too," the big man with the green jacket said.

"Me too," Sarah added.

"Thank you all," I said, "So sheriff, do you need me for anything else now that you have the whole story? My wife is waiting for me in Jacksonville, and we're supposed to go to her parents' house in North Carolina for Christmas. If I leave right now, I can just make it in time."

"I'll have a couple of things for you to sign, but why don't you call your wife?"

I went to the phone to try Jenny again, but the stupid answering machine still didn't pick up. I figured I'd just continue toward Jacksonville and try to make it before they loaded up in the Bronco and left.

The sheriff sped through his paperwork. I signed it and shook hands with him. I went to shake hands with the large man in the green jacket, and he took both of my hands in his. "Thank you so much, mister," he said to me. "You've given me the greatest gift I've received in a long, long time and restored my faith in mankind. Have a safe journey."

Sarah handed me a bag with a fresh sandwich and hot coffee, and I finally left the diner. The time was just after nine p.m. and under normal circumstances, I could be home by three a.m., but the falling snow changed everything. I wished I could have reached Jenny to let her know that I should be able to make it so she and the kids didn't leave without me. But the only thing I could do at this point was to start on my way and hope for the best.

The closer I got to Jacksonville, the lighter the snow, so my heart soared at the thought of getting home in time to take my family to my in-laws for Christmas. The thought was especially sweet, considering what I'd been through and what horrible things might have happened.

At the "Jacksonville – 3 miles" sign, I got so excited, I sang along to the Christmas carols playing on the all-night radio station I'd found. It was three a.m., and I was less than four miles from home. Hallelujah! We'd be on our way to North Carolina in no time.

It caught me totally unprepared. Black ice. When it snared my front tires, the van skidded toward the shoulder, buried under a couple of feet of slush. I turned into the swerve, the way I'd learned in driver's education all those years ago, but it didn't work. As I fought the wheel, I was vaguely aware of the Christmas presents for my family flying across the back seat and smashing against the window. But there was no time to worry about them. I had to focus on the road. All four wheels had hit ice by then and the van swerved off the road and skidded into a fallen tree at the edge of the woods. I slammed into the steering wheel at the same instant the front fender crunched against the tree. Then before the van settled into a complete stop, I felt the impact of at least one tire blowing, the force of it skewing the van's back tires off the shoulder and down an incline. I sat there for a second, dazed. When I finally got my bearings back, I tried starting the van. Five times, I turned the key and pumped the gas. With no response.

It was ten minutes after three a.m., and I was less than four miles from home. I couldn't believe how much bad luck had come my way since my shift ended on Friday morning. All I wanted was to get home to my family. Less than an hour stood between me and them leaving without me.

I needed another miracle.

I pulled my jacket tight and got out of the van to check the damage. The front fender hadn't bent all the way into the tire, so once it started, the van would still be drivable. A back tire had blown but the back of the van had slipped too far down the incline for me to be able to change the tire. I made the only decision I felt was open to me.

I had to walk. I had to make it.

I emptied my laundry bag and filled it with the presents for my family, then slung it over my shoulder Santa-style. I put on my red stocking cap and set out.

Snow blindness, I had read, could be disorienting. That wasn't the half of it. It was also panic-inducing. I tried to run but my legs got pulled into the deepening sludge and my feet numbed, so I'd hardly gotten any distance from the van when my icy breaths cut my throat as my heart worked furiously to keep up.

A truck roared past with such force, I fell through the bank of plowed snow down the side of a large ditch, my head finding a chunk of ice.

I didn't know how long I lay there before the incessant shaking jolted me. My eyes opened to the grinning face of the big man from the truck stop. "Hey, Santa," he said, "Need a hand?"

For the second time that night, the big man was my miracle.

"What time is it?" I asked, holding my breath.

"Four a.m.," he answered.

My heart dropped. Jenny and my kids were already on the road.

I swallowed my disappointment. And since I'd already missed my window, I thought I should at least get my van home so maybe I could join Jenny later.

"So listen, my van is stuck back there," I said to him. "And your trailer is empty. Any chance you could help me get the van back to my house? I don't have more money here, but I could write you a check when we get there."

"Mister, I'd be honored to help you. Let's go."

We loaded the van onto his trailer, and he gave it a cursory inspection. "Looks like your frame is bent," he said. "Probably can't drive it that way even once you get the tire fixed."

Heartsick, I gave him my address, and we drove in silence for a while. Then he said, "Listen, I want to thank you, friend. I know that fifty came from you. I've never had kindness like that before."

"You're welcome," I mumbled, embarrassed. "You would've done the same."

"That's a fact," he answered, "If I could have. Funny how it works," he added. "Those that *can* help don't always want to."

I remembered his phone conversation and felt his pain again.

After a few minutes, he asked, "Family waiting for you at home?" My stomach knotted.

"No," I answered. "They're driving to Fayetteville. My wife's whole family's there."

"You joining 'em?"

"I don't see how," I said, "There's no way I can get the van fixed in time."

"I can take you as far as Savannah if that would help."

"Thanks…but I'll…well, I don't know what I'll do right now," I said glumly.

"I'm sorry for your trouble…this your place?"

His lights shone on my mailbox. I nodded, and we worked together to remove my van from his trailer. Then I reached out to shake his hand.

"Thanks for your help," I said. "If you'll wait here, I'll go write you a check."

"No need," he answered. "And thank you for *your* help." Again, he covered my hand with both of his.

"Be careful backing out," I said, "looks like somebody has family visiting." Cars lined the street, and my eyes misted at the thought of a warm family gathering when I faced a cold house and Christmas alone. I loved Christmas and considered it the warmest night of the year.

I unlocked the door at a few minutes before six a.m.

Immediately, I was struck with a wave of unexpected sights and sounds. Embers glowed in the fireplace and sleeping bags littered the living room floor with the lights of our Christmas tree twinkling in the background. Aromas of coffee and baking biscuits tickled my nose while the sounds of meal preparation in the kitchen reached my ears.

"Daddy!" my two youngest shrieked, and my legs buckled as they threw themselves at my knees. I fell to the floor and, my two older kids and Jenny joined us—hugging, kissing, crying.

"Max, we were so worried about you. Dad and I were about to go looking for you."

"Jenny, I love you so much," I said, kissing her face, her hair. Then I pulled away and looked at her. "But…what happened? How come you're not already on the road? And…are you telling me your parents are here?"

"It was their idea, Max. Fayetteville was due for much worse snow so they worked it out for everybody to come here. Darling, let me get you out of those wet things. Are you alright?"

I held her in my arms, and the snow outside and frost on the windowpane faded away to summer breezes with her kiss. Despite the cold, the love surrounding me filled me with a warmth I could have only imagined earlier.

"I'm perfect," I said, my eyes overflowing from the love that filled me. "Just perfect."

O, Come All

M.M. Chouinard

Ye Faithful

When I was a kid, Christmas Day was my favorite part of the holiday season, for obvious reasons. Once I made it into my early twenties, mature enough to understand that what was important wasn't the presents under the tree but the people around it, Christmas Eve became my favorite part. But for the past decade or so, my favorite day of the holiday season has been Christmas Eve *eve*.

As I got older (I'm now holding on to forty-five like it's a spooked horse trying to bolt), my relationship with Christmas slipped into the *it's complicated* category. I'm married to the love of my life, and I know that makes me a hundred times more blessed than most people ever get to be. But my husband Bill and I both lost our parents young, neither of us have any siblings, and although we both desperately wanted children, that wasn't in the cards for us. For most of the year, our super-small family structure doesn't bother me; my mother always told me that God does things for a reason, and if you trust Him, you'll always get what you need. So we surrounded ourselves with friends, and usually that was enough. But during Christmas, such a family-oriented time, our friends would rightfully focus their time on their children and traditions, leaving Bill and I celebrating alone.

But Christmas Eve *eve* was different. Every year my two closest friends and I came together to have a mini-Christmas-cookie swap in St. Philomena's parish hall, then spent the evening setting up the decorations inside the church for the Christmas masses. We spent several blissful hours eating cookies for our dinner, chatting with each other, singing carols, and turning the church into a work of art. And since I'm a Eucharistic minister, I'd get to watch our handiwork cast its magic spell on the throngs of celebrants that filled the church on Christmas Eve and Christmas Day.

A few years back, after arriving first—as always—I put my cookies on the counter we used as our efficient cookie-swap assembly line. Butter spritz cookies, made with the   press my great-grandmother received as a wedding present and used for over fifty years. Walnut fudge from my grandmother's recipe, rich and addictive enough to make up for technically not being a cookie. Then my crowning glory, my mother's Italian ricotta cookies—always my favorite, both because of their soft, cake-like decadence and because making them each year with my mother was one of my favorite childhood memories.

Once I had the cookies perched and pretty, I turned to grab the half gallon of eggnog Lydia'd dropped off in the refrigerator earlier that week. I dipped and bobbed behind the other contents but couldn't find it. Then I shifted and sorted everything methodically—but still no eggnog.

Maybe she'd put it in the freezer by accident? As I rummaged through popsicles and random bags of frozen vegetables, Lydia and Sandy burst through the door, already gossiping and laughing.

"Then I said to her, 'good luck getting your money back after you did that to it!'" Sandy flipped back her blonde hair and planted a hand on her generous hip to punctuate the point.

Lydia laughed so hard she doubled over. "Thanks so much for that. I can't tell you how much I needed a laugh."

Something in her tone made me look closely at her when I reached in for our hello hug. Her brown eyes were bloodshot, and her tan skin was marred by faint dark smudges under her eyes. "Is everything okay?"

She set down the plastic bag she was holding and took a deep breath. "I don't want to spend a lot of time talking about it because I don't want to ruin our girl time. But, just so you know, Carlos was laid off Monday."

"You're kidding!" Sandy cried. "Who lays someone off this time of year?"

"A business that's barely keeping its head above water. I don't blame them. With the economy the way it is, nobody's buying a lot of new cars right now." Lydia smoothed her dark curls.

"Are you going to be okay?" I asked.

"We'll be absolutely fine, and I don't want to fuss about it so that's enough of that." She planted her feet and stood a little taller, then waved her hand at me. "Beth, look at your sweater! You'll absolutely win the prize this year."

I'm a firm believer that there's a time and place for everything, and if my friend didn't feel this was the time or place to talk about her problems, I'd respect that. So I played along by looking down at my Christmas sweater, which featured not only a reindeer with light-up antlers but also a multi-colored light-up llama and a Santa Claus on a motorcycle. "You haven't seen anything yet." I pressed the hidden disk and "Jingle Bell Rock" poured from somewhere within the polyester-cotton blend. "I went to five different stores before I found one I knew was tacky enough to win. My Susan Lucci streak ends here."

Sandy reached into the depths of her bag and pulled out the tacky twelve-inch elf-decorated winner's ribbon we awarded annually to the tackiest Christmas sweater. I pinned it to my chest with great pride, then waved my fingers at my face like I was fighting off tears.

They both laughed as they pulled out their cookies, and I leaned in to sneak peeks into their stacks of Tupperware. Unlike me, they made something different every year. "What'd you guys bring?"

Lydia produced her cookies with three flourishes. "Arlettes, because I needed something complicated to keep my mind off things last night. Christmas tree meringue cookies because I wanted to do something cheery, and cranberry and pistachio macarons to prove I could do it."

"Overachiever," I teased.

Sandy's face broke into a devilish grin. "Okay, so. These are ginger-bread men spiked with a dash of bourbon and sprinkle of cayenne." She plunked down a container. "These are thumb print cookies, but the kisses on top are caramel-filled to make them super decadent. And finally, my showstopper—" She clutched the final container briefly to her chest before revealing it. "Lumps of coal!"

Lydia and I bent forward to examine the cookies, which did in fact looked exactly like little black lumps of coal.

"Oh, Sandy, these are just adorable!" Lydia said. "What kind of cookie are they?"

"Mexican wedding cookies but instead of just powdered sugar on the outside, I covered them in a black glaze. Try one!" She held up the open container.

I grabbed one and bit into it—and groaned with pleasure. "They melt in your mouth."

Lydia followed suit and rolled her eyes. "So. Good."

Sandy pointed and giggled. "Oh, that's hilarious—your tongue is black now!"

"I'm guessing mine is, too?" I stuck it out.

Sandy nodded. "Guess I used too much food coloring. Sorry…"

Lydia crossed over to the refrigerator with a smile. "That's okay, a little eggnog will fix us right up."

"It's not in there," I said. "I was looking for it when you got here."

Lydia's face puckered. "It's not in there? That can't be." She pulled the refrigerator door farther open and bent to search. "Well, that's certainly odd. I know for sure I put it in here when I stopped by on Wednesday."

Sandy's eyes widened. "And here you guys always razz *me* for being the flighty one."

Lydia's cheeks flushed, and I hurried to smooth things over. "Ah, well, Father George probably thought it was left over from something. Nothing sweet is safe around him. But that's okay, that just leaves us more calories for cookies."

"That's what I love about you, Bethy." Sandy jumped over to the counter, grabbed one of my ricotta cookies, and waved it triumphantly. "You always find a silver lining."

Good humor restored, we pulled out our gifts bags and boxes and artistically filled them with an assortment of the cookies while we chatted and laughed and ate far more than we should have. By the time we finished and had everything tucked into our shopping bags, we were riding high on a buzz of friendship and sugar, fueled up and ready to dive into our decoration extravaganza, the missing eggnog long forgotten.

Lydia hooked up her phone to the church's sound system, and within moments "Rockin' Around the Christmas Tree" piped through. We all joined Brenda Lee in belting out the song as we dove in: wreaths on the wall hangers, red poinsettias at the end of each pew, white poinsettias around the manger scene at the base of the altar, and six huge staggered Noble fir trees all decorated in red behind it. St. Philomena's is relatively small, but when we're trying to cover the entire thing in Christmas cheer, it feels like an expansive European cathedral.

Three hours later, finally satisfied and in need of something warm to drink, we filed back out to the parish hall singing "Jingle Bell Rock" in time with my sweater. The scent of the coffee we'd set to brew greeted us and inspired Sandy to burst into an air-guitar pantomime that sent Lydia and I into peals of laughter.

"I think I've earned a few more cookies." Sandy headed straight for her brown paper bag. "Putting up all those decorations is hard work!"

"Oh, sure." Lydia laughed. "Because we didn't already eat three days' worth of calories *before* we started."

"No idea what you're talking about," Sandy said with a grin—which abruptly disappeared as she looked down. "Hey. What happened to my cookies?" She picked up the paper bag and turned it upside down—it was empty.

"There's that flightiness again," Lydia said, a little too eagerly. "You must have put them away somewhere."

The three of us searched everywhere through the parish hall and kitchen—the cabinets, the refrigerator, even the industrial oven. My cookies were safely stashed in my fabric shopping bag, and Lydia's were still in the double-bagged plastic sack she'd brought. But there were no other cookies to be found.

"I don't understand. How is that even possible?" Lydia asked, her head swiveling around.

"Maybe Father George came in and assumed someone left them for the priests?" Sandy said.

I shook my head as I dropped into a squat to check under the tables. "He and Father Pete are out delivering communion to the sick, and Father Doug is up at the prison," I said.

"Maybe they got back early?" Sandy peered out of the window that overlooked the priests' residence. "Nope, the lights are all out."

That's when I noticed my purse wasn't hanging from the back of the chair where I'd left it, but instead stuck on the floor just under the table.

I *never* put my purse on the floor. My mother always said if you do, you'll have bad luck with money, and even though I know it's a silly superstition, I also figure there's no reason to risk it. I was one-hundred percent certain I'd secured it before we left to decorate the church.

I hurried over and rummaged through the purse. My phone and keys were still there, thank goodness, and my wallet. I pulled it out and opened it.

I froze. "All my cash is gone."

Both Lydia and Sandy whirled around and grabbed their purses, then checked their wallets. "My money's still here," Lydia said. "Not that I had much to steal."

"Mine too." Sandy stared up at me. "Are you sure you had cash in your wallet? You're sure you didn't spend it somewhere?"

I cast my mind back. "I—I don't think I did."

"Maybe Bill took it before you left the house for some reason? How much did you have?" Lydia asked.

"Forty dollars." I checked the bottom of my purse to make sure the money hadn't just fallen out of the wallet, but found nothing. "But that doesn't make sense, anyway, with the cookies missing, too."

Sandy waved my objection away. "I'll bet you anything one of the priests stopped in before they left and figured the cookies were for them.

And you must have misplaced your money, because there's no way they'd take it."

Something clanged in the distance outside of the hall. Lydia pulled back the curtain on the window. "Is someone over by the dumpsters?"

I stood on my tippy-toes to peer past her but only saw shadows. I bolted back into the parish hall and out of the side doors, then cried out toward the dumpsters, "Hey, you!"

The shadow shifted, and a blob carrying another blob streaked away, rustling faintly. It flashed through one of the lights on the side of the church hall just long enough for me to catch a clear glimpse before disappearing into the darkness again, then around the corner of the church.

I pushed on the door to get back inside, but it had locked behind me. Lydia let me in.

"It was Old Man Parker and his bag of cans," I said.

Sandy's face turned into a tomato about to burst. She whirled around back to the kitchen. "I'm calling the police."

"Sandy, wait. Don't." I hurried after her. Old Man Parker was a Vietnam veteran who'd come back from the war injured physically and mentally. He lived on some sort of pension, but whatever it was, it wasn't enough, and he spent his days scouring the neighborhood for cans, bottles, and other materials he could sell at the recycling center. "I'm not sure we should."

"Beth, we all feel bad for him. But it's one thing to scavenge and another thing to steal," Sandy said.

I nodded—but something about it didn't feel right. "We don't know for sure he did it," I said. "Maybe I *am* misremembering about the money, or maybe Bill took it like you said. And if Old Man Parker took the cookies, that means he's hungry."

Lydia rubbed her upper arms. "And do we really want to have him hauled down to the police station right before Christmas?"

"Exactly." I forced a smile onto my face. "I say we divide up the rest of the cookies between the three of us and forget about it."

The flush on Sandy's face receded. "Are you sure?"

I smiled. "I'm sure. I bet when I get home, Bill will say he grabbed the money and forgot to tell me."

But Bill hadn't taken it, and the more I tried to convince myself there was an innocent explanation, the more I tossed and turned in bed that night. As I struggled to find a cool spot on my pillow at three in the morning, memories kept tugging at me—the time when I'd watched Old Man Parker rescue a frightened kitten from under an abandoned porch. The time I got a flat tire outside the grocery store, and he stopped to help me change it. Yes, he looked scraggly and scavenged around the neighborhood, but I'd never known him to be anything other than kind and compassionate. I just couldn't see him stealing.

But the other possibilities were equally as ugly, and unlikely. If one of the priests was a closet kleptomaniac, surely something would have gone missing before now—all three had been assigned to St. Philomena's for years. Could someone else with a key to the parish hall have taken the opportunity to pilfer? But we could have come into the room at any moment, and anybody who had a key would have seen the lights and known that.

Which left the possibility I really didn't want to face—that one of my friends had stolen from me. Each of us had gone off by ourselves at one point to grab more decorations or go to the restroom. Carlos had just lost his job during the most expensive time of year, and Lydia always did her Christmas shopping on Christmas Eve because Carlos got his bonus check the morning of the twenty-fourth. If Lydia couldn't afford to buy presents this year, the extra cookies might allow her to save face among her large family—she was a proud woman. Maybe too proud to admit she didn't have the money to buy the eggnog.

I tossed over on my side again. When times were bad enough, people did desperate things, even good people. Whether it was Old Man Parker or Lydia, anyone who'd steal forty dollars and Christmas cookies was in a bad situation. I fell asleep that night repeating a prayer for both Lydia and Old Man Parker, asking God to show me how to help the perpetrator if they needed it.

By the time morning dawned crisp and bright, the only solution I'd come up with was that the best, kindest thing to do was forget the theft ever happened. I didn't know for sure who had taken the money, but whoever it was needed it more than I did.

I tried to put it out of my mind and instead focus on my final preparations for Christmas Eve and Christmas Day. I made what food I could prep ahead of time for our meals so I wouldn't have to rush in between all the masses, then wrapped the few gifts I had for Bill and our friends. I did my hair and put on my dress for the Christmas vigil mass, and Bill and I headed out.

If you ask me, the Christmas vigil is the most beautiful ceremony of Advent, maybe of the whole year. It's dark outside, but inside the church is filled with the flickering glow of candles. I love how packed the church gets, standing-room only, with worshipers lined up in the back and along the walls. It's as though the birth of Christ calls to all those who've lost their way during the year, or who need an extra dose of faith. Like we're all stand-ins for The Wise Men, following the North Star that will bring us to the baby Jesus, together raising our voices in song as we wait to meet Him.

When the time came for communion, I took my position at the right front corner of the nave with my basket as strains of "O Come All Ye Faithful" urged everyone forward. The decorated altar was gorgeous to be sure, even if I do say so myself, but staring back out at all the joyful faces filling the church was even more beautiful. I had to fight back the tears that pricked my eyes, because, really, who wants to take Holy Communion from someone with a drippy face?

Once I wrestled my emotions under control, I slipped into an easy rhythm: I held up a wafer as the celebrant came forward, said 'the Body of Christ,' then placed it in either their hands or mouth depending on what they signaled. I have to admit, I much preferred to place it in their hands. I'm always worried I'll accidentally stick my fingers in their mouth when I place the wafer in, or that I'll overcompensate and stop short, dropping the Eucharist onto the floor, because I'm trying so hard *not* to stick my fingers in their mouth. And don't get me started on what you see when you look inside people's open mouths—sometimes I have to work really hard to remind myself not to judge.

As Dolly Hansen, one of our oldest congregants, stepped away from me, a little girl I didn't recognize stepped up in her place. About ten years old, her brown hair hung in greasy strands, and her clothes were smudged with dirt. I glanced at the woman behind her—Alma Ramirez, a woman I'd known my whole life, who had no children.

I held up the sacramental bread. "The Body of Christ."

The girl opened her mouth wide, and I stifled a gasp—her tongue was completely black.

I gave her communion, then watched as she drank the wine and turned away with her head down. She followed Dolly Hansen most of the way then quickly slipped among the people in the back-right corner of the church. Nobody paid any attention to her, and she didn't pay attention to them. She was alone.

When communion was finished, I gestured to Bill—I wanted to keep an eye on this girl, and I couldn't do it from the pew where I'd been sitting. His brow knit, but he nodded. I lodged myself among those standing in the back-left corner, where I could watch the girl as surreptitiously as possible.

She remained in place until just before Father Doug blessed the congregation, and I almost missed her slipping out the side door of the church. I broke away and circled around the perimeter as quickly as I could without being disruptive, then pushed through the doors just in time to see her slip into the parish hall kitchen. I put on a burst of speed to catch up with her.

When I opened the kitchen door, she was gone. I hurried through the kitchen into the hall. She wasn't there, either.

I shivered, and the hair on my arms stood on end. There was no way any flesh-and-blood human could have crossed that large hall in such a short time.

Then I remembered—the parish hall had a basement under the kitchen.

I twirled around and dashed to the back. As my hand went to twist the knob of the basement door, I froze, my heart pounding in my chest— I'd never been down there before. In fact, as far as I knew, the only time *anyone* had ever been down there was when the furnace or water heater needed to be fixed. And I really, *really* hated dark dank spaces.

I squeezed my eyes shut and told myself to stop being ridiculous—it was a basement, not the pits of hell. Was I going to let myself shiver like a scared baby when a little girl needed my help?

I planted my feet, swung the door open, and pulled the chain that hung down from the ceiling. It turned out to be connected to a single light over the stairs—not an encouraging sign. So I pulled my phone out of my pocket, turned on the flashlight, and made my way down into the dimly lit room.

I couldn't see any movement or other sign of life—I rotated the phone around the room but saw only stacks of boxes.

But some of the boxes were pushed out at an odd angle.

My heart went into overdrive again, sending blood pulsing through my ears. This was just a little girl, I told myself. She was likely far more frightened than I was.

As I neared, I noticed a gap in the bottom of the interlaced stacks. "Sweetheart, I'm not going to hurt you. I just want to help."

When nobody responded, I squatted down to peer through the empty space. The little girl crouched back against the far corner, her brown eyes wide with fear.

I sat down on the floor and turned my phone so that it lit up the enclosure of her box-fort without blinding her. "Hello. My name's Beth." I paused to smile. "What's yours?"

She hesitated. "Celeste."

"That's a pretty name. It's nice to meet you, Celeste."

"It's nice to meet you, too," she said, then pulled her knees up into herself. "Please don't make me go back."

The desperation on her face ripped at my heart. "Go back where?"

"To the Dawsons' house. The lady told me they'd take care of me, but they don't." She looked down at the floor. "They—they hurt me."

A wave of rage flashed through me, so intense I couldn't speak for a minute. When I finally did, my voice came out as a croak. "What lady?"

"The social worker. The one who put me in the foster home when my mama died." Her eyes filled with tears.

I fought back my own. "How long ago was that?"

"A month ago. She got hit by a car, and I didn't have anywhere to go because I don't have a dad and my mama didn't have any family."

"Did you tell the lady that the Dawsons hurt you?" I asked.

She looked down at her knees. "They said if I told her, she'd put me somewhere worse."

"That's scary." My eyes flicked around the small space as I tried to avoid making her uncomfortable with direct eye contact. They landed on a rolled-up jacket, then a Bible, then two of Sandy's cookie boxes.

I should have known Old Man Parker couldn't have done it, I realized—the parish hall doors swung closed, and locked automatically unless they were unlatched. But they hadn't been—Lydia had to let me back in after I went outside to check the dumpsters. I should have trusted my instincts—about both Old Man Parker *and* Lydia.

Celeste noticed me staring at the boxes. "I'm sorry I stole them. But I was really hungry."

I tried to keep my voice steady. "Of course you were. I'm glad you found something to eat."

With a shaky hand, she reached into the pocket of her jeans. "I stole some money, too. Because I wasn't sure how long I'd be able to stay."

"That makes sense." I nodded. "What made you think to come hide here?"

A tear ran down her cheek. "When my mama was alive, whenever we had a problem, she always told me to bring it to God."

Bill and I brought Celeste home that night. I called child protective services to let them know where she was, but I knew before I picked up the phone there wouldn't be any acceptable place for her to go so late on Christmas Eve. So I told the social worker that Celeste would be spending the night with me, and that if CPS had any issues with that, they could take it up with Fathers Doug, George, and Pete, and while they were at it, they could explain how they placed a newly orphaned girl with an abusive family. She didn't fight me—she sounded genuinely upset by what had happened, and the weariness in her voice told me that the department was desperately overworked. She—they—were doing the best they could.

After Celeste took a bath, I gave her one of my tee-shirts to sleep in and put her to bed in the spare room. When I came back out and spotted the Christmas tree, I panicked—Christmas morning was only a few hours away, and with everything Celeste had gone through, I just couldn't let her wake up without something special. I scrambled to find something I could give her—I had gifts waiting to be given to our friends over the next week, but nothing inside of them was fit for a little girl. I could fill my own stocking with swap cookies to give her, but they were the same cookies she'd been living on for the last two days, and I didn't want to remind her of that. So I pulled out my chocolate chips and whipped up a batch of Tollhouse cookies.

As I stood in my warm kitchen, thinking back on all my Christmas baking with my mother and my grandmother, I remembered the box of my childhood belongings stored up in the attic. It was filled mostly with junk, to be sure, but amid that junk I found the Samantha Parkington American Doll I'd prayed for and then cherished when I was a young girl. With her dark hair and eyes, she looked just like Celeste. She wasn't new, but—I hoped—she was in good enough shape to give a merry Christmas to a little girl who desperately needed one.

As Bill and I watched Celeste open that doll on Christmas morning, the social worker called. Bill saw the look on my face and nodded without me having to say a word—we both knew beyond any shadow of a doubt that none of this had happened by chance. So I asked her what we had to do to become Celeste's new foster parents.

I can still hear the relief in her voice as she walked me through it all—children in need were plentiful, but good safe homes were not, and with character references from the church, she was more than happy to allow us to temporarily foster Celeste. Before the heat of summer arrived, we asked Celeste if she'd like to become our daughter officially, and when she said yes, we legally adopted her.

That was five years ago. Ever since, on the afternoon of Christmas Eve *eve*, Celeste and I make the cookies for the mini-Christmas-cookie swap together. Butter spritz cookies with the cookie press my great-grandmother used for fifty years, which will now someday belong to Celeste. Walnut fudge from my grandmother's recipe—Celeste knows it by heart. And my mother's Italian ricotta cookies, an extra batch in fact, because they're Celeste's favorite, too. Once we've swapped with Lydia and Sandy and finished decorating the church, we light a candle together for Celeste's mother. Then we come home and feed leftover cookies to Bill while we sit around the tree.

And when I say my prayers that night, I take a moment to thank God, and Celeste's mother, for putting their faith in Bill and me.

O, Come All Ye Faithful

Mindy Steele

A Brookhaven Christmas

One

Iyla Jean Fleming stared into the portrait hanging on her coffee shop wall, framed in salvaged driftwood, whittled and scored by some forefather born in Brookhaven. It was of Bridge Street, which was the saphenous vein running nearly the length of Brookhaven. Local artist J.J. Jett had captured each brick, each stone laid so perfectly she could imagine living in that time when life was simpler. The barber shop was new, but the newspaper was old. The Coffee Stop, her coffee shop, had once been a tavern, and occasionally she would find dusty remnants of its past in her upstairs apartment. The Covered Bridge Museum was the most recent addition, replacing a parking area once meant for horse and buggies. She really needed to explore there, but who had the time? Not her. Running her own business and volunteering for church and town events like she did. She squinted. There weren't so many trees now, but if she played her hand just right come the summer charity bizarre, that would be remedied. How nice it would be to look out her apartment window and see nature bloom.

"Daydreaming again, Iyla Jean?" Sybil Jennings owned a beauty salon no bigger than the Coffee Stop's bathrooms, but because her parents owned a few jewelry stores across Kentucky and let her act in a couple commercials, she thought she was the center of the universe. Iyla Jean exhaled slowly before turning to the woman who preferred being everyone's rival.

"What can we get you today, Sybil?" Ignoring Sybil's constant preening into her phone, Iyla brushed by her. She had patrons to serve. Nearly every seat was filled this morning, thanks to the town's upcoming Christmas Festival events. Some were new, most were old, and the cash register would gladly eat every dime tossed in.

"That's no way to treat a paying customer." Sybil lowered her phone and ran her red talons down her perfectly flattened flaxen hair. "I need three Earl Greys, a half dozen donuts, and a chocolate chip muffin, but only if Nerva baked them." Aunt Nerva was a wonderful baker, but Sybil was only being difficult as usual. Everyone knew Iyla Jean did just as much baking as her aunt.

"The ladies just love Earl Grey while waiting their turn in my chair." Aunt Nerva huffed from behind the counter. It was no secret how much Nerva distrusted anyone who drank hot tea over iced. Nonetheless, Iyla paid the bills for the coffee shop building and the small cottage house down the street where her aunt and uncle lived. If Sybil wanted Earl Grey, then she got it. It was the Christian thing to do and made good business sense.

"I swear, Iyla Jean, didn't you wear that exact sweater in school?" If Sybil had thought to turn her red, it was fruitless. No one else cared what she wore as long as a smile was attached.

"It's a good sweater, still fits me just as it did in high school." Sybil caught her arrowed jab and glared.

While Nerva saw to the town's shining star, Iyla Jean refilled a cup for the local bank teller. Carla Roberts spent thirty minutes each morning updating her dating profile and drank one and one-half cups of coffee before driving to the bank.

Outside, the snow continued floating down in a steady cadence, driving in more customers than usual. Just seven days before Christmas and it was snowing. A perfect Christmas, she mused. At twenty-nine, snow still made her as giddy as it had when she was six and saw her first flakes. Sybil called her 'the transplant', but Iyla Jean had lived in Brookhaven for twenty-three years now, hardly a new face.

Next, she sought out her daily solicitors. These days, the trio spent more hours passing fish stories and deer stand locations than in summer farming months. "Another muffin, Richard?" she asked sweetly.

"When you gonna marry me, Iyla Jean." Richard Cogswell was seventy, widowed, and the closest prospect Iyla Jean had to having a family of her own. She was no Sybil, but in a town of 2, 371 souls, one would think she could have at least procured a boyfriend by now. That's what she got for putting all her focus in owning her own business.

"How does March sound," she kissed his fresh shaven cheek and turned to leave before smacking into local businessman, Travis White.

"Now Richard, you know she's saving herself for me." Travis patted her shoulder once he'd seen her steady enough and aimed for an empty chair. She was lucky she hadn't spilled coffee all over his spiffy suit.

"Now, Travis White," she said in equal banter, "I don't think your wife Beulah would agree," she cocked a hip and smiled, stirring a round of laughs.

"You look awful sweet this morning, Iyla Jean. How about bring us all some of that warm cocoa you know I love," Travis flirted as he was prone to do. Shedding his coat, he planted his rear between the older men. Who would have thought the lanky boy would grow into those limbs and become the bank's president, a town council member, and marry himself an herbalist hippy. Opposites do attract, or so she was told. Considering he always left good tips, she hurried to fetch more cocoa.

"So, Mr. White," Sybil sashayed over and ran her claws along Travis's shoulder. "I hear the next town meeting will end this ridiculous feud between citizens." Why did women change their voices when talking with some people? Iyla Jean rolled her eyes and continued to fill cups.

"The solar plant offer is a good one, but yeah, it should put an end to it once and for all." Iyla Jean cringed at his words. She wanted a solar plant marring the county about as much as she wanted a case of the scabies. Most of the town was on the same side of the fence on the matter. They wouldn't even benefit from it, considering the harnessed energy was being sent somewhere out west. It was a travesty to think anyone would consider this a good idea, and she wished someone could step in and make it all go away.

"You greedy bunch are going to be the ruin of our historic town," spouted Ben Johnston from a small table in the back. "Someone ought to take each of you over a knee." All the morning chatter stilled. He had eaten two blueberry muffins this morning, and Iyla had already called his wife to see to it that she had his insulin ready. Perhaps she should encourage him to head home now.

"We can't live in the stone ages forever." Sybil snapped in retort. But Ben Johnston was right. The big company from out west had been hounding anyone with a few flat acres for two years, and it all came down to the vote being held next week. So far, Travis would vote yes because men in high positions always voted for change. That meant Beulah would too. She might be a hippy, but she rarely went against her husband on matters of business. Katrina Eldridge, a wealthy widow who owned more land than anyone in town, would vote yes because land no longer amused her like traveling did. Then there was Peter Fulkner, who everyone knew would cave being as he was in debt up to his ears. Mack Donavon, a wealthy livestock farmer and the high school history teacher would vote for it, too. Cancer was ravaging his poor body. A deal like this could see his three children through college. Still didn't make it right, but Iyla Jean at least understand Mack's reasoning. Family first.

That left one vote to shut it all down…Graham Murphy. The handsome sheriff could, but Iyla Jean knew nothing of which side he stood on. It wasn't like she was the kind of woman he shared a thought with.

Graham Murphy swallowed back the acidy bile inching up his throat as he eyed The Coffee Stop across the street. Right now he should be sitting in a booth with his mother, eating his blueberry scone and drinking his morning coffee. Maybe even flirting with Iyla Jean and hoping today he would finally have enough nerve to ask her to dinner. He had only become Brookhaven's sheriff two years ago. At thirty-two, he considered that an accomplishment. His mother would disagree of course. She wanted grandchildren and was growing tired of his slow pace, but she was proud he followed in his father's footsteps.

Graham had only fired a couple bullets in his career, loved his mother, and protected this town. He seldom drank, for that usually ended in regret. His mother was right, but he wasn't telling her that. And Graham had a woman in mind, which he wasn't telling her either. Mothers had a habit of butting in when they shouldn't. Right now, his, who hated the cold, stood across the street waiting on her son to meet her. She hadn't a clue, that the woman she bought those dang elder flowers for the flu was being taken out of the back door of The White's Connection Herbal Shop and headed to the morgue.

"Looks like she died between 3a.m. and 6. This is not good, Murphy." Graham agreed with the local coroner about that. Today was the kickoff for the town's weekly Christmas events, and the only thing Graham knew for sure was that Beulah White wouldn't be winning the Christmas window decorating contest like she did every other year.

With Beulah's body safely in Fred Moore's hands, Graham rushed across the street to greet his mother. He took the lecture on punctually while holding the Coffee Stop door for her. He knocked wet snow off his boots on the too-pretty-to-be-knocking-off-boots-on rug Iyla had laid out. The woman had an eye for the nice things. When it came to the holidays, she had a thing for that too. The coffee shop glittered in silvery tinsel and white lights beamed in every corner with this year's theme, gingerbread men.

"I need to see to a few things. Sorry I can't join you this morning." Graham had a friend to seek out. They had played ball together, chased women together, too, but today, Graham would be the messenger who wrecked Travis's world.

"Is something wrong?" Francis finally eyed him and when her face tightened, she knew he was holding something back.

"I'll fill you in later, promise." He removed his hat and bent to offer a her a kiss on the cheek. A cop's widow, she nodded and offered an encouraging pat to his arm before moving towards their regular table. Seeing he wasn't joining his mother, Iyla Jean locked eyes on him immediately. He was a creature of habit, mostly, and seeing as this morning was different, she noticed and shot him a perplexed look. He would need to question her, later. She was the closest thing to a witness he had right now. He took in the Christmas apron, the soft strands wandering from her bun, and how she carried her special red cocoa thermoses held in one hand. Iyla Jean knew this town, its people. It was her knack for paying attention that helped him solve those string of burglaries last year. The Coffee Stop was the heart of the town. You got your coffee, a sweet, and your fill of gossip at one stop. He couldn't think of a better ally to have right now.

"Something is wrong, isn't it?" He had always liked her soft tone and all of that dirty blonde hair that hated being trapped in one place.

"Yes. I need to speak to Travis, and you as soon as I can." She glanced around at her patrons, but she didn't pry, not in public. It was a rare trait, he mused.

"He left earlier today for work. I don't close until five and have a meeting with the committee on final set-up stations for Saturday's Cocoa Crawl event." Every year, Brookhaven held the Christmas festival, but it was the Cocoa Crawl that lured in the most winter visitors. Patrons walked up and down both sides of Main Street, tasted cocoa, casted their vote, and crowned one Cocoa King or Queen by the end of the night. Graham never participated, nor would he ever unless he wanted to die by chocolate. Yeah, give him a snowman competition or ax throwing contest, something like that he could get behind.

"The window display contest is tonight. I'm also handing out the voting ballets at the starting point." Of course, she had a busy schedule.
"Please tell me their kids are okay." Beulah and Travis had a son and daughter, and it made him sick knowing what he would soon be telling them.

"The kids are okay." They held gazes. "I'll drive you to the committee meeting. We can talk then." He placed his hat back on his dark head.

"Sherriff!" Graham turned just as Pete Faulkner, retired farmer, church song leader, and beloved father, dropped dead on the floor.

Two

Pete Faulkner kissed his wife this morning before traveling four miles over fresh snow to the Coffee Stop to jaw with friends. He ate three of Nerva Fleming's much-loved Christmas cookies and drank a cup of hot chocolate. Now he was dead. Common sense told Graham it was a heart matter. Cop instinct, coupled with Beulah's recent murder, had him studying the faces of the room, a task, with Sybil Jennings gripping his arm and crying actual tears. The wannabe actress was a walking invitation which Graham regretted ever being tempted by a few years back. He called into dispatch while prying Sybil from his arm and watched as a very pale Iyla Jean try administering CPR on Faulkner herself. When help arrived, Graham watched her heart break that a miracle didn't happen.

By the time Christmas lights filled the starless night, Graham broke Travis the news and watched his children cry just as he had when he lost his father. The coroner declared Faulkner dead by unnatural causes, and Mayor Saunders declared Marcy Florence's Covered Bridge Museum the winner of the Christmas window display. All was unexpected in his quaint little town, including the autopsy and first lab reports suggesting that Pete had more than just cookies and hot chocolate in his system. Graham could only wait for forensics to confirm, but it seemed in less than 24 hours, in a town where mailbox smashing was the most menacing issue, he had two homicides on his hands.

It was late by the time Graham finally stood outside the Coffee Stop. The old brick suited a tavern, but the large front windows displaying Iyla Jean's Christmas window display of baking utensils and gingerbread men sliding on snowy hills of flour was sort of cute.

Christmas Cookies Mysteries

He knocked again. Loudly. Graham hoped, and now that he was becoming a better man, prayed she'd seen or heard something. Did she notice anything strange with Pete? The woman noticed things.

Raising a fist to deliver a third attempt, the door swung open and there stood a freshly showered and unsmiling Iyla Jean Fleming. Again, unexpected. Any more shocks to his day, and he was going to try out that last bottle of bourbon he had stashed away for emergencies.

Graham had always found the town sweetheart easy on the eyes and tried not to gawk. It's business, he coached himself. Wearing nothing but a towel, her wild dripping hair aided to the accumulating puddle on the floor, all of which didn't help him act very professional.

"Sheriff Murphy," she narrowed her glare, "I'm closed. The coffee doesn't pour this late." She started to slam the door, but Graham threw up a hand to save his face.

"I got tied up, Iyla Jean. Deputy Conley said he gave you a lift over."

"He did. He is a very thoughtful man. I adore thoughtful people." Their first argument, he mused.

"I still need to speak with you. Ask a few questions."

"I heard Beulah was shot." She shuddered and clutched the towel tighter. "Everyone knows she doesn't keep cash there. None of us do in our stores ever since those Reed boys took to making thieving a sport. Lesson learned." Graham removed his hat, waited for her to let him in. "Are you going to ask your questions or stare at me all night, Sheriff Murphy?" He wanted to do both but neither of them while standing out on the street.

"This would be easier if you were dressed." He was trying to be professional here.

"Fine, come in." She turned, and he followed her wet steps back upstairs to her little apartment.

The upstairs space reflected the woman cozy, light, and nostalgic. Light tomato-green walls trimmed in dark stained wood. Graham liked everything, even the delicate lamp with dangly crystals, and he didn't do delicate. The couch was real leather, not imitation, with pillows of color splattered about. It was a mixture of antique with a touch from the Country Sampler magazine his mother often ogled over. In a small kitchen space, he noted outdated appliances scrubbed spotlessly. He heard her fussing into some clothes behind her bedroom door. To the right, he spotted the ceiling-to-floor bookshelf, darkly stained and regularly polished by first glance assumptions. Graham walked over and scanned the selection. Edger Allen Poe, Agatha Christie, and Patricia Cornwell, popped out to him. A handful of romance novels indicated she liked cowboys by their covers. At the end of each shelf rested a bible. Some were old and worn and some new as the day. Her ironic taste made him smile.

"Did you come to view my library?" She stepped into view wearing faded jeans and a sloppy Kentucky Wildcat shirt, causing his heart rate to accelerate a little.

"How does a barista, baker, and Sunday school teacher spend her quiet nights," he jested, lifting a book entitled *Postmortem*.

"I watched Hallmark mysteries, too, and grew up on Angela Lansbury." He liked the banter that had been increasing between them. Her varied taste, he liked more.

"I grew up on Matlock." He slid the book back in place. "Did you hear anything between two and the time you opened this morning?"

"I didn't, but I didn't hear the Reed boys downstairs cleaning me out back then either." She shook her head. "I was right here. I should have heard something," she shivered again. "Is Travis alright? I can't imagine how hard that was for you to be the one to tell him and those sweet kids," her voice wobbled. Children were everyone's weak spot.

"He took it well enough. We have two murders and no leads." Ripped the band aid right off and her look matched it.

"Two? But Pete had a heart attack or something, didn't he?" Shock was followed by tears. God, he hated tears. Graham crossed the floor and urged her onto the sofa. "I'm sorry. I shouldn't have blurted it out. I think I just needed someone to listen." He wrapped an arm around her, feeling like an idiot.

"No," she sniffed, "I'm glad you didn't beat around it. I'm sorry. This is horrible." She looked up at him. Yeah, he hated tears. "I should go see his family. Oh, God, Pete was my best customer." She dropped her head in her hands.

"Iyla Jean, it's really important. Are you sure you didn't hear or see anything? Your apartment is across the street."

"Not a thing. I went to bed around ten and didn't wake until my alarm at 5." That narrowed the time frame some, he mentally stored. "And Pete...well, he was his regular self. I mean everyone knows he started dialysis last month, but he was feeling so much better for it." Graham didn't know. "Do you think the same person did this, Graham?" His name rolling off her lips had him wishing he had all the answers.

"I don't know how they are connected, yet, but I do think there's a link there." He leaned back, weary from the day and was surprised she did too.

"Beulah wasn't very old and gunshots are a crime of passion, aren't they?" She looked up at him with watery blue eyes and a wiliness to help.

"Learned that from your mystery novels?" He dropped an arm around her, and they both sat there in the quiet, pondering death and murder. It was likely a crime of passion, just as taking the time to poison an old man was.

Three

Sybil's formidable Aunt Katrina was discovered by her housekeeper Tuesday morning, twisted and cold, and very dead. At sixty-nine, the young senior spent her mornings gardening, her summers cruising the Caribbean, and always placed well in the charitable spring walk-a-thons. She was by all accounts the picture of health. Graham knew, before the coroner confirmed and Ina Martin won the one-hundred-dollar jewelry store gift certificate for winning Best Ornament in the Christmas Festival, that he had another murder on his hands. The timing was ironic since Katrina never wore jewelry. The rumor mill began to turn, and his office phones were ringing off the hook. Thankfully, his secretary and dispatcher, Bella Gentry, knew how to handle concerned citizens. The former bar-keep was well practiced in calming men from trading punches in drunken stupors as well as assuring everyone that their neighbors weren't serial killers just because they could be.

Wednesday morning, Graham took his usual coffee and scone to go and met with the coroner. There had to be a connection between the three victims.

"Belladonna is sometimes given medicinally. But if you have kidney disease like ole Pete had, it's deadly," Fred informed, "and it looks like Widow Eldridge didn't die of a hardened heart either." Blueberry scones and cadavers didn't mix, so Graham offered up his breakfast. Fred dipped a meaty paw into Graham's bag and emerged with the free meal. "I think it's safe to say somebody isn't happy with the town council." Fred took a bit unflinching, surrounded by bodies. Graham had considered that angle last night before Katrina, but her death confirmed it. Someone was killing the town council members.

"Or the solar plant vote," Graham added, "Thanks Fred. Get those next labs to me as soon as you can. I've got a man to talk to." If someone was killing council members, he, too, was a target. One name shot out to him. This man was the most vocal opposer about upcoming vote and a retired pharmacist. A man who had the backbone to pull a trigger, and the brains to know which chemicals did what to a body. Everyone who was in the Coffee Stop on Monday was a suspect, but Ben was now at the top of the list. Ben was his usual grumpy self when Graham paid him a visit, but his alibi for all three murders, in the name of one very colorful Lucille Hartley, was solid. Graham was glad of it. He really liked the old geezer.

By nightfall, Graham had helped judge the cookie contest, dealt with a dozen probing questions about the investigations, and seen one very tipsy Imogene Taylor, who had one too many mulled ciders, home. Locals were concerned, the Lady's Garden Club President was drunk, and Nerva Fleming's Christmas cookies earned the Silver Sprinkles award. Nothing unexpected at all, which Graham took as a sign that he might be able to get a few winks of sleep tonight.

Graham saw that Iyla Jean made it to her apartment safely. She wasn't a council member, but his protective nature had to see that she was safe. Then, he headed for his small humble cabin just outside of town. Graham barely made it through his door when Fred Moore called. Mrs. Eldridge's labs came back.

"Water Hemlock," Graham muttered as he eyed the google page about poisoning on his phone screen. "Two dead from poisoning and one fatal gunshot," he said to no one. Perhaps the link was severed. Could there be another connection? Before kicking out of his boots and aiming for that hidden bottle of Kentucky's finest, a knock interrupted. "What now," he growled, yanking the door open.

"Sherriff." Her green eyes were as sultry as her voice, but Graham's tastes had shifted to the more virtuous types these days.

"What are you doing here, Sybil?"

"It's a cold night." She waved his favorite Bourbon in the air. He wasn't even tempted. All he could think about was sweet Iyla Jean's bakery shop scent and that ironic bookshelf of hers.

"I'm working."

"Since when has that ever stopped you from mixing business with pleasure?"

"I'm not much on mixing things these days." On a laugh, she made a motion to step inside. "I mean it, Sybil. You should go."

"You're just as boring as all the others in this hick town." She snapped on instinct. "I know you have an eye on Iyla Jean. Don't think I don't notice. Well, she's not going to give you what I can."

"No, she can't. But considering I'm allergic to penicillin, that's not a bad thing." Graham had played ball well enough that it had paid for his college, so when Sybil flung the bottle at his head, he caught it.

"Now, Sybil, that's assault." He shook the bottle at her.

"Want to put the handcuffs on me officer?" Her ruby red lips smirked as she offered up two well-adorned wrists.

"Go home." His tone held the authority he rarely used.

"I heard Katrina and Pete were poisoned."

"I'm not talking about an investigation with you, Sybil."

"You should know that my aunt was very fond of Iyla Jean's hot cocoa. Just saying." She flipped a wrist flaunting her sparkly bracelets.

"So is half the town," he countered. It was no secret she would say anything to shine Iyla Jean in bad lighting.

"Fine. I've got my sights on someone better than you. That is, if you can keep him alive. Your record isn't looking so good right now." Graham narrowed his hazel eyes at her.

"Travis likes handcuffs too." She blew him a kiss and stomped back to her Escalade. His friend had just buried his wife this morning, and she was already sinking her talons in him. Graham couldn't think about that right now. Not with the new angle Sybil had just forced upon him. The very one he would have never seen himself.

He punched in the number and listened to the ring. "Hey, Fred. You said Pete had chocolate in his system. Just curious, did Mrs. Eldridge?"

Four

Folks art studio coordinator, Maggie Lawson, won the Christmas wreath contest Thursday evening, moments before the local elementary kids did a chaotic but cute rendition of Jesus' birth. Deputy Conley arrested the Ramey boys for stealing the Church of Christ nativity scene and hanging all the characters upside-down from the local D.Q. sign. That inflicted Mayor Saunders' sister to faint at the sight of a hanging baby Jesus and prompted a ride to the local medical center. Being a small-town sheriff was not easy, but the night wasn't a total loss because Iyla Jean shared a bag of roasted peanuts with him between her duties and his.

Friday morning, Graham sat in a pew of the Brookhaven Church of Christ beside his mother and nothing caught on fire. He and the Lord had a pact now, and if he was going to be a better man and visit more frequently than what was required, the least the man upstairs could do was toss him a few clues on who could be killing Brookhaven citizens.

On the fourth left pew sat Travis White, banker, friend, and now widower. Spouses were always the first suspect and Travis's wife knew herbs and what to do with them. But why kill off council members who were voting with you? And Graham remembered how Travis broke out just looking at poison ivy when they were kids.

Two rows back sat Ben Johnston, arms folded over his buffalo plaid covered chest and wearing his permanent frown. Multiple people could account for his whereabouts all week and whoever killed the council members knew them well enough to get close. Ben didn't suit that scenario. Sybil and her aunt weren't exactly friends, but she was in favor of the solar plant. Everyone from the bank teller to the retired farmers had alibis. That left Graham one person to consider. Everyone loved and trusted her, and it made his stomach sour.

As people filled the last available seats, and Preacher Flora settled behind the oak pulpit to offer a few kind words for Pete Faulkner, Iyla Jean and her aunt strolled passed him. Graham watched as she wiggled out of her coat, floated him a soft smile, and sat in the row in front of him. There was no way she was capable of gunning down Beulah White, but two victims had consumed cocoa, from the Coffee Shop or somewhere else, just before dying. That wasn't a simple coincidence and he would ponder this thought the rest of his day.

That evening, the Jingle Rides through town, which allowed visitors to ride on hay filled wagons and view Christmas light displays all through the heart of Brookhaven, had traffic halted from the courthouse to Flannery's Tax Office. People loved snuggling in the old tobacco wagons, freezing their tails off to see lights blink, dance, and sometimes sing. Graham would have loved snuggling with Iyla Jean if he wasn't so consumed and she wasn't possibly connected to the murders.

When he'd gathered enough volunteers to help his deputies, Graham worked his way towards the office to think. The evidence was all there, but he was missing something. As his truck plowed past the Church of Christ, Graham noted Iyla Jean's old white jeep still in the parking lot. No way would she leave it this far from The Coffee Stop. When he pulled in, he found her sitting inside.

"Need a lift?" he asked, noting how cold she looked. The engine wasn't running and she had to be freezing.

"Please," her teeth chattered uncontrollably. Graham helped her into his issued Ford Utility truck. Her rusty red and grey scarf pulled tight around her neck.

"I can have Mitch haul it over to the garage. It's probably just the battery."

"There's nothing wrong with it." She said as if she knew vehicle mechanics. Her hands were shaking just as much as the rest of her.

"Then why were you sitting in a non-running vehicle in this weather?" Her glassy blue eyes turned to him, and Graham recognized the wide-eyed look of a woman scared. In one hand she held her keys. She hadn't even tried starting the engine. Then, he noted her fisted left hand. She slowly opened it, revealing a folded piece of paper. Graham lifted it from her cold hands and unfolded it.

Stay away from him or you're next.

If Graham had thought to consider her a possible suspect before, now that theory was shot down in the breath he took to calm his temper. He should have had more faith in her, and that added guilt onto his rising emotions. Iyla Jean didn't want the solar plant to move into the area and she sold a lot of cocoa, but anyone could have poisoned Pete that day. She wasn't a council member, just someone he wanted to get closer to and for that she was being threatened. She had no enemies to speak of. Everyone adored her as much as he did. Less one, he realized.

"They're talking about you, aren't they?" she said staring out the window as Christmas lights twinkled. He reached over and took her hand. The threat could have only been written by one person.

"They are. I'm sorry you got mixed up in this." He took her other hand in hopes of warming them. "I can't let you go home alone tonight, sweetheart." She pulled from his touch.

"I...I won't be frightened off." She wiped her face and straightened before turning to face him. "I have a business to run. We have the annual Cocoa Crawl tomorrow, and I'm in charge of the caroling. I can't let some crazy person scare me, and you won't tell Nerva about this or I'll never forgive you. I have a responsibly to this town, Graham. The church ladies depend on me." God, he loved her fortitude even if it might get her killed.

"I'll keep it for now, but only if you answer one question." She nodded, and he gathered her hands back up. "So many people depend on you, but who do you depend on?" He caressed her cold cheek and waited for her answer.

"I will depend on you," she finally admitted. Graham wouldn't let her down.

"Always," he leaned forward and lightly kissed her lips. "If I'm not with you then one of the deputies will be. You will not spend one second alone until this person is locked away." She nodded. After another kiss to guarantee they were both on the same page, Graham aimed for the center of town.

"Where are we going?"

"I need to have one of my deputies try to lift some prints from your jeep, possibly from that note someone left you, and then I need to get you home and warmed up." With that thought, he cranked the truck's heater up another notch. She was still shivering but Graham had a feeling it was from fear and not the current weather.

"I can't imagine sleeping right now," she confessed.

"I'm not leaving your side," he promised. After all, it was his fault she was involved.

"I was a girl scout," she tried on a smirk. "I know how to lock doors and keep a phone handy. I will be fine." She tossed him a sheepish grin.

"And I'm still a boy scout," he winked. "You won't be alone, even tonight."

Sensing he meant that he won't let her be alone, Iyla Jean responded, "I'm not like those kinds of women you date, sheriff." Her one brow marked the line she assumed he wanted to cross. He would, one day, but this was not that day. The woman he hoped to one day marry would be treated like the treasure he believed her to be. Graham pulled her soft fingers to his lips and kissed them.

"And I'm no longer the kind of man, Iyla Jean Fleming." That had her smile widening. "That's why I'll be sleeping on the couch."

Five

The Cocoa Crawl drew in more visitors than the Summer Covered Bridge Festival. People from all over came to taste the various recipes of hot chocolate and cast their vote for the best one. Graham never held their enthusiasm, considering that he was allergic to chocolate. And this year, casting a vote might very well be a dangerous thing to do.

He and Iyla Jean talked late into the night. The threat she received placed Sybil Jennings as a person of real interest. Sybil despised her free-spirited aunt and was almost assuredly Travis White's mistress. The wannabe actress could very easily be acting when she spoke in favor of the solar plant. By Saturday afternoon, Graham had everything he needed to send Deputy Conley out to fetch Sybil for questioning. The happily married officer was one most immune to Sybil's charms. It only took an hour, considering that Sybil had no alibi for Tuesday and was present when Pete died, to arrest her on charges of murder of her aunt, and once he'd gathered enough evidence, he hoped for Pete and Beulah as well. He had his killer and his town was safe again.

"Now that I got the warrant, I need to go over to Sybil's and see how much more evidence I can get before her Monday hearing." Graham told Iyla Jean as she readied her table for the Cocoa Crawl. People were already moving about, dodging in one store and out another. Christmas shopping for him would be last-last minute this year he figured. He hoped it would make up for telling Nerva about the threat to Iyla Jean. She was still a bit raw that he had let that slip this morning over scones and coffee.

"I'll help her if you don't get back in time. Sadie might even help you serve," Travis said, zipping up his son's coat as the snowflakes grew fatter and lighter all at the same time.

"That would be great, but I know their grandparents are only staying until morning. They should spend as much time with them enjoying the festivities than helping me." Iyla Jean advised, sensible and always thinking of others. The woman made him want to be a better man.

Iyla Jean couldn't stop smiling for the next three hours as she served cocoa and chatted with visitors. It sort of made sense that Sybil was the killer. Still, there was that nagging feeling in her head that it was suspicious. Maybe she had read too many mystery novels—Sybil always got what she wanted, but did she really know anything about poisons? She and Beulah were friends, so it was possible. And Pete had sued her father for that shady land deal and won. Threatening her because of Graham made sense too. It wasn't the first time she and Sybil had been at odds over a boy. But it was Beulah's murder that had her thoughts so troubled. They were friends, and Sybil wasn't nearly as mean as she put on. She shrugged as Travis appeared. She was a baker, not a detective. What could she possibly know about?

"Got any left for a freezing man?" He teased. Aunt Nerva went to pour him a cup, but Iyla Jean stopped her.

"No, you go on home and enjoy your *Murder She Wrote*," Iyla Jean told her aunt after Trace Marshal surprised everyone by adding something spicy to his cocoa and winning Cocoa King for the year. Seeing that Travis was here, her aunt and uncle strolled away as the snow began falling in larger flakes now. The streets were so beautiful right now that one didn't even note it was only thirty-eight degrees.

"Beulah's parents are having a sleepover," Travis said in fingered quotation marks, "tonight. That leaves me at your disposal. Want me to help you with packing up?"

"That would be great. Thanks," she said as the crowds moved away to gather for caroling. "If we hurry, I can still join the carolers." She smiled. Glancing about for Deputy Crane, she couldn't spot him in the retreating faces. Then again, he was only five-nine. Graham had insisted she not be alone, but Travis was here so she should be fine.

"So, how are the children doing, you know, with everything?" Iyla began placing cups, napkins, and table Christmas decorations in one tote as Travis began filling another.

Travis shrugged. "It's been hard, on Sadie especially. She and her mother were close."

"I should stop by, bring dinner over for them or something." Travis paused mid-lift of a tote holding two large thermoses.

"They would love that. Sadie and Max have always been fond of you since you started teaching their Sunday school classes." He held her gaze for a moment before aiming for the Coffee Stop. Iyla Jean felt a shiver run through her and shook off the silly uneasiness. Travis had just lost his wife. Of course he would appreciate someone who taught his children's Sunday school lessons being around more than the regular gifts of reheatable dinners.

Christmas lights lit a path into the Coffee Stop. She weaved between tables, careful not to bump into anything.

"I told you I would carry these." Travis appeared out of nowhere. Startled by his quick appearance, the tote slipped from between her hands.

"Geez, Travis, you scared me." Iyla Jean quickly bent down to gather up the sleeves of paper cups strewn about. Travis bent down to help.

"I'm sorry, Iyla Jean." Even in the dim glow of lights she could see that he was upset with himself.

"It's okay. I'm just jumpy these days. I mean, someone out there has taken from you and threatening me. We are both a bit frazzled." Poor man, probably doesn't even know how to act these days.

He placed a hand on hers and helped her stand. "No one's going to lay a hand on you." He reached out and brushed a lock of hair behind her ear. The intimate gesture ignited her awareness.

"Travis," she started, "I'm real sorry about Beulah," Iyla Jean said, taking a step back. "But Graham is sure Sybil will in no way hurt another soul."

The laugh started low, amusingly, and grew into something hostile, causing the hairs on her neck to bristle.

"Murphy couldn't find his way home without a GPS. I know him a lot better than you. He wouldn't even be sheriff today if not for his daddy."

"He's your friend," she reminded him. "That's not a nice thing to say about a friend."

"Neither is trying to make moves on another man's girl." His dark eyes narrowed down at her.

"I don't understand." He wasn't making any sense.

"God, I love how naive you are, Iyla Jean," he moved closer and she took another step back.

"Travis, what are you doing?"

"I'm walking to you." For each step he took, Iyla Jean backed up two. Still, he was growing more visible. She glanced at the front glass door hoping the deputy was nearby.

"Graham will be here any minute," she warned.

Travis laughed. "No, he won't. Sybil has so much evidence in her house, it will take him all night to process it. You know she hated you with a passion." He shook a finger at her. "Seems like all the women I like prefer Graham and are jealous of you."

"Why would you think that?" She needed to keep him talking.

"She tells me that all the time. A weak woman, that one. Do you believe Sybil actually stood me up to visit him? The man doesn't even own his house. He has so little to offer a woman."

Graham had told her about Sybil's unsolicited visit, but she hadn't a clue Travis and Sybil had been seeing each other. He was married. Her breath quickened with every clue being dealt to her.

"Travis, you're wrong. Sybil would never be jealous of me." The wrong person was in jail.

"Of course she is. We all love you. It's just that some of us are willing to go to further lengths for you."

Tears blurred her vision as she recognized that the real killer was standing before her. "What are you talking about?" Iyla Jean felt the panic from her toes to her fingertips.

"Graham was always better at basketball, baseball, and women. I've spent a lifetime trying to beat him at something, and then he set his sights on you." He moved closer, and she felt the counter dig into her shoulder blades. If she could just keep him talking until Graham returned, perhaps even find something to defend herself in the meantime. "There are rules between friends, and I saw you first." *Where was the deputy, Graham?*

"But Beulah…" Outside, Iyla Jean could hear the distant sound of carolers making their way up the street towards the courthouse. If they hurried, perhaps some of them would see her.

"Was a woman that tricked me into marrying her. I mean really, Iyla Jean, we married just six months before Sadie was born. And the door is locked sweetheart, so don't think any of those howling carolers are going to pop in."

"You…you killed her…" *A weapon. Find a weapon, Iyla.*

"Like Sybil, she was a jealous woman. She simply couldn't understand that I could never love her like I do you. You're not like them. You are jealous of no one."

"Travis, you don't love me. We're just friends," she tried to reason with him.

"Friends don't flirt like we do. Friends don't feel what I feel for you." He ran a slimy finger down her damp cheek.

"You killed Pete." Just the thought of poor Pete brought on fresh tears and surprisingly, anger.

"I was aiming for Mack, but Pete drank his cup. Greedy old man." Travis placed a hand on each side of her, pinning her in place.

"Mack is dying with cancer, he has children. Why would you even want to take what little time they had left together from them?"

"Exactly, and he is leaving behind more in life insurance for them, dead. The solar plant deal is a good deal, but you don't want it." He leaned closer. "I could never vote for it if it made you unhappy. I can make you happy, Iyla Jean." He cupped her face and when she tried withdrawing from his touch, Travis gripped her chin firmly. Acidy bile rose up and singed her throat. "We can live anywhere. Beulah had a nice insurance policy. The kids want Florida, but you get to decide if our family will stay or go."

"Travis, I don't love you. We are not a family."

"We will be." He pulled her towards him and assaulted her delicate lips with his. She pushed and shoved and yet the man didn't budge bruising and stealing from her.

"God, I always knew you would taste sweet." His dark eyes danced devilishly, and she could see an uncertain future in them.

"Don't touch me!" She smacked him open handed. "Help!!!" Travis quickly pulled her to him and slapped a hand over her mouth.

"How about we slip upstairs, discuss the details." Iyla Jane jerked again to free herself. That's when she felt the cold metal at her side and slowed her rebellion. He was going to kill her if she didn't comply.

She was going to die.

He breathed her in, and she felt his hot breath on her neck as he urged her towards the stairs. "God, I have always loved your scent."

"I'm pretty fond of it myself." Graham appeared in the shadowy doorway. She was so glad he insisted on having a key now.

"Graham, he has a gun in my side," Iyla Jean quickly warned.

"He's also got something that doesn't belong to him. Come on, Travis, let's not make this ugly." Iyla Jean noted the glint of metal in Graham's hand as well. These two powerful men were both armed and the only thing between them was her.

"You always got the trophies and the girls. I'm keeping this one thing. This," Travis pulled Iyla Jean against him, "is mine." Nothing felt more wicked or stomach turning than being pawed by evil. She whined as Travis continued to handle her. "She's the mother of my future children."

Travis lifted his weapon but remained shielded behind Iyla Jean. Graham wouldn't risk a shot. "Pretty clever leading me towards Sybil." *Keep him talking, Graham.* Seeing Iyla Jean in danger had sent all kinds of alerts over him.

"Sybil doesn't mind being used. Shouldn't you be processing the evidence, sheriff?"

"I should, but when Mack Donavon paid me a surprising visit, I realized my first suspect was the right one all along."

"He meant to kill Mack, not Pete," Iyla Jean blurted out, earning her a tighter hold.

"Mack said you bought everyone drinks Monday, and considering he had his fill already, Pete swallowed his down."

Outside, carolers neared. He nearly forgot about the tree lighting. Ironic, Graham thought, that 'O Come all Ye Faithful' was being sung while his oldest friend held the woman he loved, hostage. He could use some of that divine intervention right about now. Time was running out and he had to act.

"Iyla, do you trust me?" Her eyes widened but when her head made a slightest nod, Graham knew he had to take the shot before the crowd outside realized what was happening. Travis was too desperate not to shoot his way out of Brookhaven at this point.

"It's been fun chatting, Murphy, but we need to be going," Travis released the safety and aimed.

"Left!" Graham didn't hesitate when Iyla Jean yelled one word. He pulled the trigger. One shot, that was all he had, and it was all he needed.

Six

They stood under the tree among the people they had come to love. "You know, this has been the longest week of my life." Graham said.

"What's going to happen to Travis?" She liked the way he looked at her now, like a man satisfied and ready to commit.

"He'll get a trial, but he won't get out of jail until it comes time to bury him." She leaned against him, and he laid an arm around her.

"When the carolers came, I thought he would kill one of us," she said looking up.

"Where was that faith of yours, then? Don't you know that the good guy always wins?" He kissed her forehead. "'O Come all Ye Faithful' is now my favorite Christmas Carol."

"Mine too." She smiled. "Graham?"

"Yes."

"When I yelled left…how did you know it was your left and not mine?" He had pondered that himself, after.

"I don't have an answer to that. I'm just glad I was right."

"Five…Four…Three…Two…One!" The countdown finished as the tree on the snowy courthouse lawn lit up, and all of Brookhaven cheered.

The End